RED TYPHOON

The Adventures of Captain Hunt

Gabriel Rabanales

CONTENTS

1. YUYUAN GARDEN

As she entered the ancient Chinese city, under the diminishing light of sunset, a grim thought forcefully invaded the mind of nurse Mary Ann Taylor, to the point of making her shudder. Something bad was going to happen. Something very bad.

Narrow and tortuous streets led her to the garden where she was to find the strange man who had asked for her help that same afternoon. No, she corrected herself. Who had *begged* for help. Mary Ann mechanically made her way through the dozens of fortune tellers, jugglers, calligraphers and artisans who offered their services and products to the pedestrians. He passed by food stalls, animal shops, cloth merchants and dens where opium was obtained at a low price. Groups of children played with fireworks on street corners.

One of the streets, crowded with people, led to the *Yuyuan*, the Garden of Happiness. From there, following a gravel path flanked by trees, it reached the central pond. The striking *Huxingting* tea house stood in the middle of the water, fastened on several wooden stilts. Its walls were painted in shades of bright red and the ceiling had the eaves finished in tips curved upwards. Inside were lit a score of paper lamps also red – the color of good luck – that hung from the ceiling, whose glow slipped to the outside through the half-open wooden blinds.

A zigzag bridge, with balustrade railings, crossed the pond from both ends of the tea house. According to Chinese mythology, evil spirits could only advance in a straight line, so the landscapers who designed the garden wanted to make sure that the pond would be free of those demons. Much to her regret, Mary Ann smiled as she remembered that story. At that moment, she would have liked to feel protected from demons, even though her own were quite real. She went deep into the bridge and rested her elbows on the edge of the railing, tense from the wait.

Shanghai was a divided city. Foreigners lived in one of the international concessions and very few of them ventured into *Nanshi* district, the truly Chinese area. Most foreign residents could spend their entire lives inside the concessions, having known nothing of the authentic life and local culture. The British were particularly reluctant to assimilate any aspect of that place, as Mary Ann knew from experience. Although her compatriots had been settled in the city for eighty years, during that time they had concentrated all their efforts on recreating their own lifestyle within the limits of their territory.

There they had pubs, gentlemen's clubs, golf courses and even equestrian circuits. Mary Ann assumed that that was because Britain had forcibly imposed its presence in China and its representatives knew that, to this day, they were not welcome there.

Mary Ann, on the other hand, used to told herself she was in Shanghai to help. Her fellow missionaries had come inspired by a divine mission, but her intentions were far more mundane. The only ambition that had motivated her to travel to the other side of the world was to use her knowledge to help the Chinese have a better quality of life. When she heard the sermons in the Protestant church in her neighborhood, which she went to after her work at the hospital in London, she knew she had to travel immediately to the remote Asian country. She was only twenty-two years old, single, and left no family behind. Her nursing knowledge would be better used in the Far East than in the capital of a modern country.

According to preachers, sanitary conditions in China were deplorable. After three years living in Shanghai, Mary Ann had found that what they said was true. Outbreaks of cholera and other infections ravaged entire regions of the country; opium addicts numbered in the thousands; leprosy and tuberculosis were widespread, and the horrendous practice of foot binding had not yet been banished, especially among the peasants. The missionaries' hospitals could not cope with treating the local population, not to mention the distrust that the Chinese showed regarding Western medicine.

Mary Ann worked at Shantung Road Missionary Hospital, located in the International Settlement, the oldest concession in the city. It had been founded by a doctor of the British Missionary Society in 1844; the same institution administered it until today. The first to arrive in that region were the evangelizers of the Protestant religions, who had preceded even foreign merchants. However, their efforts proved very limited until the European powers, along with the Americans, forced China to open its ports in the 1840s. Originally, the local government only allowed the presence of a few missionaries in Canton, in the south of the country, but after the First Opium War, in 1842, access was also allowed to the ports of Amoy, Foochow, Ningpo and Shanghai.

A dozen Protestant missionary organizations, in addition to some Catholic ones, had more than three thousand volunteers who preached the word of God throughout China. Before, the number had been higher, but after the Boxer Rebellion in 1900, and with the Great War that had swept Europe, missionary momentum waned. It was able to flourish again at the beginning of the 1920s, with the constant arrival of volunteers and the construction of new churches, schools and hospitals. An important part of the Christian effort was devoted to the health of the new faithful. Like Mary Ann, doctors and nurses traveled from Europe and the United States to work in the modern missionary care facilities.

On her work at the hospital, Mary Ann was to oversee two patient recovery wards. One was of men and the other was occupied only by women. The Chinese did not mix both sexes in their health care and, in addition, local women did not allow themselves to be examined by male foreign doctors. All missionary hospitals had to have women with medical degrees to care for the female population. Dozens of female doctors preferred to work in Asia rather than in European or American hospitals, where they were discriminated against by their male colleagues.

During her visits to the men's ward, Mary Ann only checked the conditions of each patient, without approaching them or talking to them, so as not to provoke conflict. That's why she felt confused when that day, in the middle of the afternoon, one of the patients tried to talk to her. She was about to finish her round and suddenly saw that a young man, covered in sweat and with his face shaken, made desperate gestures to get her attention.

After hesitating for a moment, Mary Ann approached the patient.

"Where am I?", the man asked, in a raspy voice. He spoke a hesitant English.

Mary Ann held out a glass of water and responded with the name and location of the hospital. Knowing that he was in the International Settlement, the man seemed relieved.

"How long have I been here?", he insisted.

The nurse looked at the pages with medical notes resting on a bamboo table, next to the simple cot. That man had arrived dying three days earlier, after being shot in the chest. The doctors had operated on him urgently and now he was languishing on that bed, given to his fate. The hospital could not spend supplies and medicines on a poor unknown patient. They had not even reported the crime to the police.

Mary Ann informed his situation to the poor man.

"Three days!", the Chinese exclaimed, horrified. "I must get out of here."

He tried to push the sheets away, but the abrupt gesture caused him to bout in pain. Mary Ann forced him to lie down.

"You English woman?", the patient asked in a rudimentary way.

Mary Ann nodded, surprised by the question.

"I friend of the English," he said. "Good Christian of missionary school".

She smiled and told him to rest. When she

tried to continue with her round, he grabbed her hard by the wrist. Mary Ann was shocked but did not want to make a fuss. She took the patient's sweaty hand and pulled it away with a firm gesture.

"What is your name?", she asked.

The insistence of the Chinese was making her curious.

"Wang Min."

Mary Ann knew that in Chinese usage, the family name came first and then the given name.

"Listen, Mr. Wang. You have a strong infection that causes fever and dizziness. But if you rest for several days..."

"No! I must warn the English. Nurse should help me."

"Warn?" Maybe that man was delusional. "You suffered a major injury, Mr. Wang. You have a concussion and..."

"Listen!", Wang ordered, half sitting up. He looked around at the other patients and lowered his voice: "I was attacked for being a friend of the English. I want to warn of danger that will fall on them."

Mary Ann was astonished at what the patient was saying. Although he was disturbed, he did not seem to have lost his mental faculties. Amid the sweat-soaked and trembling face, his eyes remained fixed on the nurse. More than looking like a madman, Wang looked only desperate.

"Very serious danger, nurse! Please help me get out of here. I go home and give help to English."

"It is not possible for you to be discharged, Mr. Wang. Doctors say you should stay hospitalized for several days."

"You take home, and I will give help you!"

Mary Ann abruptly turned away from the man. Now he did seem to have lost his mind.

"If you want to leave, I can talk to the director of the hospital," Mary Ann said in a forceful tone. "But I can't..."

"Men who attacked me must look for me now," Wang interrupted. "Soon they will kill me again."

"It's impossible for anyone to attack you inside the hospital," she said, shaking her head.

The Chinese laugh between throes of pain.

"You don't know who they are, nurse. I'm leaving here now. If you don't want to help, I will find someone else."

That was crazy. The missionaries were to take care of their patients and the Christian faithful, but without meddling in their affairs. Mary Ann could not only lose her job but would surely be expelled from the British Missionary Society. She would have to return to England humiliated and out of work. However, Wang Min's gaze told her that the man was serious. What if there really was a danger looming over the English community? Shanghai was a violent city, without a clear government, populated by revolutionaries, gangsters and criminal societies. It was unwise to ignore such a warning.

"All right," Mary Ann said, after a moment. "I will help you."

To the girl's surprise, a couple of tears slipped down the cheeks of the badly injured patient.

"Thank you," he whispered.

The nurse continued her round to the women's ward. It took her an hour to check on the patients and then she went to the dispensary. When she was left alone in the room, she took bandages, compresses and an orderly apron. She took the package directly to the male recovery ward and came to Wang Min's cot. Most patients slept and some complained of pain or raved in their beds. No one noticed the care that the nurse provided to Wang. Mary Ann put a compress over the bruised chest wound, crudely sutured after surgery, and then bandaged it around the torso.

"Put this on," she whispered to the patient. "I will wait for you at the back exit of the hospital."

Mary Ann immediately went to the service access of the establishment. On the way she came across a couple of fellow nurses whom she barely greeted. Her body was shaking, and her throat was dry, gripped by fear. While treating Wang's wound she had seen several tattoos on his body. That man was a criminal, no doubt a member of some secret society. No wonder he had been shot. The girl was sure she was getting into a tremendous mess.

Wang appeared after an eternity, dressed in the orderly apron. Most of the assistants of the hospital were Chinese, so no one had noticed him, despite his gaunt appearance and erratic gait. Mary Ann gestured to him to follow her, and they ran down a corridor to the back street of the hospital. From there they took a detour and went back to Shantung Road. They walked to a corner and there the girl stopped a rickshaw.

Those two-wheeled passenger carts, pulled by human traction, were the most common means of transport in Shanghai and in most cities in the Far East. However, it was highly unusual for a European woman and a Chinese man to travel together in the same vehicle. Mary Ann lifted the lapels of her coat and pulled on her nurse's cap while Wang Min gave instructions to the runner in the local dialect.

The cart headed south, immersed in the heavy traffic of the afternoon. Dozens of rickshaws competed for street space with private motor cars, buses and trams. Shanghai was one of the largest cities in the world and its narrow avenues were totally collapsed by vehicles and pedestrians. Mary Ann took advantage of the slow movement of the vehicle to study askance her forced companion. She estimated that he would be about twenty-five years old and that he was originally from the region near the city. In her three years living there, the nurse already distinguished the local dialect from the other variants of the Chinese language. That country was so large that dozens of ethnicities and languages coexisted in its territory, that had little in common with each other.

According to what he himself had said, Wang had studied at a missionary school, where he converted to Christianity and learned a little English. It was a pity that he had ended up becoming a criminal, but the girl knew it was a very frequent situation. Young Chinese were destined to become servants of foreigners, who despised them even if they were educated and spoke their language. Therefore, many preferred to integrate into secret societies, which provided them with easy money and a life of adventure. There were few who managed to continue their education and develop a profession. One of them had been Dr. Sun Yat-Sen, who had studied Western medicine in missionary institutions and later founded the nationalist Kuomintang party, becoming the first president of the Republic of China.

The rickshaw arrived at the intersection with Avenue Edward VII, a wide thoroughfare that crossed the city center from east to west, marking the boundary between the International Settlement and the French Concession. From that point on, the street through which they circulated was renamed Rue Vincent Mathieu. At the end of this was the Boulevard of the Two Republics, which separated the European territory from the ancient Chinese city. Until ten years ago, the district of *Nanshi* was protected by an old defensive wall, but the governor of the new republic had ordered its demolition to replace it with a modern circular avenue.

"You know *Yuyuan* Garden?", Wang Min asked as they got off the rickshaw. Mary Ann nodded. "Wait for me there. I must go home looking for something for you."

Before the girl could reply, the Chinese disappeared in the middle of the crowd that packed out the alleys of the old district. A few minutes later, she was by the central pond, watching the red paper lamps glowing inside the teahouse.

"Nurse!", called a voice from the end of the bridge.

Mary Ann startled but managed to calm down a little when she saw that it was Wang. She went to meet him and followed him as he went through the paths of the garden. The walls that separated the different sections of the park were crowned by imposing figures of dragons that looked up at the sky with their jaws open. In the growing darkness, the mythological creatures cast fearsome shadows over the landscape. Mary Ann felt a shudder.

"What's wrong, Wang? Where are we going?"

"My house guarded, but I manage to get in."

The Chinese guided the girl to the Grand Rockery. Mary Ann had been there before. That section of the garden consisted of a fourteen-meter-high formation built with more than two thousand tons of limestone rock brought from the Wukang Mountains in Chekiang Province. The rocks were joined with rice gum and recreated a small landscape of cliffs and gorges, crossed by tortuous passages. Considering the garden was built in the mid-sixteenth century and the rocks had to be transported two hundred kilometers to Shanghai, the result of the work was simply spectacular.

Wang went into the rocks until there was no one in sight.

"Take this," said the Chinese.

He placed a small glass vial in the girl's hand. The nurse lifted the vial into the light to better see its contents. The inside was filled with small reddish crystals that flashed as the container was removed.

"Put it away!", Wang Min ordered.

"What is this?"

Mary Ann kept looking at the red flashes emanating from the vial.

Wang was trembling. His face felt feverish, but the girl was sure that the shudders were due to another reason. The Chinese man was terrified.

"Bad men look for the blood of the dragon to launch the typhoon over England," said the man, speaking in a hurry. "Many people will die if you don't stop it."

"Wait a minute," said Mary Ann, her hands up. "Blood of the dragon? Is it a kind of disease?"

"The crystals!", the man exclaimed, in a desperate voice.

"Do you mean what's in the vial?"

Wang nodded vehemently.

"I don't know why," he said in a voice of anguish, "but crystals are important."

"Oh, God, I don't understand anything!" Mary Ann was on the verge of tears. "Who are those bad men? Why would they do anything against my country? There are no typhoons in England!"

Mary Ann knew that in China they called 'typhoon' a tropical storm. She had suffered the onslaught of a typhoon the previous year during a visit to the coast, but she couldn't imagine that anyone could trigger a storm somewhere or at a certain time. She stared at Wang to force him to give her a coherent answer, but he was not paying attention to her.

Wang had become tense, and his features were stiff. He looked up as he turned his head. To Mary Ann it seemed as he was pricking up his ears, but she could only hear a gentle breeze sneaking through the huge ornamental rocks.

"Hide," he whispered, in a trembling voice.

"Do not make noise."

He grabbed her arm and pushed her unceremoniously towards the rocks. She wanted to protest, but the man's gaze left no room for doubt. Mary Ann went inside the false cliffs and was soon enveloped by the shadows cast by the erect rocks. When she looked back at the passage where Wang was, she saw that there was someone next to the Chinese. Mary Ann blinked in her hiding place. Where did that figure come from? Not even a moment ago Wang had been alone in the middle of the gorge.

The newcomer was wrapped in a robe and covered his head with a hood. Mary Ann couldn't see his features; she couldn't even tell if it was a man or a woman. Apparently, the mysterious figure was talking to Wang, because he was shaking his head. After a moment the man tried to walk away, but the hooded figure stretched out one arm and put a hand on Wang's chest. Mary Ann couldn't quite see what was happening, but it seemed to her that agile fingers were tapping on the man's body, as if playing a strange melody on an imaginary piano.

Wang then fell to his knees with his arms hanging on the sides of his torso. The figure muttered something that the nurse could barely hear. Wang was stiff and no longer spoke. Mary Ann supposed that the man was paralyzed by terror. Or was it something else that kept him motionless? The figure stood behind Wang, and with a swift gesture unsheathed a long sword that had been hidden under the cloak. Mary Ann hadn't even seen the weapon under the stranger's robes, but now a shiny blade was towering over the kneeling body, throwing a metal hiss as it cut through the air.

The girl put a hand in her mouth so as not to scream. She bit her knuckles in fear and felt her teeth dig into the delicate skin. However, she could not take her eyes away from the scene that took place a few meters beyond, in the narrow passage between the rocks. The figure holding the shining sword stood in front of the kneeling Wang, but he did not move or say anything. Mary Ann couldn't believe that the man didn't show any reaction to an impending attack. What power did the executioner have over a young, hardened man like Wang?

With a slight whistle, like a soft chime, the sharp blade cut off the night air, and then stopped, trembling slightly. For an instant it seemed that nothing had happened, but as the dark figure sheathed the elegant weapon again, Wang Min's head leaned forward and stood there suspended, as if the man had fallen asleep. Then the head separated from the body and rolled on the ground until it stopped next to a rock.

Mary Ann felt a spasm so hard that she thought she was going to vomit and faint at the same time. But her survival instinct was superior to terror, and she managed to remain still in the shadows, a few meters from the decapitated man. At that moment the killer turned to the rocks, as if he had heard something. His hood was directed toward the hiding place for a moment, but to Mary Ann it seemed like an eternity. After a few seconds, the figure crouched next to the corpse and checked his clothes. The girl heard an exclamation of anger and the next instant the killer was no longer there. He had disappeared as furtively as he had arrived.

Mary Ann remained hidden for a long time, as the night progressed. Her feet hurt from standing in an awkward position. Nausea invaded her in wild waves, but she was reluctant to move or make any sound. Only the tears that slipped down his cheeks showed the true horror that had taken hold of her body. At last, exhausted and on the verge of exhaustion, she managed to gather the strength to go out into the narrow passage and pass by the grisly remains of the man she had barely come to know.

Without looking back, she ran in desperation and aimlessly. She would only stop when exhaustion threw her to the ground.

2. THE BUND

The imposing buildings that lined the boardwalk, facing the Whangpoo River, were a faithful testament to what their presence in Shanghai meant to foreign powers: thriving businesses, freedom to operate without the influence of the Chinese government, and the imposition of their permanent lifestyle in the heart of the Far East. While walking along the promenade by the river, Captain Peter Hunt counted more than twenty corporate headquarters from great western companies.

Most of the buildings were recent constructions that had replaced the previous structures, built during the time of European settlement in the city. The current buildings were larger and more modern than the original ones, whose objective was not only for renovation, but also intended to demonstrate the glorious splendor of their owners. The constructions were designed in different architectural styles, although those of 'revival' predominated: neo-Romanesque, neo-Baroque and Neoclassical.

The row of buildings also served as an advertisement for Shanghai's 'who's who'. There stood the large luxury hotels, the headquarters of the powerful international banks and, especially, the head offices of the gigantic companies that controlled production and trade in that corner of China. None of them belonged to local capitals. It was enough to read the signs located on the main entrances to find British, French, German or Japanese businesses.

The boardwalk along the river, located in front of those symbols of economic power, was called the *Bund*. This term was not of Chinese origin but came from Persia, probably adopted by the first British merchants who settled in the city, who already traded in India and the Middle East, where the people called 'band' or 'bund' the banks built on the edges of the rivers. The Chinese knew the boardwalk, simply, as the "outer bank". Such was the splendor of that river walk, that it had no rival anywhere in Asia. To mention the term without any adjective, or when writing with a capital letter, the *Bund,* was understood to refer undoubtedly to the boardwalk of Shanghai.

Hunt walked the promenade from north to south, under a warm and humid afternoon. Hundreds of people passed through the boardwalk, forming a very heterogeneous mixture of people that was only seen in that city. There were British businessmen, elegant French ladies, American servicemen in glossy uniforms, demure-looking Scandinavian missionaries, poor Russian expatriates,, and mysterious Japanese who always seemed to be in a hurry. Among them were several Settlement police officers, another heterogeneous group of men, though they came mostly from the British colonies of Southeast Asia.

Turbans, top hats, peaked caps and folk costumes of a dozen countries were mixed on the street. While passers-by went to or from their jobs and others just strolled by the river, or gathered to secretly conspire unnoticed in the crowd, there were also a few impoverished immigrants trying to sell their belongings to pedestrians, at any price.

The Bund was the heart of the twenty-three square kilometers that formed the International Settlement, where about twenty thousand foreigners lived. More than eight hundred thousand Chinese also resided there. Another two million of their compatriots lived outside those boundaries, in Greater Shanghai. Despite the enormous disproportion between natives and foreigners, the few Chinese who could be seen along the boardwalk were nothing more than rickshaw-pulling coolies or young *amahs*, the maids of wealthy families. In the Public Garden, located at the northern end of the boardwalk, the presence of the local population was expressly prohibited. This form of obvious discrimination had given rise to the myth about the existence of a sign displayed at the entrance of the park that supposedly indicated: 'No dogs or Chinese allowed'.

Hunt advanced among that sea of people, oblivious to the differences of classes and nationalities, with his gaze fixed forward. His mind was concentrated on his own reason to find himself in that land, more than nine thousand kilometers away from his native England. The multitude of colors in the streets, the aromas of the meals that were prepared outdoors, and the dozens of languages that were heard everywhere, had amazed him when he arrived in Shanghai. But at that moment he could only think of his mission.

Hunt had been working for six months for the British Museum as an investigator in one of its departments. His trip to China was aimed at acquiring a valuable piece for the Museum's collection. However, he was not an archaeologist, nor did he have any academic degree. For its part, the artifact had not been dug up from an excavation nor had it been found in an old trunk, let alone had it been taken down from a ruined wall. Hunt wasn't even going to acquire the piece from another museum or an authorized dealer. But he would have to pay for it. And, no doubt, it would be too high a price. And it wasn't just about money.

He checked his trench watch to see how much was left for his appointment. The watch, which had been provided to British Army officers during the Great War, had a design like pocket watches. It had a hinge cover on the dial, made of reinforced glass, but also had a pair of metal lugs that allowed a leather strap to pass through them and fasten it to the wrist. According to the luminescent radium hands, the meeting would not be for half an hour. The captain bought a copy of the *North China Daily News* and sat on a bench to read the newspaper.

The main news still concerned the sudden death of American President Warren Harding and recounted his state funeral and the succession of Vice President Coolidge. In Germany, the economic crisis was worsening, and a far-right party called the National Socialist German Workers' Party was gaining more and more support, particularly in Bavaria. The rest of the articles were devoted exclusively to foreign businesses taking place in Shanghai and in the other treaty ports.

Hunt used the newspaper's extended pages as a parapet to stealthily watch the neo-Renaissance façade of the Palace Hotel, which stood on the other side of the Bund. He searched the crowd for furtive-eyed men, suspicious walkers or parked cars with their occupants on board. When he saw that there was nothing out of the ordinary, he left the newspaper on the bench and crossed the street. The hotel doorman opened the door for him, and Hunt went to the lobby restaurant. He picked a table located in a corner, from which he dominated the entire hall, and there he prepared to wait.

Some twenty tables were displayed in the form of a crescent around a central stage. More than fifty diners were distributed among the tables, dining and chatting relaxedly. On stage, a beautiful singer played a melody by Ivor Novello, oblivious to the hustle and bustle of the diners. Hunt sought out his contact among the bankers, businessmen and diplomats who occupied the room, but could not guess if any of them were the negotiator of the sale. The current owners of the piece that the museum wished to acquire were Chinese, but the captain assumed that the transaction would be carried out by a white man. A Chinese would draw attention inside the luxurious lobby of the Palace.

He ordered a glass of Glenlivet whisky, neat, and drank it slowly while watching the restaurant. He tried to remain calm, resisting the temptation to check the time constantly on his trench watch. After a while he forced himself to relax his muscles and leaned back on his chair. He stroked the outline of the revolver he was carrying in a holster under his jacket and felt confident. The Webley Mk VI had pulled him out of various troubles before and now, if necessary, it wouldn't fail him either.

During his first mission for the British Museum, at the beginning of that year, Hunt had been on the verge of losing his revolver forever.

He only managed to recover it by miracle. The singer's pleasant voice allowed him to forget the tension of the moment and his memory set him back to Cairo, where he had traveled to investigate a murder. His inquiries led him to come across the plans of a fearsome sect of worshippers of a mythological god of Ancient Egypt. In the end, he had confronted and eliminated them all.

Despite the time that had passed, the captain still remembered his amazement at discovering the existence of Department X, a secret unit of the museum tasked with collecting and investigating artifacts and works related to paranormal phenomena. The man killed in Egypt worked for the Department, whose chief had recruited Hunt after finding that the captain also showed interest in the occult sciences. Both the chief of the Department and Hunt were members of the Price Club in London, where British gentlemen who wished to explore such arcane knowledge met.

The Webley was the old service revolver that had been issued to Hunt during the war. The captain took it with him to Cairo, suspecting that the assignment might get dangerous. During his mission, he had lost it by fighting with one of the sectarians in the basement of the Egyptian Museum. The police raided the place after the sect was defeated, thanks to Hunt's own efforts, and seized the evidence found, including an old military revolver. By then, the captain was still in the country, convalescing from the wounds he had suffered in his confrontation with the cult leader, under the care of a beautiful girl who had helped him thwart the plans of those fanatics.

Now, as he sipped the whisky, he smiled remembering the skillful and courageous Emily Everhart. For two weeks they had enjoyed an intense and joyful romance, fueled by the attempt to leave behind the vicissitudes that happened together at the hands of their enemies. However, they both knew that the relationship would end as unexpectedly as it had begun. So, when Emily announced she was to return to her job as a pilot at the ailing airline she owned with her father, Hunt prepared to take a steamer back to London as soon as possible. However, just the day before his departure, he received a message from Cairo's police chief, a British official, to come to a little meeting.

He had assumed that a lengthy interrogation awaited him about his involvement in the sect affair, especially regarding the disappearance of a renowned local businessman who turned out to be the high priest of that party of mad men. For such an eventuality, he had already prepared a series of evasive answers and half-truths. To his surprise, Russell Pasha, the police chief, simply thanked him while winking at him. When he added that Sir John Connelly was sending greetings, Hunt understood that the senior official was also aware of the activities of Department X.

"I understand that this is yours," said the official, holding out his precious revolver.

Hunt immediately grabbed it and put it in the back of the trouser waist. He said goodbye to Russell with a nod of his head and reserved a hug and a long kiss for his beloved Emily. True to her style, the girl saw him board the train at Cairo station and then walked away without looking back.

Applause abruptly returned Hunt to the present. The singer had finished her number and was walking around the tables greeting some acquaintances. Soon the conversations of the diners resumed, as well as the metallic tinkling of the cutlery and the bursts of the corks of the bottles of champagne. Waiters brought elegant china dishes to the tables and the stage light went out. Hunt gave a fleeting glance at his watch and cursed in his mind the seller's delay. He thought about ordering a new glass of whisky just as the singer sat on the chair on the other side of his table.

"Thank you. You are very kind in inviting me," she said, aloud. "I think I will accept a drink."

Hunt concealed his surprise and just nodded, giving a hint of a smile.

"Let me guess," he said. "Champagne. Moët et Chandon?"

The girl laughed discreetly as he called the waiter. While the order was being brought to them, Hunt took the opportunity to take a closer look at his new companion. Brown hair combed in waves covering the side of the face, large green eyes with long eyelashes, a pointy nose and thick, seductive lips. He guessed that she would be about twenty-five years old and that she came from Central Europe or perhaps the Balkans. Her accent was almost imperceptible.

When they had the glasses of bubbly liquor in their hands, Hunt lifted his own to the girl.

"You have an excellent voice, Miss..."

"Call me Ilsa."

"Well, Ilsa, to what do I owe the pleasure of your company?"

"Business. How much are you willing to pay?"

The girl had a serious grimace; her head tilted, and her gaze hidden behind the waterfall of hair. Hunt kept the glass halfway from his mouth.

"I'm sorry, but I haven't come here looking for that kind of services."

She pulled her hair away so Hunt could see her eyes blazing.

"I'm not a prostitute," she replied angrily. Her Central European accent became more pronounced. "I mean the piece for sale... Captain Hunt."

He cursed himself for his lack of

imagination. He had waited for a man, perhaps someone rough and threatening, but at the same time eager to strike quickly a deal. Instead, a beautiful girl recognized as a singer had appeared. Now he understood why the sellers of the artifact had insisted that the appointment take place at the Palace Hotel.

"Sorry. It is hard for me to imagine you as an associate of the triads," said the captain.

Chinese criminal organizations had begun to be called 'triads' by the British settlers of Hong Kong, in the nineteenth century, because they used secret triangular symbols due to their mystical beliefs regarding the union of heaven, earth and humanity. Several of these organizations operated in Shanghai, in addition to other criminal groups that rivaled each other. As Hunt had heard, the local policemen were becoming experts in the fight against organized crime.

"I'm just doing a favor to a friend," replied Ilsa, shrugging.

She put a thin cigarette into her mouth and lit it with a lighter that was on the table. "So, how much are you willing to pay for the piece?"

"I thought you would set the price."

"It's a very valuable object," she said, trying to look like an expert.

Hunt deduced that, on the contrary, the girl surely had no idea about the true value of the artifact. The captain didn't say anything. He just looked at the young lady with a neutral expression. The girl gave a few nervous puffs to the cigarette and suddenly threw it:

"A thousand dollars."

"Americans? That's a lot of money."

"Mexicans," she clarified. "Silver."

As China did not have a unified monetary system, in most international ports the Mexican peso was used as a form of payment. This silver coin, minted in the North American nation, had replaced the dollar of the former Spanish Empire, also called *'real de a ocho'*, of great circulation in America and the Far East. In Shanghai, all businesses were traded under that denomination.

"First I must verify the authenticity of the piece," Hunt explained. "Can I see it?"

"It's upstairs, in my room."

"Well, let's go, then."

"I hope you bring the money, Captain. The business is only valid for tonight."

It was a trap, obviously, but Hunt had to move on. Not in vain he had traveled almost a month by ship just to obtain the piece that was in the possession of the Chinese triad. He released the button of his jacket so that he could easily access his gun. Then he followed the girl. The sequined dress was tight to her body and Hunt could see how she swayed her hips as she walked down the aisle. He sighed and concentrated on his mission.

They boarded a gleaming elevator with a grid door. Ilsa informed that they were going to the top floor. The operator manipulated a lever that put the cabin in motion. Hunt and the girl just looked forward, saying nothing to each other. The six-story journey became eternal. Hunt wondered if a couple of thugs would be waiting for him upstairs to steal his money. When the elevator stopped, the captain opened his jacket and brought a hand to the gun. He smiled forcibly at the operator and walked out into the hallway behind the girl.

The corridor was illuminated by several lamps hanging from the ceiling at regular intervals. The floor was covered by an elegant and thick carpet. The place was deserted, but the doors that opened on both sides of the corridor seemed to enclose more than one threat. Hunt moved forward cautiously, not detaching himself from the girl, until they reached the door at the end of the hallway. That walk seemed to Hunt like the death row of a prison. He felt the adrenaline running through his whole body.

Ilsa hold the handle and opened the door, which was unlocked. Hunt followed her without taking his hand out of the inside of his jacket. The door led to a spacious, soberly decorated room with a private bathroom. Hunt abandoned all pretense and set out to search the room until he was convinced that no one was in there. The girl cracked a fake smile as he returned to her side.

"Don't you want to search me too, Captain?"

"I imagine your weapons are of another kind," Hunt said. "Where is the artifact?"

The girl scrutinized him with her gaze, somewhat resentful of his lack of interest. After a moment, she pointed her chin at a sideboard next to the wall. On its cover was laid an object that was just under a meter long, hidden under a velvet cloth. Hunt pulled the cloth away and held his breath.

A human arm, made of terracotta and slightly curved at the elbow, clung with its long fingers the base of an armillary sphere of a size somewhat smaller than a football. The arm, molded with great detail, was a color between ochre and brown, although it was quite worn. It was sectioned at the height of the union with the shoulder, but it was noticeable that it had belonged to a life-size sculpture of a man dressed in a robe. On the edges were still the remains of the original painting, made with natural pigments.

The celestial sphere, on the other hand, was made of several concentric brass rings, held by small rivets. The rings were covered with rust, but their measurement marks were intact. Hunt picked up the piece with a delicate gesture and examined the sphere more closely. If the artifact was authentic, he thought, it was more than two thousand years old.

Armillary spheres were used to measure celestial objects. They had been invented, at the same time, by Chinese and Greek astronomers, shortly before the beginning of the Christian Era. Its rings represented celestial longitude and latitude, in addition to other astronomical phenomena. But that particular sphere did not measure the distances from the sun or the other planets near Earth. In fact, their marks did not correspond even to the rest of the solar system. According to the sources available to Department X, that device allowed its user to calculate the distance, and travel time, to the far reaches of the galaxy.

"Where was it found?" Hunt asked, though he already knew the answer. He just wanted to make sure the story was consistent.

"Near Sian, in Shensi Province," replied Ilsa. "They say that there are hundreds of terracotta statues buried in an imperial tomb."

"Yes, I've heard about it," Hunt replied, turning to the girl. "I wonder how the piece got into the hands of the triad."

"Does it matter? My client wants to sell it and yours wants to buy it. We must agree on a price that is...*fair*."

The girl's voice had become velvety, and her eyes looked at the captain with obvious intention of seducing him. Hunt realized the turn of the negotiations. He left the artifact on the sideboard and approached the girl.

"How will we achieve that agreement?" He asked, following the game.

She took one of the thin straps of the dress and dropped it down the side of her shoulder. The neckline of the tight garment opened several centimeters, revealing the deep valley of her breasts. Hunt swallowed.

"I'm very good at negotiating," Ilsa said.

"I have a limited budget," the captain explained. "Believe it or not, I work for a museum."

Ilsa laughed, but to Hunt it seemed a fake laugh. Only one of the girl's eyes was visible, while the other remained hidden behind her hair, which covered half of her face. Hunt thought the eye had a special glow, but his instinct indicated that it was not one of passion, but rather of restlessness. The thick-lipped mouth also had a tension rictus. The captain was sure that it was not his presence that provoked it. His internal alerts were immediately activated.

When a light breeze stroked the side of his face, he squatted sharply. The bludgeon directed to his neck passed over him and only hit the air. Hunt stood up right away and turned at the same time to face his opponent, a sinister-looking Chinese who again brandished the thick black bludgeon. This time Hunt was prepared. He dodged the blow by quickly pushing his body away. He immediately threw an accurate kick to the attacker's shin. The man cursed in his language and threw himself over the captain with all his weight. The bludgeon hit Hunt on his shoulder before he could pull away. The captain couldn't stop a grimace of pain from peeking out on his face. The Chinese man gave out a malevolent smile.

Hunt blocked a new blow by raising his sore arm, causing a wave of pain that spread through half of his body. But he managed to immobilize his opponent. With a cry of fury, Hunt drove his right fist into the side of the Chinese's torso and dealt the edge of his left hand on the back of the man's neck. The thug snorted and fell to his knees to the ground, half hunched over in pain. However, he was not yet defeated. He tried to get on his feet immediately, but Hunt hit the back of his neck again and this time threw him face down on the carpet, where he lay unconscious.

The captain stood in front of the girl and looked at her with a furious expression. He lifted a finger up at her in a gesture of reprimand.

"Don't move, Captain!"

The man who gave him the order had entered the room quickly through the window, which opened onto a small balcony. In his hand he was holding a large pistol that was pointed at the center of Hunt's body.

Hunt deduced that both thugs had hidden on the balcony while he searched the room. Ilsa had not only led him into the trap, but then kept him distracted so that the criminals could enter surreptitiously. Hunt wished to give the girl a lesson, but first he had to confront the armed Chinese.

"Give money now!" the gunman demanded.

He spoke English with an atrocious accent and wore a long mustache with fallen tips that reminded Hunt of the celebrate literary villain Fu Manchu. The captain put his right hand inside the jacket.

"Slowly!" shouted the Chinese.

Hunt stood next to the girl, almost brushing her shoulder. Ilsa did not take her eyes off the gun that the intruder wielded. The captain made wild gesticulations with his right hand while pretending to rummage through the inner pocket of the jacket. At the same time, he slowly moved his left hand to the girl's back and then made it ascend, without touching her, to the shoulder. Still distracting the gunman, Hunt hooked a finger on the only strap holding the dress and gave it a strong tug.

The top of the dress fell forward, revealing Ilsa's upright breasts. Then the rest of the cloth slid down the girl's body and fell to her feet, before she could hold it. Fu Manchu opened his eyes wide and licked his lips in a reflexive gesture, while Ilsa tried to cover her breasts with one arm and the crotch with the other hand. Hunt didn't even look at her. He pulled out his Webley revolver like lightning, aimed at the hypnotized Chinese, and shot him in the eyes.

The gunman jumped back and fell to the ground. At the same time, Ilsa let out a scream of horror and leaned back. She fell on her back on the bed. Hunt threw himself towards the armillary sphere and terracotta arm, covered them with the velvet cloth, and put them under his arm. He immediately went to the open window, but as he passed by the bed, he looked at the girl with a stern expression.

"If I had time, I would give you a good spanking," he said.

She just shrank between the sheets.

Hunt stepped out onto the balcony, which overlooked an inner courtyard behind the hotel building. Above the courtyard, at the height of the roof and no more than one meter from where the captain was, several electrical cables crossed from one building to the other. Hunt took off his belt, ran it over the nearest cable, and formed a handle. He pulled hard down and found that the cable was resisting. Without stopping to think about it, he climbed over the balcony railing and threw himself out.

His own weight propelled him over the courtyard, hanging from the thick leather belt. The journey lasted only a few seconds, but going suspended over the void, six stories high, to Hunt seemed endless. He clung with all his strength to the makeshift hook and firmly held the valuable piece. Reaching the opposite end of the courtyard he propelled himself to another balcony and fell cleanly on the small platform. The belt was smoking from friction and was about to be cut into two halves. Hunt breathed a sigh of relief, but his heart was beating wildly.

From the balcony he jumped into a metal fire escape that zigzagged down the outside wall of the building. He ran down and when he reached the ground, he went through a portal that led to a garage. The other end of it opened to the street. Hunt held the sphere and terracotta arm clinging against his chest and continued without stopping until he turned the building around and returned to the Bund. There he paused for a moment, somewhat disoriented in the crowd. It was already the dead of the night, but the high traffic of vehicles and people had not diminished.

A sleek, slender Duesenberg Straight Eight touring car, which had the rear door open, stopped next to Hunt with a squeak from its hydraulic brakes. Hunt climbed into the running board and from there threw himself into the interior of the car, which departed as quickly as it had arrived. Hunt curled up in the back seat and regained his breath.

"Do you have the piece?" Sir John Connelly asked from the next seat.

For every answer, Hunt handed him the artifact.

The director of Department X of the British Museum was an aristocratic-looking man, fresh into the sixties. He had gray hair and beard, but he stayed in good shape. His energetic walking and an uptight bearing gave him a vitality that betrayed his true age. Sir John was a historian and university professor, although today he devoted all his time to the study of paranormal phenomena.

"It seems that the negotiations were arduous," he said in a phlegmatic voice as he looked askance at the captain.

He then removed the velvet cloth and examined the sphere and arm between the swings of the car, which was speeding away from the Palace Hotel. Hunt fixed his clothes and controlled the rhythm of his hectic breathing.

"The sellers were asking for a price impossible to pay," the captain said, for all accounts. "Fortunately, I was able to prevail in the haggling."

"Judging by the smell of gunpowder emanating from your jacket," Sir John said, "I guess the sellers didn't take it very well."

"They were not in a position to complain."

Sir John nodded with an almost imperceptible gesture, understanding the meaning of those words. However, he did not make any comment. The members of the triads were ruinous villains, and no one would miss them.

Hunt didn't say anything else either. From an inner pocket of the jacket, he extracted a small canvas bag, filled with Mexican silver dollars, and handed it to his boss. Sir John launched a funny laugh.

"The Board of Directors of the Museum will appreciate your efforts, my dear friend. And now, let's go eat something to tell me the details of your adventure."

"Maybe I should go to sleep," Hunt replied. That day started to feel too much long. "I can tell you the story on the journey back to London. We will have plenty of time."

"I'm afraid it won't be possible, Captain."

Hunt turned to his boss and looked at him with a surprised gesture.

"Won't we go back to London? We have passage on a steamer that departs tomorrow."

They planned this way the return trip to get the armillary sphere out of China as soon as possible. The Shanghai triad had acquired the piece suspiciously, to say the least, and in addition there were several secret groups and organizations that were also behind its powers.

"Only I will return on the steamer, Captain," Sir John reported. "Another matter awaits you."

Hunt raised an eyebrow.

"Our representative in the city, the same one who warned us of the sale of the sphere, contacted me this afternoon. He delivered an urgent message."

"Did another artifact appear for the Department's collection?" The captain asked.

The Chinese had an interesting and long

history of studies in the occult sciences. Sir John shook his head.

"This time it's not about that," the director replied. "I'm afraid it's a pretty serious matter." After a pause, he added: "Someone plans to launch a full-scale attack on England."

Hunt assimilated the news for a second. Then he commented:

"I don't doubt that it's a serious matter, but how does it relate to us?"

"The attack will be carried out with a magic weapon capable of destroying an entire city."

Sir John said it as if it were the most natural thing in the world.

3. HONAN ROAD

In 1843, at the end of the Opium War, of which it had been victorious, Great Britain obtained from China, the defeated, the right to establish settlements in several of its ports, including Shanghai, in order to trade with the increasingly demanded local products, such as tea, silk, and porcelain. At the same time, it allowed the British to continue selling opium to the Chinese, who consumed it in large quantities, although clearly that part of the deal was not reflected in the Treaty of Nanking, which ended the conflict.

Under the terms of the agreement, the territory granted in the treaty ports was subject to British law, and property within such settlements could be rented in perpetuity by foreign traders. The following year, the United States signed a similar treaty with China and established a concession in Shanghai, located north of the British. Later, to the south of it, the French also settled, having arrived in the city in 1848.

In 1854, the three powers created the Municipal Council, in charge of the management and regulation of the joint government of the concessions. However, France withdrew from the agreement in 1862 and continued separately. A year later, the American and British settlements merged to form the International Settlement. Sixty years later, the city of Shanghai had become a prosperous and huge metropolis, still controlled by foreigners, and devoted entirely to trade. Today there were more than a dozen nations that were part of the concession, which had its own laws, police force, military corps, postal service and even a symphony orchestra.

The settlement had all the goods and comforts that could be found in any large European or American city. There was everything from movie theaters and jazz clubs to luxury stores, where you could buy the same products just put on sale in London or New York. At the same time, for those tourists who wanted to take a souvenir of their trip, or for the more serious collectors looking for select items, there were also dozens of locals who sold Chinese products of the most different qualities.

The most distinguished antiques dealers had their shops on Honan Road, a small street in the center of the concession, parallel to the Bund. Captain Peter Hunt and his boss, Sir John Connelly, arrived there early in the morning. The rented Duesenberg, with chauffeur service included, left them in front of a discreet place whose bronze plaque only indicated Peng's in

English and in Chinese, Japanese and Cyrillic characters. Signs written in multiple languages were the norm throughout the concession, from road signs to advertisements.

A bell hanging by the door announced the entrance to the premises of the two British men. The interior was sparsely lit by multicolored silk lamps hanging from the ceiling. The place consisted of a spacious hall decorated with elegance, although in an abundant way. Ancient engravings, sets of porcelain plates, jade ornaments of various sizes, lacquered vases, tapestries with drawings and calligraphy, and military items, ranging from armors to swords, crowded all the available space. A soft scent of incense flooded the air of the shadowy hall.

A tall, slender middle-aged Chinese man watched the newcomers from behind a counter at the back of the store. It was so still that at first Hunt mistook him for a statue. But then the man bowed his head and gave them a wide smile as only the Orientals could hint.

"Welcome," he said in impeccable English.

"Captain Hunt," Sir John said, "let me introduce you to Manchester Peng *xiānshēng.*"

Peng would be about fifty years old and had a fully shaved face and head. He wore a traditional *changshan* costume, made of a long, loose jacket of embroidered blue silk and wide black pants. On his head he wore a round and flat cap, also made of silk, which covered his bald crown.

"A pleasure, captain," the antiques dealer greeted. "Please call me Chester."

Hunt raised an eyebrow. Then he stretched out his hand to him. Peng smiled again.

"My mother was English," he explained, using a tone of voice that showed he had had to tell that story countless times. "She came to the country as a missionary but fell in love with my father and adopted a Chinese lifestyle. However, when I was born, she felt homesick and wanted to remember her hometown."

The last part he said laughing. The two Englishmen smiled politely.

"Imagine my family and friends trying to pronounce that strange name," Peng continued. "Everyone called me *'Man Che Teng'*. When I discovered that many Americans bore the name "Chester," I also began to use it."

Hunt knew that the Chinese who lived in the treaty ports used to use a Western proper name next to their real surname, since their language was very difficult to pronounce by the *Laowai,* or foreigners. In Peng's case, such a difficulty extended even to his own countrymen.

"Fortunately, your mother didn't come from Wales or Cornwall," Hunt said. "You would have been in serious difficulties."

Even Sir John laughed at the occurrence, imagining someone named 'Llandudno' or 'Truro'. Peng smiled broadly and bowed his head again in agreement.

"It is also a pleasure for me to meet you, Chester *xiānshēng*," the captain added, using the local treatment equivalent to 'sir'.

"Just Chester, please," the antiques dealer insisted. "Come with me, gentlemen."

On the way from the Astor House Hotel, where they were staying, Sir John had explained to Hunt that Mr. Peng was the representative of the British Museum in China. Thanks to his invaluable services, the Department of Oriental Antiquities had acquired precious artifacts of the local culture, such as paintings, jade and lacquer objects, ceramic and bronze pieces, as well as dozens of scrolls and coins. That was his official function, at least. Secretly, Peng worked for Department X.

Thanks to this clandestine work, the antiques dealer was in permanent contact with secret and occult societies throughout the country. It was in this capacity that Peng had learned of the discovery of the piece of terracotta holding the armillary sphere. Among mystics and other enthusiasts of paranormal phenomena, rumor soon spread that the celestial sphere did not measure the solar system, but other distant worlds in the galaxy. Understanding that he had a good business on his hands, the owner had put the piece up for sale to the highest bidder.

Peng immediately sent a message to London, addressed directly to Sir John Connelly, who was very interested in acquiring the artifact. While the director was preparing for the long trip to Shanghai, his agent told him that he had discovered an important detail: the sellers of the piece were none other than the members of a triad. Undeterred on altering his plans, Sir John decided that he should be accompanied on the journey by his principal investigator, Captain Hunt. While the antiques dealer made the preliminary negotiations with those criminals, with the tact and discretion that only the Chinese themselves could use when relating to the societies of the underworld, the two English crossed half the world to put the artifact safe.

However, although he did not demonstrate it openly or express it verbally, Hunt had found it impractical to travel a month by ship to be only a few days in China and then make a similar return journey. He assumed that in dealing with the triad the matter could become dangerous, but he had not thought the effort was justified. That is why he was glad that his services were required for a new matter.

The antiques dealer guided them to an office located in the back room. Hunt took a seat next to Sir John, in front of a small carved desk, while Peng stood behind it. Both Englishmen leaned forward, ready to listen carefully to what that man was going to say.

"A couple of days ago a young missionary girl came to me," Mr. Peng began. "British, by the way.

He told me a fantastic story, hard to believe, but not entirely impossible."

Sir John pulled out his pipe and hung it from his lips. The antiques dealer picked up a silver lighter from a side table, but the professor shook his head. Hunt knew his boss no longer smoked, but he needed to hold the pipe to concentrate on the matters he deemed of great importance.

"Why did the girl come to you and not to the authorities?" Hunt asked, taking advantage of the pause. "Our consul or the City Council?"

"When I tell you the story, you will understand."

Peng then narrated to his visitors everything that nurse Mary Ann Taylor had told him, trying to repeat the same words that the girl had used in her nervous account of what happened that night in Yuyuan Garden. As the Chinese spoke, Hunt had leaned further and further forward, as if the story was physically catching him. Sir John, for his part, squeezed the pipe until his teeth were marked on the mouthpiece.

When Peng finished speaking, the two visitors looked at each other with an astonished gesture.

"That beheading... Would it be an execution?" Hunt asked. "I guess this man, Wang Min, belonged to some triad."

"It's most likely," the antiques dealer said. "However, in our country beheadings are frequent. In the Chinese part of the city,

Republican soldiers cut off the heads of any enemy of the government, from ordinary criminals to communist sympathizers."

"That means Wang's death must not have attracted attention," Sir John concluded.

Peng nodded.

"I'm sorry, Chester," Hunt said, this time cautiously. "But I can't understand why that woman came to you."

"Do you mean because I'm Chinese?"

Hunt tried to clear up, but Peng interrupted him with a wave of his hand.

"No, no, that's okay. I understand that, in other circumstances, the girl had trusted only in some of her compatriots, or at least, in a white man."

"However, many of the British missionaries know me quite well and trust me," he explained, without false modesty. "I was raised in the mission where my mother worked, I am a Christian, and I contribute large amounts of money to hospitals and missionary schools. Also, everyone knows that I am half English."

"I didn't mean to offend you, Chester," the captain hurriedly said. Peng repaid the explanation with a bow of his head. "Did you know the girl personally?"

"No. But she said she had seen me several times at Shantung Road Missionary Hospital parties and events. It is one of the institutions to which I contribute."

"And besides," Sir John ventured, "it is possible that she was aware of your occult activities."

"Probably. I am afraid that among the missionaries there are quite a few rumors about my... other interests."

"So did the girl come here directly after fleeing the garden?" asked Hunt, who was trying to reconstruct the events in his mind.

"On the night of Wang's murder, she hid somewhere and only came to see me the next morning," Peng continued. "As I said, this local is known among the British missionary community."

"Miss Taylor was very upset and asked me several questions before telling her story. First, she wanted to confirm that I *really* understood supernatural matters. Once she was convinced, and told me what happened, I told her that I would take care of the matter and recommended that she hide in a safe place.

"You say the girl was carrying a vial with crystals," Hunt said. "Do you have it with you?"

"She didn't bring it with her that morning," the antiques dealer explained. "I guess she didn't know if she could trust me. In any case, it was not necessary for me to see the contents of the vial."

"Because you knew already what that man... Wang?... was talking about", Sir John intervened.

Peng nodded solemnly.

"I'm afraid so. The reference to the "blood of the dragon" or *longxie* was unmistakable." Both Englishmen looked at him expectantly. "It is an alchemist compound made of cinnabar and other secret components. This element, in turn, is used to create another substance, called *taifengdan*, or "red typhoon," Peng said. "It is an ancient explosive weapon that is manufactured using a very complex spell developed by the Taoists. At present it is believed that its formula is lost."

During the long ship voyage from England, Sir John and Hunt had been instructed themselves in various subjects related to their place of destination, from the political situation in China in general, and that of Shanghai in particular, to the beliefs, mythology and occult practices of local secret societies. Most of the texts they had read mentioned Taoism, a religious and philosophical tradition that sought the harmony of the human being with the Tao, 'the way', or natural order of the universe.

As part of that harmonious quest, the Taoists of antiquity practiced alchemy to purify the body and spirit in order to achieve immortality. Over the centuries, Chinese alchemists had managed to develop powerful compounds and elixirs whose formulas were kept strictly secret, recorded in unique scrolls that only some *daoshi,* or Taoist monks, knew.

"How does that 'red typhoon' work, Chester?"

asked Hunt.

If that matter concerned a weapon, the captain's military training, and his experience in intelligence work during the war, would allow him to assess the threat. Magical or not, that weapon could be studied and countered.

"I don't know for sure, Captain. You must understand that the records of that time were very inaccurate, and reality was mixed with myths."

Peng rested his elbows on the surface of the desk and put the tips of the extended fingers of both hands together. His face remained impassive, as if he were practicing Zen meditation. After a moment, he said:

"Apparently it was gunpowder of great power mixed with the blood of the dragon (the compound of cinnabar), which was prepared by performing an alchemist spell."

"Hmm, interesting," Sir John said. "Gunpowder was invented here in China during the 9th century of the Christian Era. Therefore, I imagine that this *taifengdan* must be contemporary, or later, than that compound."

Gunpowder was another find of Taoist alchemists, who had invented it by accident by experimenting with their mixtures to achieve immortality. However, they soon understood that this element had better potential if it was used as a weapon.

"It is likely that the red typhoon developed

in the 11th century of the Western calendar," Peng said, nodding. "At that time, around the year 1040, the famous compendium *Wujing Zongyao* was written, a treatise describing the military technology of the time, including the formula of gunpowder. However, *taifengdan* is not mentioned there."

"Which indicates that its invention is later than the treatise," Hunt surmised.

"Or that it was such a secret weapon that its composition could not be revealed," Sir John said. "Are there accounts of the proven use of this weapon or was it just a theory?" he asked the local agent.

"There are Taoist texts that mention *taifengdan* at the time of the Song Dynasty," the antiquarian noted. "There are also some historical works describing the use of the weapon in the wars between the Song and the Jin dynasty of the Jurchen, which occurred between the 12th and early 13th centuries. But they are usually novelesque stories rather than exact chronicles of the war.

"Anyway," Hunt insisted, "I would like to know what was said about the weapon."

Peng nodded as he rummaged through the shelves of the office, from where he extracted old rolls of beautifully painted paper. Hunt recalled that paper was another Chinese invention that had been used long before it was brought to Europe in the 13th century. The antiques dealer unrolled the texts on the desk, with reverential care, and slowly examined their characters and drawings.

"Here it is," he said, after reviewing several passages of the scrolls. He read quietly, first in Chinese, and then translated it aloud to his guests:

"The author describes a sudden fireball thrown into the air, which exploded with great destructive power when it hit the target. According to some witnesses to the attacks, the *red typhoon* could destroy an entire village or wipe out an entire cavalry company in a matter of seconds. Other accounts describe it as a fiery wave of intense red color that reduced everything to ashes in its path."

The Englishmen looked at each other, astonished. If such an explosive could still be manufactured, and used against their country, it would cause destruction and death like never before.

"Oh my God!" Sir John exclaimed. He was impressed, even though in his life he had known not a few gadgets intended to create chaos and terrorize people. "Apparently, it is a weapon similar to the Greek fire used by the Byzantines in the Middle Ages."

"This is much worse," Hunt added. "Greek fire was a fiery liquid that was thrown at enemies through pipes or flamethrowers. Although it was very powerful, it was a material that only generated combustion. The *red typhoon,* on the other hand, is capable of detonating or generating an explosion of great magnitude."

Peng and Sir John looked at Hunt silently, admired for his knowledge of the subject. After a moment, the Director of Department X smiled.

"I knew I had to bring you with me on this trip, Captain. Somehow, I assumed things would get *hot.*"

Chester Peng approached a stove in a corner of the office and brewed *pu-erh* tea in a Yixing clay teapot. He let the hot water act on the copper-colored fermented leaves and then he poured the infusion in lidded porcelain bowls called *gaiwan.* While drinking the tea, Hunt continued to inquire into the missionary's extraordinary account.

"The crystals, this 'blood of the dragon', do we know where they come from?"

"It is likely that Wang obtained them from an alchemist," Peng said. "A Taoist monk, perhaps."

"Stolen, you mean. I imagine that cinnabar and the other compounds must be expensive and hard to come by."

Cinnabar was a sulfurous mineral like quartz, but reddish in color, composed of mercury and sulfur. Peng explained that it was widely used by Chinese alchemists, who made it burn to extract the 'liquid silver' with which they made their elixirs. The antiques dealer added with a serious tone that many monks, nobles and even emperors had died of mercury poisoning in search of their immortality.

"We must assume that someone is making this 'blood of the dragon'," the captain said. "And that he plans to create that *red typhoon* to use against England, or the English."

"That's the strangest thing," Sir John mused. "Who could be behind this matter?"

"To quote Wang's words," Hunt said, "'bad men'."

"Have him referred to his own companions in the triad?" asked Sir John, self-absorbed. He didn't stop puffing the pipe as if he were really smoking. "From the girl's description of that man Wang, he looked like an ordinary criminal."

"Yes, it's hard to imagine a triad performing alchemist rituals," Hunt agreed. "Although they took quite a bit of trouble to make sure they silenced their accomplice."

"Wang's murder was not the work of a triad," Peng denied, shaking his head. "At present, gangsters are limited to shooting their opponents. Based on what the girl described, I estimate the beheading to be a ritual death."

"The hooded figure who attacked Wang was a skilled swordsman, a true warrior," the antiquarian continued. "Only a martial artist can thus wield a *jian,* the traditional Chinese sword."

"According to classical Chinese accounts, martial warriors often help people," Hunt said.

"They are not hitmen."

"I see you've read some *wuxia* stories, Captain Hunt," Peng said, smiling.

He was referring to Chinese fantasy literature, whose tales spanned several centuries. These stories told the adventures of chivalrous warriors who traveled the country saving the oppressed thanks to their extraordinary combat skills.

"But I'm afraid that in real life," the antiques dealer insisted, "there are not only knights-errant. Assassins can also wield a sword."

"Wang arrived at the Missionary Hospital with a gunshot wound," Sir John reminded them. "Perhaps the triad tried to kill him, and failing, they sent this hooded warrior to complete the mission."

"Martial artists and alchemists," Hunt reflected. "What a combination."

"Welcome to China, Captain," Peng said.

Again, he had his fingers put together on the table and looked at him with a serious expression. Hunt poured himself another cup of *pu-erh* tea and his boss gestured to him to refill his *gaiwan* as well.

"I think we are overlooking the most important thing," Sir John said, after sipping the infusion. "Why do these men want to attack our country?"

"In Shanghai they don't want us," Hunt said. "Our settlement rights are called *unequal treaties* by the Chinese. Many argue that the agreements were imposed on the emperor and that the new republic should terminate them as soon as possible."

Peng nodded imperceptibly, for he knew that the captain was right. The Qing Dynasty had been humiliated after the Opium War and forced to surrender several free ports for trade, but in 1911 the empire was overthrown during the Xinhai Revolution and the republic was established. Both nationalists and their communist opponents constantly denounced the excessive privileges of foreigners in China and demanded their expulsion. In Shanghai there had been numerous massive demonstrations against the treaties and several foreign nationals had been killed.

"You, Chester," Sir John asked, "do you think this issue could be of a *political* nature?

He uttered the word almost with aversion, as if he found such a motivation more incredible than the use of a magic weapon to achieve the goals of its possessors. Peng, for his part, maintained his Zen expression as he replied:

"No, gentlemen, I don't think so. Right now, China is in chaos, without a united and strong central government. All parties are ruled by warlords. In Shanghai, outside of foreign concessions, criminal gangs and conspirators are on the rise."

"But none of them would be able to obtain

these ancient secrets or achieve martial training like the one that was told to me. No, I am convinced that this is the work of a more intelligent and subtle enemy. And, therefore, much more dangerous."

The English remained silent for an instant, not knowing what to say in the face of the logic of what their host had exposed. After a moment, Sir John got up and began to walk around the office.

"How I would like to smoke again," he said, looking wistfully at his extinguished pipe.

Hunt also stood up, unable to continue sitting. He felt the adrenaline running through his veins and his body was asking for action.

"We must find out who is behind this affair and when they plan to carry out the attack. They are already three days ahead."

Sir John consulted a pocket watch he extracted from the waistcoat of his suit.

"It's getting late. I must return to the hotel to collect my luggage. The steamer will depart within a few hours."

"Don't worry. I will continue with the investigation," Hunt announced. "With the invaluable help of Chester *xiānshēng,* of course."

The antiques dealer bowed slightly.

"Just Chester, captain."

"Call me Peter, dear friend."

"I know I leave this matter in good hands." Sir John stepped forward and shook hands with both men. "Keep me informed, Captain Hunt. The steamer will stop at several ports where I will be able to pick up mail."

"I hope to have this affair solved before your first stop," Hunt said, showing a confidence superior to what he really felt at that moment.

He still did not know where his inquiries would begin, but he was sure that he would not waste a single moment in starting his task. Together with Peng they accompanied Sir John to the waiting car and then returned to the office.

"Do you drink, Chester?" The captain asked. The antiques dealer looked at him in surprise. "We will need something stronger than *pu-ehr* tea if we want to be prepared for our mission."

Peng nodded with his usual solemnity. He approached a cabinet and extracted a bottle of whisky from inside. Hunt smiled at the sight of the Glenlivet's label. The antiques dealer poured two full glasses and raised his own, saying:

"'If you know the enemy and know yourself, you need not fear the result of a hundred battles'. Sun Tzu."

"*The Art of War,*" Hunt said. "Very appropriate."

4. FRENCH CONCESSION

A huge and gleaming Hispano-Suiza H6 luxury sedan headed with an elegant rhythm down a narrow street flanked by tall shade plane trees, whose tops intertwined over the roadway, forming a pleasant green canopy that protected from the afternoon heat. The quiet neighborhood, made up of modern houses surrounded by large gardens, could have been found perfectly in any of the distinguished residential districts of Paris. However, it was located more than nine thousand kilometers from the French capital.

To the south of Avenue Edward VII, which ran through Shanghai from the Bund to the west, extended the territory granted to France shortly after signing an arrangement similar to that of the British. Initially, the concession was much smaller than that of its neighbors, but it had expanded through some complementary treaties. Now occupied the entire area to the north and west between the International Settlement and the ancient Chinese city. The expansion had favored the construction of new residential sectors, desired by foreigners and wealthy Chinese.

The car stopped in front of a sturdy wooden gate that crossed a high brick wall, crowned in turn by a thick bush of bougainvillea. Behind the wall loomed the flowering branches of a magnolia, which almost completely concealed the magnificent four-story house that stood inside the property. The driver, a burly former officer in the Imperial Russian Army, gave two short touches to the car's deep horn. Almost immediately, a couple of Chinese opened the gate pushing its two doors with great effort.

The Hispano-Suiza crossed the entrance as soon it had barely enough space to pass. The servants stood on the opposite side of the gate and pushed back to close it. Even if there had been a curious bystander passing through the street at that time, he would not have been able to see more than a brief glimpse of the interior of the property. The owner was a man very jealous of his privacy. Not even the neighbors knew his identity, because he rarely saw him. He only entered and left the house in a car with the windows covered by curtains.

The heavy vehicle rolled slowly along the access road, crossing the well-kept garden until it surrounded a large fountain that launched delicate jets of water. Finally, it stopped by the front door of the house. The driver got off and opened the back door of the car. He wasn't supposed to look closely at the beautiful girl who descended with graceful movements from the inside, but he admired anyway her curves with disguised desire.

On the face of the young Chinese woman, about twenty-five years old, stood out large eyes with long eyelashes that flickered like the delicate wings of a butterfly. Her hair, black and silky, was held by a jade *fa-zan* pin. The girl wore a tight *cheongsam,* the traditional Chinese dress, made of pastel white silk and adorned with flowers embroidered with golden threads. The girl's delicate arms and toned legs were exposed, while the rest of her voluptuous body struggled against the tight fabric. From her right shoulder hung a small black leather bag.

A uniformed butler opened the door for her without her knocking. With a wave of his hand, the butler motioned for the girl to move into a spacious lobby. The interior of the house was sumptuous and was decorated with exquisite Chinese antiques. It would have been tasteful had it not been for the fact that the pieces were stolen or smuggled in. The owner of that house was one of the most notorious criminals in Shanghai and eastern China. The girl, aware of such a situation, waited with a low gaze for the appearance of her host.

"Mei Ling *xiǎojiě* has arrived, master," the butler announced loudly.

Then, without even looking at the girl, he left leaving her alone.

Although the man had called her "Miss,"

her cold welcome meant that he had not been fooled by her appearance. Mei Ling was a 'sing-song' girl, a courtesan trained to entertain her male companions through singing and dancing, as well as providing her sexual services. In many circles, these girls were considered true artists. However, for the more conservative Chinese, they were no more than mere prostitutes.

A few minutes later the sliding doors of an imposing study opened, and the owner of the house came to receive the beautiful girl. Tony 'the mountain' Lu, businessman for the public and leader of the Green Gang for his acquaintances, was a gigantic and thick man who made a great impression with his mere presence. He wore a luxurious silk robe printed in various colors and covered his bald head with a round black hat. His narrow eyes, almost hidden by the fat cheeks, opened widely at the sight of the girl. His mouth made a disgusting grimace that appeared to be a smile.

"The beautiful Mei Ling," the gangster greeted in a shrill voice. "Finally, a pleasant break from business."

Behind that mole were several men inside the study, all of them of reprehensible appearance. They argued loudly and gesticulated at each other. Two bodyguards closed the doors again, and the noise of the study became an unintelligible murmur. Lu came to the girl and looked at her with ardor.

"Let's go to the bedroom," he ordered.

With a thunderous slap on her butt, he led Mei Ling towards the stairs. She laughed like a little girl and preceded the mighty man to the second floor. He ascended with his eyes fixed on the undulating movement of her hips. The bodyguards were going after their boss, but he barked at them an order before entering the bedroom next to the girl. The two men quickly vanished.

The room was huge. The bed, which was twice the size of an ordinary double bed, had been specially designed to accommodate the great humanity of Mountain Lu. Next to the bed, a bedside table held a lit lamp that provided the only light to the room. The curtains were drawn, and the rest of the room was in darkness. In the center of the chamber was a normal-sized therapist's stretcher that looked unable to bear the weight of the gigantic gangster.

Lu closed the door behind him and pounced on the girl. His fat hands ran over the beautiful body, squeezing it with desperation, but somehow the courtesan managed to get away from her enormous client. He looked at her in surprise.

"First the massage," she said, with a professional tone.

The Green Gang was Shanghai's main criminal organization. Its origins dated back to an obscure sect of river transporters founded two hundred years ago, during the Qing Dynasty. Today, its activities included opium trafficking, extortion, gambling and prostitution. The dual jurisdiction of the city's foreign concessions made proper administrative and police regulation difficult, which favored crime and smuggling. At the height of that underground empire was Tony Lu, the fearsome 'Mountain', a man who took orders from nobody, whose fury was legendary against those who made him angry.

However, inside his room he obeyed meekly. Mei Ling was his favorite sing-song girl and the most expert of all those who attended to him. He knew that all good things would come if he knew how to wait. He threw the hat on the ground and took off his robe with a resigned expression, giving quick slaps, until he was completely naked in front of the girl. Concealing her disgust, Mei Ling smiled as if she was contemplating a work of art.

Lu lay flat on his face on the stretcher, which bended and creaked under his weight. Mei Ling left the bag on a side table next to the stretcher and extracted oils, lotions and sticks of incense. For several minutes, the girl arranged the bowls with the scented substances and prepared several towels to dry the body after applying them. Then she lit the incense and waited for its scent to flood the interior of the room. Finally, she took a breath, taking care that the giant on the stretcher did not see the gesture of apprehension, and got to work.

She covered the gangster's wide back with oil and proceeded to massage the man's hard skin with gentle and efficient gestures. The body, tense and sweaty, was covered with tattoos and scars. Lu Ho Teng had been born fifty years ago in a miserable village in the inner region of Shanghai, from which he had made his way to the big city thanks to his imposing bearing and exceptional cruelty. His whole life was linked to crime and secret societies, in whose ranks he had risen quickly and ruthlessly. His dead enemies numbered in the hundreds, and his current minions in the thousands.

Mountain Lu was the most powerful man in Shanghai, as well as being the most feared. However, Lu knew that among foreigners his mere presence was not enough to be accepted, even if he had to do business with them. On the contrary, his fame only brought him discredit. To achieve even a patina of respectability, he called himself Tony and contributed to charity through his legal dealings, which allowed him to attend the meetings of the Municipal Board of Directors of the French Concession, where most of his foreign contacts operated.

Such a man had no rest and could not live in peace. His only moments of relaxation were the weekly visits of Mei Ling, who massaged or danced for him before taking him to bed and showing him her true talent. Those delicate hands worked wonders on his hardened body. The tension subsided and Lu soon fell into a state of drowsiness. The girl noticed that the muscles were softening and that the hoarse breathing became rhythmic. She raised her hands on the man's back and looked down that indecent body as if inspecting an ancient map. A moment later her fingers searched for the points she had traced in the imaginary drawing, and she was squeezing the skin following a pre-established order. With rapid movements the fingers covered the area between the shoulders, the base of the neck and the center of the spine. When the finger dance was over, the most powerful man in Shanghai was completely motionless and couldn't even speak.

Lu woke up suddenly and had a feeling he hadn't experienced for many years: fear. His brain sent commands to his limbs and muscles, but these did not respond. It was as if they weren't there. He opened his mouth, or so he thought he was doing. He cried for help, but unless his ears had also disappeared, he could not hear the words he had formed in his mind. His heart raced from terror and his skin was covered with cold sweat.

"You're paralyzed," the girl explained. Although it seemed like an obvious information, she wanted him to know that it had been her work. "Try to breathe normally and nothing will happen to you."

The huge gangster snorted, unable to remain still. His face twitched in a strange grimace; his features hardened.

"I know you have a safe in this room," said the girl. "Show me with your eyes where it is."

Lu couldn't believe what was happening. He had known the girl for months and had never taken her more than for a prostitute. Beautiful and talented in the arts of love, but a courtesan after all. Now, instead, Mei Ling had another attitude. Confident, cold and ruthless. Even her voice was different, more serious and authoritarian. The Mountain evaluated his possibilities and directed his eyes – he could not move his head even a millimeter – towards a painting that hung on the wall, next to the bed. The girl picked it up and revealed the door of the safe.

"The key?"

Lu blinked to remove the sweat from his eyes and showed her with a glance that the key was in a drawer on the bedside table.

The girl used the key to remove the security lock and extracted the contents from inside the safe. On the bed she threw documents, drug caches, money in currency from various countries and some jewelry. She then pushed both hands to the end of the safe and carefully took out a finely engraved vermilion-red lacquered wooden chest. She opened the chest, about thirty centimeters long, and from inside she extracted a roll of paper tied with a leather ribbon.

Mei Ling unrolled the manuscript, almost a meter wide, and examined it sitting at the foot of the bed. It was beautifully painted, with bright drawings and classic calligraphy. The paper creaked as the sheet spread, revealing its antiquity. The girl smiled. Before her was the Spell of the Red Typhoon. However, she showed no signs of anxiety or of being in a hurry to leave.

From the stretcher, Lu looked at her with exorbitant eyes and cursed in his mind. The insults he imagined only emanated from his mouth in the form of a thread of saliva that ran down his chin. After a moment, Mei Ling came to him with the roll in her hand and held it in front of the giant's face.

"I'm going to let you speak. If you yell or say something I don't like, I'm going to kill you. You know I can do it, right?"

Lu blinked violently until he saw her nod. Then she leaned over him and he felt she touched some points on his back with her fingertips. Suddenly, he felt a breath of air filling his lungs. He coughed and managed to articulate a few words.

"You're a damn thief!"

The sharp slap that pierced his face was not expected. Despite the thickness of his cheeks, he felt his face burn with pain.

"You'll speak when I order it!"

The girl waved the roll in front of Lu's eyes.

"You were commissioned to obtain this manuscript," she said, reminding him of the assignment. "But instead of honoring your contract with the client, you had a better idea, right? You were thinking of selling the roll to the highest bidder."

Lu made a choked sound, and his body shuddered. Who was really that girl? The gangster understood that he had underestimated the man who hired him to locate the scroll. Lu had assumed that he was a mere wealthy collector who could be fooled, but now he realized that the client was more cunning than him. He had infiltrated the girl into his inner circle to keep an eye on him and make sure he got the merchandise he had bought. Lu felt humiliated and knew that he had made too big a mistake.

"No!" he babbled, "it's not true..."

Mei Ling hit his face again. Lu's sight became cloudy, and he felt a tooth loosen. He said to himself he wouldn't make it out of there alive, but terror kept him from screaming for help. He knew that the scroll was valuable, *very valuable,* but nothing mattered anymore.

"Damn stupid!" Mei Ling exclaimed, in a voice full of contempt. "You never knew what you had in your hands."

The girl shook her head and leaned back over

the gangster's motionless body. It didn't matter what he might say. She had already fulfilled her mission. Then she played her macabre dance with her hands, going through the strategic points of his back. A sharp pain swept across Tony 'The Mountain' Lu's body.

The girl took a few steps away from the man so that he could see her well. She again adopted her submissive position as a sing-song girl and threw out one of her silly laughs that he was used to.

"Oh, Master Tony, how sorry I am! I hope you enjoyed your last massage. Too bad that your tired heart did not resist Mei Ling's caresses."

The gangster was about to faint as a result of the fear that invaded his body, but the girl's deadly technique acted faster. The blood that ran through the veins started to boil and circulated at high speed through the interior of the body, returning to the heart faster than what the organ managed to send back. The heart swelled, it couldn't keep pumping more blood, and finally burst out. A trail of blood flowed from Lu's mouth, through his nose and ears. After one last rattle, the body of the Mountain was motionless on the stretcher.

Not deigning to look at the corpse, Mei Ling fixed her hair and straightened her dress. She kept the roll inside a towel and then stuffed it into her bag. She walked out of the room quietly and slowly closed the door behind her. One of the bodyguards was leaning against the wall at the end of the staircase. He was a short, brute man who called himself the Bear.

"Master Tony is sleeping," the girl explained. "He ordered no one to disturb him."

"You left him exhausted, huh?" The Bear commented, with a lascivious smile on his lips. "It didn't take long for you this time."

She showed a restrained expression and lowered her gaze. The other bodyguard was at the opposite end of the hallway. He was tall and taciturn. The other guards called him the Tiger. Mei Ling saw from the corner of her eye that the Tiger was heading to the door of the main bedroom.

"The boss is asleep," the Bear explained, in whispers.

"I'll just check that he's okay," replied the Tiger.

He opened the door and peeked inside.

Mei Ling took advantage of the distraction of the Bear, who stared at the bedroom, to pass by him and go downstairs at a brisk pace. She was halfway by the stairs when she heard the Tiger's cry of horror. The Bear was startled, but immediately turned to the girl.

"Hey, you, stop there!"

Mei Ling ran away. The guard jumped down the steps and caught up with her before she could reach the first floor. The girl turned around and punched him in the face. The Bear didn't expect it. The blow broke his nose, and he began to bleed copiously. However, he was a strong man and did not pay attention to his wound. He recovered from the blow immediately and threw himself towards the girl. He tried to grab her arm, but Mei Ling moved so fast that the Bear blinked believing it had been his imagination. The girl stood by his side, grabbed him by the arm and left him trapped in a hold. The man howled helplessly — like a wounded bear, she thought — and used his brute force to break free. The girl squeezed his arm to immobilize him and then pushed him face first against the wall. The guard's head slammed with a sharp noise. Mei Ling let go of the body, which fell disheveled rolling over the steps.

The Tiger appeared at the top of the stairs, with a gun in his hand. He ran down as he raised the gun to point at the girl. Mei Ling came to the lobby and threw herself to catch a luxurious ceramic vase adorning a side table. She raised the vase above her head and threw it directly towards the Tiger, who was already coming down the middle of the stairs. The guard stretched out his arm to shoot, but the vase hit him in the hand and the shot was deflected. The Tiger continued his race and came to the lobby.

From there he aimed at Mei Ling again and fired several times, launching screams of fury. The girl rolled on the ground, got up again, and ran over a sofa. Then she threw herself onto a table and ran over it. The Tiger turned his body with the gun raised and kept shooting, trying to catch up with the girl with its sights. But she was moving very fast. All the shots fell short. In the lobby, ornaments, lamps and a window burst. The guard continued to pull the trigger until he emptied the magazine, not realizing that only a few metallic clicks could be heard.

Mei Ling rushed to her opponent, who just watched her, dumbfounded. The girl jumped, threw a kick while in the air, and fell behind the guard. The Tiger only saw a shadow coming over him and then his head burst into wild pain. His body took a turn and went backwards. Blackness engulfed him and he was unconscious before falling with his back to the ground, several meters from where the girl was. She only allowed herself a second to catch her breath and then headed for the exit.

Mei Ling slammed open the front door of the house. On the other side he found the Russian driver, who was on the entrance porch with his Nagant M1895 revolver in his hand. The man, surprised, stepped back to raise his gun. The girl squatted down, and the shot went over her head. She immediately stood up again and threw herself on the Russian. He fired again, but the young woman had already taken his hand and with all her weight forced him to lift it. The shot departed into the sky. The driver tried to push the girl away, but she twisted his arm and then jumped over him, without letting go. A shuddering crunch was heard as the arm split, as the body turned in the opposite direction. Mei Ling landed on the ground again, behind the staggering Russian, and hit him with the edge of her hand at the base of his neck. The man fell to his knees, his head down, and stood there motionless, like a penitent who was asleep.

The young woman walked hurriedly towards the Hispano-Suiza that was parked next to the water fountain. She jumped behind the wheel, started the engine, and rolled back down the road to the outer gate. The two servants at the entrance looked at her in fear. She leaned out the front window.

"Open the gate if you don't want to die!" she shouted at them.

The two men ran to push the heavy wood doors. The girl accelerated the car, passed through the opening, and got lost down the street.

It was already dark. Only a few cars and one or another tram circulated through the quiet streets of the residential district. Rickshaws pulled by coolies did not usually arrive in that area, nor were many pedestrians seen on the sidewalks. However, Mei Ling knew that the Hispano-Suiza was an attention-grabbing car. She abandoned it shortly after in front of a large mansion. Anyone walking around would assume that the vehicle belonged to the property owner.

The girl continued the rest of the way on foot. Although her short dress was eye-catching, not to mention how unusual it was to see a Chinese woman walking alone during the night, she managed to go unnoticed during her journey. She stayed away from streetlights, used narrow alleys and avoided crossing paths with the few pedestrians who wandered at that time. Finally, she arrived at a luxurious apartment building of recent construction, located in the western sector of the French Concession, in which exclusively wealthy foreigners lived.

After inspecting the building for several minutes, to make sure that no one was watching, Mei Ling went around it and approached the back. The courtyard was silent, and light could be seen only in some of the windows. A metal fire escape climbed zigzagging through the center of the brick wall. The girl went up the stairs in complete silence, lighter than the gentle breeze blowing that night. She stopped on reaching the top floor and opened the sash window overlooking the staircase, sliding the panel slowly so as not to produce any noise. She snuck inside and crouched behind a huge sofa, while analyzing the situation.

She was in a spacious living room decorated with antique and heavy furniture of European style. A floor lamp dimly illuminated the room. The tobacco smell permeated the air and somewhere a gramophone played an opera at low volume. Mei Ling moved forward stealthily, her back leaning against the wall. Adjacent to the living room was an office containing several shelves and a large central desk. The only light came from a table lamp with a green screen.

Sitting behind the desk was a middle-aged man, dressed in a smoking jacket, inspecting an open book with the help of a monocle. His hair was beginning to gray, but the pointed beard and mustache with erect ends remained a gleaming black. A cigarette was burning next to him, on a Bohemian glass ashtray.

"Well?" The man suddenly asked, in English, without looking up.

Mei Ling was startled but remained motionless. She guessed that she hadn't been quiet enough, after all. As if the man had read her thought, he added:

"The cigarette smoke trembled with the breeze coming through the window," he explained. He raised his head and looked at the girl directly. "I would never have been able to hear you. Even less so during *Siegfried's Funeral March.*"

With a nod of his head, he pointed to the gramophone located in a corner. The girl nodded almost imperceptibly and walked over to the desk. The man gave the *cheongsam* a scrutinizing look but said nothing. Mei Ling knew that he never lent himself to frivolities and he would never insinuate to her. However, she was sure that he found her attractive anyway.

"Well?" The man repeated. "Do you have it?"

The girl stood in front of the desk and with both hands stretched out the roll towards the man, while bowing.

"Here it is, mister consul."

5. LONGHUA TEMPLE

Following Sir John Connelly's departure, Captain Hunt decided to renew the lease of the Duesenberg tourer. Only this time he preferred to do without the driver to be able to drive the car himself. The day after his meeting with Chester Peng, he picked up the antiques dealer at his Honan Road shop early in the morning. From there they headed south, following Peng's directions. They traversed the French Concession and the old Chinese city and continued to the suburbs of Shanghai. At the end of a dusty road, not far from the Whangpoo River, stood a magnificent Buddhist temple in the village of Longhua.

The temple complex occupied an area of more than twenty thousand square meters, surrounded by beautiful gardens designed by renowned classical landscapers. The original temple dated from 242 AD but had been rebuilt several times throughout its history. The current structure followed the architecture of the Song Dynasty, which ruled China from the middle of the 10th century to the end of the 13th. The main buildings were arranged on a north-south axis, almost two hundred meters long. From the entrance there were five large halls, a bell tower, the main library and, at the end, an imposing seven-level pagoda.

"The abbot is a good friend of mine," Peng explained as they got out of the car. "He will certainly be able to guide us on the trail of that mysterious murderer."

"I believed that Buddhists monks were only engaged in meditation," Hunt said.

"To a large extent, yes. But some of them are also experts in other areas of knowledge. Come on, you'll see."

They entered through a high portal, beautifully decorated, which opened into the perimeter wall. From there, an extensive tiled courtyard led to the first hall. A few monks roamed the gardens, but no one paid attention to the visitors. They took a gravel road that ran along the side of the buildings. The path was flanked by statues of religious motifs and peach trees that cast a pleasant shade. The visitors left behind the first two halls and finally went to the third of the buildings that made up the axis of the constructions.

The main hall of Buddhist temples, called *Mahavira,* was the largest and most important building in each complex. Like the other halls of the temple, the *Mahavira* of Longhua had the walls painted a vivid orange-yellow color and was covered by a roof of long eaves whose tips were curved upwards. As the antiques dealer had explained to the captain, as they made their way to the complex, Buddhist temples were built to inspire inner peace and represent the purity of Buddha's surroundings.

Visitors took off their shoes at the entrance of the building and entered barefoot into the hall. The interior was decorated with three large golden statues of Buddha, in different manifestations, along with two effigies of his disciples. In addition, there was a bas-relief depicting Guanyin, a female manifestation of a *bodhisattva*. At the back of the hall stood sixteen golden statuettes of the chief *arhats,* disciples who had reached the maximum state of understanding, or nirvana. The place was silent and only the distant singing of some monks could be heard. Chester Peng lit some incense sticks that he extracted from a dispenser located next to the entrance and deposited them at the feet of a large figure showing Buddha sitting in the lotus position.

A moment later they were approached by a *bhikkhu* monk. He had his hair cropped very short and wore a simple dark grey robe, called *jiāshā,* wrapped around his body. Hunt did not attempt to shake his hand and kept his arms to his back. Monks performed purification rituals and could not be touched by strangers. Peng spoke to the monk in the dialect of Shanghai. Then he turned to the captain.

"The *fangzhang* cannot receive us now," he

explained. He was referring to the abbot of the temple, the superior of the other monks. "He's leading a *wushu* training."

"Do you mean *kung fu?*" asked Hunt with interested tone. "I would like to observe the training, if possible."

In English, Chinese martial arts were known as *kung fu.* These disciplines had been practiced for many centuries in various styles of combat and self-defense inspired by ancient philosophy, religion and legends. One of the most renowned techniques was the one that had been developed by *Shaolin* Buddhist monks.

Peng translated the captain's request. The monk just nodded, turned around and started walking. The visitors retrieved their shoes at the entrance and then set off behind the monk. The *bhikkhu* guided them to the last building of the complex, a splendid pagoda with an octagonal base, forty meters high. The tower consisted of seven levels surrounded by red balustrade balconies, covered with curved-pointed roofs. As they approached it, the antiquarian explained that the pagoda had been erected almost a thousand years ago and had long been the tallest structure in Shanghai.

At the foot of the tower stretched a large courtyard where *kung fu* training took place. On one side of the field, it had been arranged a stand in which a dozen older monks were seated. Behind the stand stood the *sāmaṇera* novices of the temple. Hunt saw that there were from young children to teenagers. Only at the age of twenty could a novice become a monk. They all wore simple grey robes wrapped around their bodies.

In the middle of the courtyard, about thirty monks performed in unison exercises with arms and legs. All of them dressed in loose robes that gave them freedom of movement to practice punches, kicks, grips and projections. All the fighters were moving at the same time, training in complete silence, with their features contracted by concentration. To Hunt it seemed like a perfect choreography of a dance corps.

A few minutes later the group disbanded. The monks arranged themselves in pairs to practice the fighting. Suddenly the fighters were locked in fast and fierce fights, hitting with their hands and feet at an incredible speed. However, the rivals managed to stop and deflect the attacks with ease, as if they knew the movements in advance. The fighters moved with great fluidity and their bodies twisted in positions that defied the laws of physics. When a wrestler failed to land a fist punch, he used his legs and arms to catch the opponent and spin him in the air. Hunt saw several monks get thrown away by an opponent's projection maneuver.

When the round of combat was over, the winners of each fight formed new pairs between them. Training resumed immediately, with none of the monks showing symptoms of fatigue. After a while there were less than ten fighters left on the field, who continued to throw fierce blows and kicks, jumping on their opponents and clinging in tight holds. Little by little some of the fighters fell and new couples emerged immediately, without rest. Hunt was in awe about the endurance of those men. He imagined that they had to train constantly and brutally, to the limit of exhaustion.

Finally, the last two monks engaged in the final combat. Both were young, agile and tough. The fighting was intense and relentless. They immediately attacked with fierce punches and hit the opponent with the outstretched edge of their hands, but the impacts did not seem to have an effect on them. The strong kicks they received only ripped out faint grunts of pain. At one point one of them was trapped by the other, but then it was this one that was throw away projected by the first one. However, none of the opponents fell. The exchange of attacks was so rapid that it was difficult to follow the course of the fight.

Hunt felt his heart beating fast, anxious to know which of the monks would win. Each of them turned on and dodged the opponent, while continuing to attack with fierce onslaughts. None stopped looking the other in the eye, letting fists and feet act almost on their own. For a moment, the captain thought that those men could go on like this for hours. Until one of them was distracted only a second and the other took advantage of the slightest opportunity. He took his rival between his legs, lifted him over his own body, and with a twist threw him on his back. The other wrestler tried to fall on his feet and almost succeeded, but his opponent anticipated the move and jumped and kicked him in the chest. The rival burst forth away and rolled on the hard dirt floor.

The *sāmaṇera* novices erupted in applause. The *fangzhang* gave them a look over his shoulder, and the jubilation was immediately silenced. The winner of the match went with a submissive attitude to the abbot, bowing his head to him as a sign of respect. From that position he whispered something in the ear of the superior. The abbott pondered for a moment, and then nodded with an almost imperceptible gesture. The same *bhikkhu* who had guided the visitors to the driving range approached them on the side of the courtyard. He spoke in his language in a solemn voice, addressing Peng. The antiques dealer then turned to Captain Hunt.

"Monk Li Chen wishes to demonstrate his art to the foreign visitor," Peng announced.

Hunt gave a look to such Li Chen, who was waiting standing in front of the stand of the senior monks. Then he said to Peng:

"I have never practiced this discipline."

"It would be impolite if you declined the

invitation, Captain," whispered the antiques dealer. "It is an honor to fight a monk."

"Yes, of course," he muttered in turn. Then he swallowed and forced his best smile. Out loud he said: "It will be a pleasure to accept the offer."

Hunt took off his suit jacket and tie and rolled up his shirt sleeves. Li Chen was waiting for him in the center of the training ground, in front of the stand occupied by the older monks. By standing in front of the winner of the match, Hunt was able to study him well for the first time. He was tall and nervy, with an undaunted face and cold eyes. Like the other Buddhists, he sported his hair close-cropped. Hunt calculated that he would be in his early thirties.

The captain asked to himself if the monk had invited him to the demonstration just to humiliate or mock him. It was known that in China they did not want foreigners. The older men sitting in the stands looked at the white man with a neutral expression, but Hunt noticed frowns on some onlookers. Among the *sāmaṇera,* on the other hand, there was tension by the unusual combat. Several young men murmured among themselves until the *fangzhang* ordered them to shut up. The rest of the monks watched from the other side of the courtyard, in the shade of the pagoda. Hunt noticed that the abbot was staring at him intensely and deduced that the combat was a kind of test for him, though not just of a physical type.

During his time in the army, Hunt had practiced boxing and some wrestling. He hoped that his knowledge would serve to defeat, or at least contain, that monk. He raised his fists in front of his face and prepared for the onslaught. Li Chen greeted him with a brief bow and immediately attacked him. Hunt managed to deflect a couple of accurate blows that his rival threw at him with his hands, but he neglected the lower part of his body and Li took immediate advantage. The monk crouched down and performed a swift sweep with his legs. Hunt lost his balance and fell backwards on the hard dirt floor.

Several laughs were heard among the novices. Hunt stood up as worthily as he could and greeted the victor with his head. Li Chen instructed him to stand in front of him again. Hunt maintained a serious expression but wondered how long that trance would last. It was evident that it would be very difficult to defeat his opponent. His agility and speed were astounding. Hunt hadn't even managed to throw a punch and the Chinese had already beaten him. Resigned, the captain again adopted a position of defense and prepared for the confrontation.

This time the fighting lasted a little longer, but it still didn't come close to the extent of the fighting that had taken place between the monks. Hunt managed to retreat to Li's leg attacks, but when he punched the monk, he grabbed his arm with a hold and used his own body as an impulse to throw Hunt over him. Hunt slammed hard into the ground. Pain swept through his body and his suit was dirty and ruined. This time even the other monks laughed. The captain stood up with difficulty, but to the amazement of the onlookers, he stood in front of Li Chen again. Now Hunt was angry.

The monk gave a hint of a minimal smile. Hunt understood that the bastard was enjoying his humiliation. He thought that on the third attempt he would have to act faster if he did not want to be beaten again. When Li attacked, Hunt anticipated his movements and deflected both hand punches and kicks. Silence fell sharply on the training ground. All the spectators saw that the foreigner was learning. Li also noticed. Hunt discovered that the monk's gaze was more cautious, and his maneuvers became slower. The Chinese was also studying him.

Hunt decided to wait for the other to attack. If he threw himself into confrontation, he was lost. After a moment, Li resumed his attacks, faster and fiercer. It was no longer a simple demonstration. Hunt tried to surprise his rival with a few blows when he approached him, but the monk diverted them easily. For his part, the captain received several hits in his torso and arms. He cursed silently and held back the pain. He tried to sweep his opponent with his legs, but the monk avoided it by jumping and twisting over him. Hunt turned immediately, but Li grabbed him from behind and immobilized him.

The captain understood that only in physical strength did he surpass Li. When he tried to knock him down, Hunt pushed himself back, his body loose as a dead weight, and dragged the Chinese in his fall. Using a wrestling hold, he grabbed his opponent and carried his full force on him. Li couldn't stop Hunt from falling on him. Both were left lying on the ground. The monk scrambled furiously, but Hunt stretched out his arms and legs and kept him trapped under his body. He waited a full minute, while his rival struggled unsuccessfully, before releasing him and standing up.

The monks who had been witnessing the fighting advanced towards the fighters, but a gesture from the abbot stopped them. The novices were speechless and silent, expectant at the consequences of what they had just seen. Li Chen, for his part, looked at the ground and kept his head down towards the victor. Hunt approached him, without touching him, and bowed to him.

"Excellent combat, Master Li. It was an honor to fight you."

The monk looked up at him with an expressionless gesture. If he felt anger, he disguised it very well thanks to his Zen teachings. The abbot stood up and gave three sharp but loud applause. The young *sāmaṇera* relaxed and applauded respectfully. Then the *fangzhang* dissolved the group, and all the monks moved away from the field. Peng and the abbot went to meet Hunt.

"Captain," said the antiquarian, "I'd like to introduce you to Abbot Tsuan Cho."

The monk was an old man of beatific and simple appearance. He wore the same gray and worn robe of the other monks, which made him indistinguishable from those. However, his eyes gave off great wisdom and a contagious calm.

"You are a great warrior, Hunt *shàngwèi,*" said the abbot, using the Chinese equivalent of 'captain'. "But you wouldn't be a good Buddhist. You let your fury surface to win the match."

"Didn't Li Chen do the same?"

The *fangzhang* smiled.

"No. His mistake was to show arrogance. A few weeks of meditation in his cell will help him expel those impure thoughts."

He said it without irony, but Hunt felt that some annoyance loomed over his words.

"Now come with me to my chambers," he said, starting to walk. "My dear friend Peng says you need my help."

One of the temple buildings was dedicated exclusively to the abbot's use. However, his rooms were small and sparsely furnished. A novice brought a washbasin filled with water for Hunt to remove the dust from his face. He would have willingly preferred to take a bath and send his clothes to the hotel laundry, but he would have to wait. Another monk brought them a frugal meal and the three men sat in a circle on cushions.

Peng told the abbot what he knew about the attempts to recreate the spell of the *red typhoon,* beginning with the murder that occurred in the garden of the old city.

"Maybe you should have tried a Taoist temple, my friend," Tsuan said. "Those monks are given to the experiments you mention."

"I thought you could help us on the swordsman, Tsuan *fangzhang,"* Peng replied.

"Do you say that the beheading took place in Yuyuan Garden? Only a barbarian would do such a thing."

The abbot looked upset. In his religion there was no place for acts of that nature. A Buddhist would not even be able to imagine such a thing. However...

"You think the killer has *shaolin* training, don't you?" Asked the abbot.

Peng nodded. Hunt said nothing but deduced that the monk was an expert in martial arts. No doubt he had also learned to fight in the distant and famous Shaolin Monastery, the Zen Buddhist temple located on Mount Song, a thousand kilometers away from Shanghai.

"The hooded man you are looking for is not a monk," the abbot said. "Zen Buddhism would never train assassins."

"Couldn't it be some renegade?" The captain asked.

Tsuan gave him a reprobate look, but his tone of voice was forgiving.

"The monks of the Shaolin temple studied martial arts to defend themselves against bandits, esteemed *shàngwèi.* When it was necessary to use a weapon, they only used a *gun* staff."

"Who uses swords then?" Hunt insisted. "They call them *jian,* don't they?"

"You learn quickly to be a *laowai.*"

The old monk had a funny expression in his eyes.

"A foreigner," the captain translated. "I know. And well, Reverend Abbot, what do you think?"

"I think it's a Wudang swordsman."

Hunt raised an eyebrow. It was the first time he had heard the term. Peng quickly explained that it was another martial arts school, almost as old as *Shaolin,* which had also originated in a remote mountain temple.

"The Wudang Mountains are sacred to Taoism," the antiquarian said.

"There *taijijian* is practiced, a style of sword combat, based on *tai chi,*" said the abbot. "Moreover, several Wudang warriors know the technique of *neijing,* the mind control of life energy."

"That's what immobilized Wang Min when

he was attacked by the mysterious figure," Hunt ventured.

The abbot nodded.

"No doubt the killer attacked Wang with a vibrating palm blow or *dim mak.*" Seeing the captain's expression of surprise, Tsuan Cho added: "The human body has various pressure points that could be manipulated to cause pain, dizziness, fainting, paralysis or even death. These points of the body are also used in Chinese medicine and acupuncture."

"And to cause that effect, a simple touch of the hand is enough?"

"Well, it's not that simple, Hunt *shàngwèi,*" the abbot replied, giving one of his looks of reprobation. "But yes, just one touch is enough."

The abbot's hand cracked like a whip towards Hunt's arm. He only noticed the swift movement when he felt the old monk's fingers squeezing three points of his wrist. Although the pressure was light, he suddenly felt his arm burning and then he lost all his strength. A feeling of lack swept through his body, as if his limb had been amputated. Tsuan let go of his wrist and suddenly Hunt felt his arm again.

"As I said, a little touch is enough."

Hunt rubbed his wrist, which still felt numb.

"So *dim mak*, ¿eh? ¡Damn!"

Chester Peng couldn't hold back the laughter. After a moment, Hunt also laughed. Tsuan, for his part, maintained his Zen expression. To be sure, he didn't joke about his knowledge.

"Do you know where we can find this Wudang warrior?" The antiques dealer asked.

Tsuan Cho didn't look at his friend, but at Hunt. His dark eyes were nailed to the captain.

"What will you do when you find this man, *shàngwèi?*"

Hunt hesitated for a moment, but then he told the truth.

"If what that man, Wang Min, said is true, then I must stop the murderer and his accomplices." Hunt kept the abbot's gaze and spoke in a firm voice. "I will not allow strangers to attack England without provocation."

The abbot nodded. His gaze was lost, immersed in his reflections.

"You have set yourself a noble mission, Hunt *shàngwèi*. I respect that."

"So, will you help us?"

To the amazement of the two visitors, the old monk shook his head.

"Sorry, my friends. I don't know the whereabouts of such a powerful warrior."

Hunt felt his heart sank. Had the trip to the temple been in vain? The abbot had given him spiritual advice, but he needed a concrete clue, a way to follow. Hunt looked at Peng willing to leave, but then the old master raised a hand to stop him.

"But I can tell you *how* to find the murderer."

He said it with an ominous voice. Hunt looked at the abbot with an intrigued expression.

"You must make a journey, Captain," said the *fangzhang,* in a solemn tone.

"A trip? I would say that the killer is still in Shanghai."

"Oh, yes, that's right," Tsuan confirmed. "That is why you must travel to the dark realm and find there the link that bind you with the murderer."

"Which link?"

"You and the killer are two opposing forces, but bounded, Hunt *shàngwèi.* Taoists call it 'the yin and yang'. That point of binding will allow you to find your other half."

Hunt wasn't seduced to feel attached to a mysterious killer, but he knew he had to transform into his nemesis if he wanted to find him. The abbot understood his feelings, for he pointed a finger at him and spoke with a tone of hope.

"Your *qi* is strong, my friend. You proved it on the training ground."

Hunt had already heard that expression, which meant "life energy." As he understood, Chinese philosophy and its various religions revolved around *qi.* However, the captain didn't know what to say, so he looked at the abbot silently. It was evident that he was not referring to a physical journey, but rather to a mystic one. Tsuan Cho in turn looked at Hunt for quite a long time, as if he were measuring him inside, trying to calculate whether his *qi* would really withstand that journey he was talking about. In the end he said:

"Look for the link, Captain, and come back right away. The dark realm has many paths, and it is easy to get lost inside."

Hunt was afraid to ask what the dark realm was, but he still did. The old man looked exhausted when speaking.

"*Diyu.* You would call it... hell."

Suddenly, Hunt felt his throat dry.

"What will happen if I get lost in that place?"

Somehow, he knew it, but he couldn't help but shudder at hearing the monk's answer:

"Your *qi* would be trapped forever outside your body." Tsuan closed his eyes, with a gesture of bitterness. Without opening them, he added: "You would be a living dead man, Hunt *shàngwèi.*"

6. THE DARK REALM

He was still in Shanghai, or so it seemed to him. The streets were dark and deserted. Where before there had been color and noise, now only a gray landscape was seen. An artificial and oppressive silence reigned everywhere. Trams and rickshaws were gone. Crowds could no longer be seen on street corners and the luminous neon signs no shone above the clubs and department stores. Nor were perceived the aromas that usually flooded the air of the city, whether they were pleasant or repulsive: the fetid vapors that the breeze dragged from the river, the fried and spicy food of the open-air markets, the incense that emanated from the temples, the perfumes of the ladies who walked through the Bund.

It was Shanghai, but at the same time it wasn't. The city was stopped in time, abandoned from all traces of life. Black clouds covered the sky, threatening with some storm that refused to come. The air was dry and when he breathed it, it made his throat sore. Even the warm breeze that used to blow in the evenings had transformed into an icy, thick breath. He wandered the deserted streets and looked towards the confines of the city, but only a cloak of blackness could be seen. Suddenly he felt dejected and tired. His legs failed him, and he had to stop. He looked at everything around him and wondered how he got there.

A memory poked into his mind but disappeared immediately. It was just a flash. A blurry and distant image. A bathtub with hot water, a glass of whisky on the edge, the bottle on a bedside table. His beaten body that was submerged in the water... after the combat in the Buddhist temple! Yes, it was him in his room at the Astor House, returning from his meeting with the abbot. After his *kung fu* fight with the warrior. Then another image, another flash. Chester Peng talking from the other side of a table. Among them there were several dishes and a few drinks. Yes, both having dinner that same night. Something in the back of his brain told him that that hadn't happened a long time ago. So how did he get to that cold, gray place? He suddenly remembered where he was.

In hell.

After dining together, Chester Peng had led Captain Hunt to a discreet street in the district of Nanshi, the old Chinese city. There they crossed an anonymous portal, guarded by an immense sentinel who moved aside when he saw the antiques dealer and let them pass. The visitors descended a narrow staircase and, after walking through a short corridor, came to a solid-looking door. Peng gave a single blow with his knuckles. Immediately a peephole opened on the door, and a reddened eye inspected them for a few moments. Then there were heavy bolts running off and the door opened.

"Ah, Master Peng! It is an honor you visit us tonight."

The man who welcomed them, middle-aged and with obsequious manners, spoke in English automatically upon seeing Hunt. After making great gestures towards his visitors, he told them to enter his establishment.

It was a large basement that was divided into compartments by thick red curtains that went from the ceiling to the ground. A few paper lamps that hung from the ceiling, of ubiquitous red color, cast a faint illumination onto the cavernous hall. A dense cloud of smoke covered the upper half of the room, further thinning the environment. In each of the cubicles that formed the curtains, one or more men lay on large cushions. Some of the customers were holding long pipes in their hands, while others seemed to sleep a hectic dream. Silent employees went from one cubicle to another carrying trays with the paraphernalia of the business.

Hunt had read about opium dens in Sherlock Holmes or Dr. Fu Manchu stories, but now he thoughted that reality surpassed fiction. The sweet smell of the drug permeated the clothes and slipped through the nose. The sleepy men showed a sickly appearance, and the gloom created a bleak panorama. Hunt had to make a great effort to suppress his urges to leave immediately.

"Hsie's place is one of the most reputable of its kind," Peng whispered.

It was true that the place was clean, and the clientele wore luxurious clothes, but it was nothing more than a den of perdition. Hunt had heard that opium addiction was widespread in the country, but he never imagined it would be at such a high level. Now he understood why Shanghai was called 'the vice capital of the world'. Thinking that Britain had fought two wars in the last century to impose the opium trade on the Chinese, Hunt felt ashamed.

"I don't want to know what the disreputable places are like," he murmured.

Peng did not answer. He approached the owner and put a hand on his shoulder to speak to him in a low voice.

"We need the special mixture, *yāpiàn huǒ*. My friend must go on a journey."

Hsie looked at the captain with a serious expression. After a moment he nodded and gestured to them.

"Come here," he said.

He took them to a private room located at the back of the establishment, separated from the hall by a solid door. Inside there were also cushions to lie down and a side table with the implements to smoke opium. Hsie asked them to wait a moment and left them alone. Hunt sat on the cushions and tried to get comfortable.

"What is that special mixture?" he asked.

"They call it *yāpiàn huǒ,* 'opium of fire'. It is a very potent version of opium, mixed with hallucinogenic substances, which produces a catatonic state in the smoker."

Hunt looked at the antiques dealer in alarm. He liked that affair less and less.

"I hope it's just a hallucination," he said. "The abbot said that I could die in that place."

Peng raised his hands to his chest height and put the tips of his stretched fingers together. With an expressionless face, he quoted:

"'Cowards die many times before their true death; the brave taste death only once'."

"¿Confucius?"

"Shakespeare. *Julius Caesar.*"

Hunt laughed. His joy ended abruptly when the owner of the den returned. His expression seemed to indicate that he was on his way to a funeral. In his hands he carried a small lacquered wooden box. From its interior he extracted a dark ball of porous texture. Hunt deduced that it was an opium pill. Hsie knelt in front of the central table and began preparations for Hunt to embark on his 'journey'.

With a long match he lit a silver lamp decorated with cloisonné. A sweet smell emanated from the small glass chimney as the almond oil began to burn without smoke. Hsie took a pipe made of ivory and placed the pill in the jade bowl that was mounted near the end, in a piece of metal. Then he held the mount over the heat of the lamp, so that the opium would slowly evaporate. The pill immediately acquired an orange-red hue of intense brilliance, and then began to dissolve. Hsie handed the pipe to the captain.

"Go slowly, noble sir. Your journey will take you to the brink of death."

With those ominous words, Hunt put the mouthpiece of the pipe into his mouth and began smoking the opium of fire. His throat stung for a moment and his nose filled with smoke, but he was soon overwhelmed by an irresistible dream. Then, blackness enveloped him, and he didn't feel his body when he fell lying on the cushions. At first, he had his eyes open, although he didn't see anything. His heart accelerated sharply, and the whole body began to tremble, but he didn't even notice. Peng and Hsie held him by the arms and then the owner of the establishment wiped away the copious sweat that had bathed his face.

"He's already there," Hsie said. "In *Diyu*."

"The dark realm," Peng muttered.

Hunt wandered for hours through the streets of hellish Shanghai. Every time he turned in a direction that was familiar to him, he would eventually reach the same starting point. It took a long time to understand that he was inside a labyrinth. A distant memory in his brain told him that he should let himself go. He ran into several high walls that suddenly emerged from the ground and prevented him from continuing his way. He tried to leave his mind blank and just kept moving forward. His instinct guided him.

After long hours of walking, he felt his body tired and his mind dull. Above, the sky was dark on an eternal night. The clouds, gray and throbbing, barely let in some light. In that strange place not even time passed normally. Hunt looked toward the horizon, down a long avenue he was on, and only spotted darkness at the end of the road. It was impossible to determine what time of day it was.

Suddenly he found himself in a place full of musty trees, ruined walls and crumbling rocks. He stopped abruptly. He said to himself he knew that place. He rummaged through his brain for some memory that would tell him where he was, but he couldn't find any ideas that would reveal his whereabouts. His mind was emptying. He understood that soon he would not remember even his name. He went into the trees and into the middle of the rocks, until a flash struck him, and an image appeared inside his head. He and Sir John Connelly were talking to a Chinese man... Peng! And he described to them an incident that occurred in a public garden... Yuyuan, that was it!

Along with the name of the place also

came a certainty. He was in the place where the criminal had been executed. Or at least in the hellish version of the same garden. Hunt continued along the rock formation and later saw two ghostly figures appearing behind a bend. Startled, the captain hid behind a large rock that was still standing tall and from there watched the scene. One of the figures, dark and with blurred contours, fell to his knees in front of the other apparition. Hunt understood that it was the spirit of the dead man, Wang Min.

At that moment the kneeling specter turned to Hunt and motioned for him to approach. The captain felt an intense chill running down his whole body. However, he plucked up the courage and approached the two figures. Wang's image opened a black and shapeless mouth, but he couldn't speak. A metallic glow flashed in the air and with a shriek the spectral figure of the gangster dissolved. A howl of pain followed; a scream that pierced Hunt's heart and froze his blood. However, the other figure did not seem to hear it. He just stood there, staring at the ground as if his victim's body was still at his feet.

Hunt hesitated for a moment, but seeing that the figure was not moving, he approached the specter slowly from behind. A gentle breeze swirled the creature's robes, which seemed to be made of tatters, dark and old. The sky was still covered, and the landscape was getting darker and darker. The thin and long blade of the sword shone as if it produced its own light. As he approached, Hunt saw that the figure was suspended in the air, without touching the ground. The captain moved forward slowly, trying not to make any noise, but he still retained his corporeal shape, and the pebbles on the ground creaked under his feet.

The figure of the murderer turned quickly when perceiving the intruder. Hunt was petrified, his heart beating as if it wanted to escape his chest. The ghostly figure wore his head covered and under his hood only an infinite blackness could be seen. Hunt didn't budge, doubting whether the specter knew he was there. In a burst of courage, the captain took a step until he was next to the figure. She put her hands to the hood and removed it from her head, revealing the beautiful face of a young woman with Chinese features. Hunt was immediately captivated. His dull mind told him that he had never seen such beauty.

Then the young woman spoke to him.

"Who are you?"

She spoke In Chinese, but somehow, he managed to understand the language. However, the voice sounded like a metallic and cold squeak. The captain felt the words pierce his chest. He took a step back and babbled something, but no sound came out of his mouth. He just looked at the spectral beauty floating in front of him and wondered what the link would be that united him with that young woman.

The figure stretched out one hand and grabbed the captain by the wrist. At the instant she touched him, it felt like a thousand mirrors were broken at once. A burst of shattered glass invaded everything around him and a deadly cold ran through his veins, as if they had been injected with an icy liquid. Intense pain swept through his body, and he found that he was screaming from the bottom of his bowels, as if swallowed by an endless dark abyss.

Peng and Hsie jumped back at the same time. The captain's body, free from the hold of the two men, began to twist. His face was deformed by pain. The antiques dealer managed to react and threw himself on his friend, trying to contain the spasms. The body was frozen like a corpse.

"We are losing him," Hsie said, in horror. "Someone is attacking him on the other side."

In the dark realm, Hunt was about to fall to his knees as a result of the ghost's icy touch, but his will managed to ignite a spark of sanity and he remembered what the abbot of the Buddhist temple had told him. His *qi,* the life energy, was powerful. He gathered all the mental strength he had left and pushed his arm away in one fell swoop. The sudden movement caught the figure off guard, who let go of her deadly touch. Hunt regained his fortitude but felt exhausted and weak.

"What are you doing here, foreigner?" The

spectral woman asked in her squeaky voice. "This place is not for you."

"Who are you?" He wanted to ask her.

A moment later he understood that he had said it out loud, in perfect Chinese language.

"Do you dare to question me?" The figure screamed, as it soared through the air.

Her eyes sparkled and were fixed on the intruder.

"Your name is Peter Hunt," the woman whispered suddenly, in an accusatory tone. "I know everything about you!"

The specter floated towards the captain; her sword held high. He tried to dodge her but found he couldn't move.

"I'll go get you, Peter Hunt!"

The bright blade whistled in the air and fell on Hunt. He was immediately invaded by darkness.

"Wake up, Captain!" Shouted a distant voice.

It sounded dull, as if someone was calling him from underwater.

Then he understood that the situation was the other way around. He was underwater and the voice was calling to him from the surface. He tried to swim there, where a tiny ray of light pointed the way. He closed his mind to any thoughts and ascended with precise and fast movements. His *qi* seemed to run out quickly. He felt weights on his legs pulling him down, as if strong hands were holding him to prevent him from leaving. He made one last effort and propelled himself towards the surface of the sea of darkness.

Hunt opened his eyes and was flooded by a blinding light. A few seconds later the brightness decreased in intensity and Hunt discovered that he was still in the private room of the opium den. The lighting came from paper lamps hanging from the ceiling, but the light they projected was enough to make Hunt's eyes burn. He tried to sit up, leaning on his elbows, but felt that he was invaded by strong convulsions in his stomach. He turned sideways and vomited a dark bile on the wooden floor.

"Captain... are you okay?" Peng asked.

Hunt managed to sit on the cushions and saw the two Chinese looking at him dumbfounded. He tried to smile to encourage them, but only managed to make an ambiguous grimace.

"How... how long was I there?"

"Less than an hour," Hsie replied. "We almost lost you, noble sir."

"What happened?" asked Peng, who had regained his Zen expression. "Your body suffered severe spasms and became icy."

Hunt nodded to himself, remembering the supernatural cold that had invaded him. In Western culture hell was depicted as a fiery place, in eternal flames. But the dark realm, *Diyu,* was an icy, gray site. Hsie served a concoction to the captain, and he drank it slowly, recovering his body temperature and the color of his cheeks. As he recovered, he told them everything he remembered of his journey to hell.

"Do you say that spirit... *did it touch you*?" Peng asked, in a trembling voice.

Hunt nodded and stretched out his arm.

Hsie stepped forward and discovered Hunt's wrist. On the skin was a burn in the shape of several fingers. Hunt was speechless. In his mind everything seemed like a hallucination, but the scar was very real. He touched his skin and felt it numb where contact with the spectral figure had been marked.

"After touching me... the specter knew everything about me!"

"You must leave immediately," Hsie said, standing up. Peng and Hunt looked at him in surprise. "You said it, noble sir. That creature knows where to find you. That means she will come *here*."

The den's owner trembled, and the words came out in spurts. Hunt understood that the Chinese was terrified. He looked at Peng for help. The antiques dealer nodded.

"Hsie is right, my friend. We must go."

From outside the room came the noise of a commotion. Hsie hesitated for a moment, but then opened the door. Several men were flocking through the hall's main door. Customers who were not too lethargic by the drug began to complain and several female employees screamed in shock. Hunt saw that the intruders were armed with machetes and daggers.

"They are coming for us," he murmured.

The guards of the establishment tried to stop the intruders, but they acted with ferocity, brandishing their weapons unceremoniously. Cries of panic and pain flooded the rarefied air of the den. The attackers spread out inside the hall and searched all over the cubicles, tearing the curtains and kicking the cushions. Anyone who got in his way was beaten or stabbed. Soon the wooden floor was covered with blood.

Hunt draw his revolver and pointed it at the attackers, but his arm was shaking, and he couldn't focus his vision. He tried to concentrate on one of the intruders, but after a moment he discarded the idea and put the weapon back away. Chaos had unleashed in the hall. Customers and employees ran back and forth, escaping from the attackers, who threw stabs and punches left and right. Hsie had a pale face and looked about to faint.

"Is there another way out?" Hunt questioned him. The owner didn't even look at him. "Hsie, listen to me! We must flee *now!*"

He shook the Chinese and Hsie looked at him with a lethargic expression.

"Back exit," he muttered. "There."

With a trembling finger he pointed towards a span that opened on the back wall of the hall, covered by a beaded curtain. Hunt and Peng ran away. The owner of the establishment forgot about them and threw himself screaming towards the pandemonium.

The span overlooked a large pantry whose walls were lined with shelves filled with pipes, lamps and opium boxes. Hunt thought that this place would be the paradise of a drug addict. For a moment he wanted to set the place on fire, but he knew he had no time to waste. He stumbled forward, still exhausted by the effort, followed by Peng. On the opposite wall of the pantry was a low, narrow door. Hunt charged at it with his shoulder and slammed it open. He crouched down to pass through the doorframe and found himself in an equally low and dark tunnel.

"Come on, Chester, hurry up!" He whispered to his companion.

They ran blindly, with their hands outstretched in front of them so as not to hit the walls. The tunnel was narrow and wet. The smell that floated in the air, a mixture of dust and opium, became unbearable. Hunt advanced with his body shrunk for several minutes, until he understood that the passageway stretched for several hundred meters. He wished to hurry up, but the blackness was absolute.

Shortly after, both fugitives heard noises coming from the beginning of the tunnel. They stopped immediately and remained silent. The captain assumed that the attackers had discovered their escape route and were preparing to light a lamp so that they could follow them. Indeed, an instant later a light appeared further back, where they had come. Hunt pulled out his revolver and pointed it at the lamp. He waited for the intruders to go into the passageway and then fired.

They heard some curses in Chinese and the light stopped moving. Hunt fired again. This time the shot was followed by a cry of pain. After that there was another attempt to follow them that was answered with a new shot. The light fell to the ground and after a moment it became extinct. Surely it was a kerosene lamp. Hunt grabbed Peng by the arm.

"Let's move on!"

They restarted to run, fleeing in desperation. Hunt grazed the walls of the tunnel several times, scratching the palms of his hands, and nearly fell on more than one occasion when he tripped over loose rubble. After several minutes, he could make out a fading light later and understood that they were reaching the end of the tunnel. A pungent musty smell invaded the air inside the passageway, followed by creaks and taps that increased in intensity as approaching the exit.

Hunt deduced that the noise was produced by the hulls of boats when they collided with each other, rocked by the sway of the waves. He deducted they were on their way to a dock.

A moment later he emerged to the surface and found himself in a modest dock in which there were moored some fishermen's sampans. The underground tunnel connected Hsie's establishment, through hundreds of meters below several streets of Nanshi District, with the Whangpoo River. No doubt the owner used it to discreetly supply his den. In the faint light of dawn, Hunt saw that beyond the precarious pier were several larger boats anchored in the river or moored to cargo jetties.

"Help me release a sampan," the captain said to Peng, who came out of the tunnel a moment later. "If someone comes through the tunnel, they will believe that we have left on the boat."

Between them they loosened the moorings and pushed the boat with all their strength until the current began to move it away from the shore. Without wasting any more time, they set out to walk at a brisk pace along the edge of the river in a northerly direction, towards the territory of the French Concession.

"They found us very quickly," Hunt said, in a tone of amazement. "Within minutes they were upon us."

"By touching you," Peng agreed, "that woman must have established a psychic link with you, Captain."

"The binding works both ways, I guess."

"Now you both are permanently bound, my friend. You are yin and yang."

"I shouldn't have gone to the dark realm," Hunt lamented, rubbing the scar on his wrist. "It only served to get our enemies to discover us."

"Didn't you manage to discover anything in return?"

Hunt shook his head. Suddenly he noticed the cold of the night and shuddered. He hurried his steps.

"Believe it or not, I asked her directly who she was," he said. "That made her angry," he added, "and she threw herself at me with her sword raised..."

He stopped sharply and put a hand on his partner's arm.

"You must not fear, Captain," the antiques dealer tried to comfort him. "The danger has passed."

"It's not that. Now I'm remember something!"

He approached the earthen edge of the boardwalk and with one finger traced on the ground several crisscrossing lines. In the end the drawing resembled a couple of *hanzi* characters from Chinese writing. Peng watched the strokes carefully.

"Are you sure this is what you saw?" He asked.

"Yes, yes. The girl had it tattooed on the back of her right hand. I saw it when she raised her sword to attack me. What does it mean?"

Peng pondered for a few moments. Then he

nodded.

"*Mudan,*" he said. "The flower of the peony."

7. THE HOUSE OF WHITE PEONY

At the western end of the International Settlement, not far from the residences of Shanghai's richest men, stood an elegant three-story house surrounded by a beautiful rose garden. Its white walls were dotted with windows whose balconies were enclosed by wrought iron grilles. On the street, in front of the property, a dozen luxury cars lined the curb, watched by their drivers as they smoked in small groups on the sidewalk. All the windows of the house had the curtains drawn and no sound came from the inside. At first glance, it was impossible to guess what was going on in the house.

Hunt left the Duesenberg with the other cars and headed to the house without worrying about the curious looks that the drivers gave him and the splendid vehicle. He crossed the garden along the gravel path that ran between the manicured rose bushes and knocked on the door. It was immediately opened by an impeccably uniformed Chinese butler. Before the servant could say anything, Hunt deposited in his hand a wad of high-value bills, following the advice he had received from Chester Peng a couple of hours earlier. The butler made the money disappear inside his jacket as if by magic.

"Good evening, sir," the man greeted, in perfect English. "Welcome to the House of White Peony."

It had taken Peng two days to find out the meaning of the tattoo worn by the woman in the vision that the captain had experienced during his journey to the dark realm.

The girls of the "white peony" were the most famous and exclusive courtesans in Shanghai. Several dozens of them received their wealthy clients in that discreet and elegant house, where they could enjoy their services comfortably and safely. Paying an additional cost, of no small entity, some client who wished to maintain his privacy could ask one of the adorable sing-song girls to visit him in his own home or the place of his convenience. In this regard, in those days there was a rumor that an important Chinese businessman was accompanied by one of those select young ladies when a quick and violent death occurred to him.

Peng had gathered quite a bit of information on the matter, considering the reserved nature of the activities taking place in that house.

"The courtesans receive a very rigorous training, after which a tattoo is made on their hand to identify them," explained the antiques dealer. "This demonstrates the authenticity of each girl and avoids deception."

"Oh my God!" Hunt exclaimed. "It seems that we were talking about an antique porcelain set."

"These girls are not so fragile, but they are just as valuable," Peng said.

They were gathered in the Chinese man's office. Hunt gestured in the direction of the liquor cabinet and Peng nodded. The captain poured two glasses of whisky.

"We must go tonight at the house in question," Hunt said.

Peng simply drank from his glass with a shocked gesture.

"I'm afraid I won't be able to accompany you," he announced.

The captain looked at his friend in disbelief. Peng was a resolute man and a valuable ally. Hunt guessed that in the sing-song house there would be no more danger than in the opium den. Peng emptied his glass in one sip and explained to Hunt that it was unthinkable for a European to go to a place like that next to a Chinese. It was not necessary to add that the antiquarian, as a devout Christian, disapproved of the activities carried out by those girls and did not even wish to imagine what happened in establishments of that type. Hunt understood his friend's apprehensions and left alone in the car.

The butler led Hunt into a beautifully decorated hall with antique furniture, fine tapestries and porcelain vases that could had passed as any of Belgravia's palatial houses.

However, there ended the resemblance to the residences of the luxurious London district. Scattered around the living room were several armchairs and sofas occupied by wealthy-looking men, dressed in dinner jackets, mostly in their fifties. They were all foreigners. Among the clients walked about twenty semi-naked girls of great beauty. They were all Chinese.

The place was illuminated by several table and standing lamps. When Hunt accustomed his eyes to the gloom, he could deduce that among the crowd were English bankers, American exporters, French diplomats and a few Japanese whose profession was impossible to elucidate. Some of the girls frolicked on the couches, others brought cocktails from the corner bar, and a few leaned against a wall and chatted with each other with a boring expression.

Hunt searched for an empty armchair and found one that was somewhat separated from the others. As soon as he had sat down, he was approached by one of the girls who were wandering around the room. She had a vivacious face and was short of stature, but she had a voluptuous body. She wore a red silk negligee, which showed off her firm bare breasts, and a suspender belt over French knickers. She introduced herself as Lotus Flower.

"Can I offer you something to drink, mister..."

"Captain," he corrected. "Peter Hunt."

"It's an honor to have you in our house, Captain. What can I bring you?"

He asked for a Glenlivet neat. The girl walked away swaggering her butt and went to prepare the drink herself at the bar in the corner of the hall. She returned immediately and sat unceremoniously on the captain's legs. He drank slowly, looking around the living room. Lotus Flower ran her fingers across his arm, as if groping his muscles.

"I've never seen you around here, Captain. First time in the house?"

"Yes. I recently arrived in Shanghai."

"Did you enlist in the Volunteer Corps?"

The girl was referring to the private army of the International Settlement, made up mostly of former British officers.

"No. I work on my own," he replied, as ambiguously as possible.

"Oh, there are many opportunities in Shanghai!" The girl exclaimed.

She seemed to know everything about local businesses. Hunt assumed that she had learned something from her clients.

"Are you looking for any of the girls in particular?"

Hunt looked up smiling at Lotus Flower.

"Of course not, my dear. I'm with you, isn't I?"

"It's that you don't stop looking around the room," she said with a tone of feigned reproach, making a grimace of anger. "I thought you liked my company."

"Of course," he said, patting her butt. "You are a very beautiful girl."

Lotus Flower smiled broadly. Then she leaned towards the captain and kissed him. Hunt sighed and let himself be taken care of. After all, in a place like that, acting differently would have attracted attention.

Shortly after, when the girl went to bring him another glass, Hunt took the opportunity to inspect the room once again. He could not find the woman of his vision, but he could see that the atmosphere of the place was increasingly relaxed. Many of the customers were already without a jacket, with the bow tie untied and some of them even had taken off their shirts. The state of nudity of the hostesses had also increased and the situation threatened to spiral out of control soon. A catchy music animated the show from a hidden phonograph and tobacco smoke flooded the air.

Hunt took the glass from Lotus Flower's hands and motioned for her to come over to speak in her ear.

"Is there a more private place we can go?" He asked, bringing his mouth a few centimeters from her ear.

She threw a funny chuckle.

"Ah, bad captain!"

She took him by the hand and led him

upstairs. Other couples were also going up. A couple of men greeted Hunt with a bow of their heads, as if they were all in the same business. Well, in a way we are, the captain thought. Some girls crossed paths with them as they returned to the hall, but none of them were the woman of his vision. Hunt thought it had been a mistake to go to that house, but he still followed Lotus Flower to one of the rooms on the second floor.

The room was furnished only in a practical way. There was a double bed next to a bedside table, a wooden chair and a washbasin with water. The splendor of the first floor was not necessary up there, where customers were passing through and did not notice what surrounded them. Lotus Flower lit some candles that were on the bedside table and coughed slightly, indicating with the chin a lacquered tray. Hunt hesitated for a moment, but then he understood the girl's gesture. With his face flushed, he left a generous amount of bills on the tray.

Lotus Flower laughed happily and made a gesture to remove the negligee. Hunt stopped her and asked her to sit at the foot of the bed. She looked at him with an expression that mixed equal parts disappointment and distrust.

"Don't be afraid. I just want to talk."

"Just talk?" She insisted, with grimace of strangeness.

What her clients did the least in that room

was talk. Hunt left more bills on the tray and squatted in front of the girl.

"I need you to help me. I'm looking for someone. Another of the girls in the house."

"I knew it!" Lotus Flower exclaimed. Now her tone was one of annoyance. "I thought you liked me, Captain."

"Er... of course, my dear. But I need to talk to this other girl."

Lotus Flower looked at him with a frown.

"Do you just like to *talk* to girls?"

Hunt tried not to laugh at such a question. He approached the young woman and kissed her to reassure her.

"Will you help me?" He insisted, while caressing her mechanically.

"Okay," she replied with resignation.

"You see, the other girl..." he hesitated about how to describe the woman in his vision. There all the girls were similar. "She is tall and very beautiful, er..."

"You mean *Meihua*, Cherry Blossom," she immediately said. "She is the most beautiful girl in the house. She has dozens of admirers."

She said it with annoyance, as if she was tired of being compared to her partner's celebrity.

"It's not her real name, right?"

The girl laughed eagerly as she shook her head.

"Here we are all beautiful flowers, Captain.

It's our... *artistic* name.

"I see. Is Meihua here tonight?"

"I haven't seen her. I think she hasn't come to the house for a few days."

"Do you know where she lives?"

She shook her head.

"Some girls rent rooms in a nearby *shikumen,* but I don't know where it is. The rest of us live right here, on the top floor.

Shikumen were terraced houses located along an enclosed alley called *longdang,* which was accessed by a stone portico or *paifang.* Hunt had read about them during his long boat trip from England. He knew they were the most favored residences by the local inhabitants of the city. The problem was that there were more than nine thousand of those alleys scattered all over Shanghai.

Hunt sat next to the girl on the edge of the bed. On his face was reflected disappointment. Lotus Flower pressed against him and kissed him again.

"Don't be sad, Captain. I can make you forget Meihua."

"I don't doubt it," he murmured, somewhat embarrassed.

Despite the advances of the beautiful young woman who accompanied him, Hunt made his best effort not to forget the reason that had led him to the House of White Peony.

"Is there anything else you can tell me about

Meihua? Maybe she's friends with another girl she trusts?"

"No lady friends," said Lotus Flower, shaking her head. "Only male friends who give her good gifts. *Very good* gifts."

Hunt assumed that the courtesans of the house had several sponsors who bought them clothes, perfumes and perhaps invited them to some show where they could go without their wives.

"Any special friends?" He asked finally, without much hope.

The girl put a finger on her lips while thinking.

"Hmmm, I don't know. I think *Ko Zul* is her best customer. At least he fancies her."

Hunt stood up again in front of the young woman.

"*Ko Zul?* Is he Chinese?"

"No, he's white like you, Captain. Very good customer, although he always asks for Meihua," explained the girl, with a tone of envy. Then she added, with an air of reverie: "I have tried to attend to him, but I cannot hold him back much until he asks for her. And I always show him my *mīmī.*"

She pulled the lace that held the negligee at the height of the neck and opened it in the two halves of cloth, exposing her breasts. Hunt looked up at the ceiling to forget about the beautiful *mīmī* of Lotus Flower. She let out a suggestive giggle.

"Can you show me if *Ko Zul* is here tonight?" he asked in a trembling voice.

The girl led Hunt out of the room, not bothering to close the negligee again. Both stopped at the top of the staircase, from where much of the hall was dominated. There a boisterous and uncontrolled spree had been unleashed. Most of the customers were drunk, laughed loudly, and chased the girls with their pants tangled at the ankles. Others occupied the sofas with their companions, enjoying more pleasant, but no less noisy activities.

Lotus Flower looked around the crowd without a hint of surprise, because that was the usual atmosphere in the house during the nights. After a moment, she pointed her finger:

"*Ko Zul.*"

A man in his fifties was standing in a corner of the hall, talking to a Chinese woman of a similar age to his own, dressed in a silk robe. Hunt assumed it was the *amah,* the madam of the house. *Ko Zul* wore an impeccable dress coat and sported a beard and mustache that was somewhat old-fashioned, but which gave him an aristocratic air. He seemed totally oblivious to the decadent spectacle that surrounded him. The *amah* bowed constantly to him and seemed to give him unsatisfactory explanations, judging by the angry rictus in the man's face.

"I'm sorry, my dear," Hunt said to Lotus

Flower, "but you'll have to find another friend for tonight."

"Maybe I manage to conquer *Ko Zul.*" She laughed and went downstairs.

Lotus Flower had no luck. As he descended, a Chinese servant approached the *amah* and spoke in her ear. The woman showed a radiant expression and turned to the distinguished client again, making new and exaggerated curtseys. The man nodded once and turned to head towards the stairs. There he crossed paths with Lotus Flower, who looked at him with a seductive gesture. The man passed by without looking at her. Hunt, for his part, delved into the shadows of the corridor that ran along the upper floor from one end to the other. *Ko Zul* approached a door at the end of the corridor, called once with a sharp knock, and entered the room closing again behind him.

The corridor was deserted. Hunt went through it at a rapid pace and stuck his ear on the door that the man just went through. He seemed to hear a male voice inside, but the noise of the bacchanal on the first floor prevented him from clearly distinguishing what was being said. He cursed in a whisper and tried the next door. It was unlocked. He snuck inside and found himself in another room intended for customers. It was evident that it had just been used. The bed was unmade, and the air was permeated with cheap perfume and sweat. Suppressing a sense of disgust, Hunt walked to the window and opened it wide.

The window led to a balcony surrounded by a wrought iron railing. Hunt passed over the railing and swayed precariously on the narrow outer edge of the balcony. From there he stretched out one leg and managed to set foot on the next balcony. With a little momentum, he threw the rest of the body over the separation between the two balconies and finally circumvented the adjoining railing. Then he approached the window and through a crack between the cast curtains he managed to see in part what was happening inside the room.

A young Chinese woman dressed in a bright red *cheongsam* walked around gesticulating, while the man in the dress coat stood still and stiff in place. Hunt immediately recognized the woman of his vision. Fortunately, she and the foreigner communicated in English. Hunt managed to hear some of the conversation through the window glass.

"... wait a long time," the man was saying. "Why didn't you want to receive me?"

"The killers of the Green Gang are looking for me," the girl explained. "They want to avenge the Mountain and they know that I work here."

"So, it's not a good hiding place. You can use my apartment. They won't find you there."

Although the man said it in a casual tone, the young woman looked at him with a suspicious gesture. However, he did not react.

"I can easily get rid of them," she said, in a contemptuous voice. "But I don't want to draw attention. We must also worry about the Englishman."

Hunt shuddered to realize that they were referring to him. He stuck his back to the wall next to the window and pricked his ear.

"The other night he managed to escape, didn't he?" Now the man sounded upset. "It's a complication."

The so-called *Ko Zul* came to the girl and looked at her harshly.

"You were going to take care of that after the Englishman appeared in that... *vision*."

"My men attacked the den immediately!" she exclaimed, indignantly. "Next time I will go after him myself."

"We shouldn't have resorted to the Green Gang to get the spell," *Ko Zul* lamented. "Somehow, what Wang Min found out reached the ears of the English."

"There was no one with him when I..."

Suddenly the girl stopped and, in her eyes, appeared the shadow of a doubt. His accomplice gave her a scrutinizing look, but she ignored him.

"We must tie up all the loose ends before proceeding with the next stage of the plan," the man said. "If the English find out what we propose..."

He didn't finish the sentence but looked

intensely at the girl to demonstrate the implications of what he had meant. She nodded with a sharp gesture.

"When will we go in search of the element that we lack?" She asked, in an anxious voice.

For the first time, the man gave the hint of a slight smile.

"Come to the reception tomorrow. There we will discuss it."

"*Shì, zhǎngguān*. Yes, sir."

The man called *Ko Zul* turned around and left the room. Hunt quickly returned to the adjoining balcony, in the same way as he had come, and then ran to the door of the empty room. He opened the door and spied on the hallway. A moment later he managed to spot the man, who was going down the stairs. He waited for a moment and went out to the corridor ready to follow him stealthily.

"You!"

Hunt froze in the middle of the hallway. Turning back, he saw that the young girl was looking at him from the doorframe of the room where she just had met *Ko Zul.* The captain deduced that his options for following the mysterious man had vanished. He resolved to try an approach with the girl.

"Hello, Meihua," he said as he made his way to her. "It's a pleasure to meet you... *in person.*"

The young woman was even more beautiful than she had appeared in his vision. Her eyes were captivating, and she had a sinuous body that would dizzy if one tried to follow her curves. Not even the gesture of her face, halfway between stupor and fury, managed to take away one speck of her beauty.

"So, you have found me, Peter Hunt," she snapped.

"I just followed the link that binds us together," he said. "We are yin and yang."

She let out a sardonic laugh.

"Do you really think you are the same as me? You are nothing but a nuisance, foreigner."

"But here we are," Hunt insisted.

"Then, it will be your farewell."

She made a gesture to back off, but he foresaw her movement. He stepped forward and grabbed her wrist.

"Go to hell!"

"I've already been there," Hunt replied, without loosening his prey, "and I didn't like it."

The girl struggled to free herself from the captain but was immobilized in the doorframe. Hunt remembered that the girl's sensual appearance was just a deception to hide her martial skills. If he didn't reduce her soon, she would manage to beat him easily. A sudden twinkle in the young woman's eyes showed him that she was thinking the same thing. Hunt used the weight of his body to press her against the door. She stirred furiously. She wore an intoxicating perfume, and her red painted mouth was half-opened in a sensual gesture. Despite the scuffle, he smiled.

From the first floor came the noise of a loud commotion, followed by running steps that ascended the stairs. Two burly Chinese appeared down the hallway and ran towards Hunt and the girl. When they saw them, they shouted some orders at them in their language. Meihua replied to them with a submissive tone and his head down. She had assumed again her sing-song girl personality.

"Is something wrong, folks?" Hunt asked in an innocent tone. "I'm just saying goodbye to my girl."

To reinforce his role, he bowed his head and kissed the young woman on the lips. To his surprise, she responded enthusiastically.

"Get out!" ordered one of the men, in hesitant English.

He was the older and burlier of the two. Hunt approached him with an innocent gesture.

"Hey..."

The Chinese put a hand on his chest to stop him. Hunt didn't have to fake his outrage.

"Take your hands off me..."

"Shut up, damn *laowai!*"

The younger Chinese, who was located further back in the hallway, took a hand inside the jacket and drew a pistol. He only managed to show the butt, as the other Chinese shook his head. He was the boss. His gesture made it clear that there were too many people to start a shooting. Hunt also carried his gun in a holster, but he also didn't want to use it, for the same reason. The henchman put away the gun, but in its place appeared a gleaming dagger that he brandished furtively. The other Chinese looked at Hunt and cracked out an evil smile. Those men were not afraid to kill him; they were just trying to avoid scandal.

Hunt sighed and threw a heavy punch in the belly at the biggest of the gangsters. The man bent over himself from the unforeseen impact, but thanks to his corpulence he soon recovered and charged. Hunt dodged him with a feint and drove his elbow into the man's back. The gangster hunched over the pain and Hunt took the opportunity to give him several blows in a row on the side of the torso, under the ribs. The man pulled out a rubber bludgeon and wielded it hard at Hunt, who was hit in the shoulder. A twinge of pain ran through his nerve terminals and clouded his sight. Almost blindly, he hit the Chinese again and managed to hit a strong blow to his chin. The gangster rolled his eyes and collapsed next to the girl.

Meihua let out a hysterical squeal. Hunt winked at her to congratulate her on her performance. He saw that she was not looking at him directly but was watching something beyond his shoulder. Hunt crouched down and the younger gangster's stab went just over his head. Hunt recalled the fighting tactics of Buddhist monks and used a sweep of his legs to take down his opponent. When he had him on the ground, he threw himself on the gangster and began to hit him in the face. The gangster tried to raise the dagger, but Hunt grabbed his wrist and slammed his hand to the ground several times, until he released the weapon. Hunt then pressed his arm against the man's neck and pushed with all his weight there. The gangster gasped for air as his face turned redder and redder, until he let out a moan and fainted.

Hunt stood up, panting and sore. There was no one in the doorframe. He entered the room and saw the night breeze was rocking the just drawn curtains on the window. He stepped out onto the balcony he had been on minutes before and looked towards the manicured rose garden. The beautiful girl with the red *cheongsam* was running along the gravel road towards the street. Somehow, she had jumped to the ground from the second floor. Very reluctantly, the captain smiled and smelled the perfume that still flooded his nose.

He stood there on the balcony, thoughtfully, until he noticed that something was sticking to the palm of his hand. He ran a finger and found that it was makeup powder. Then he remembered that on the back of Meihua's hand had been exposed the tattoo that she covered with the substance: two Chinese characters that meant "peony". He leaned on the railing and said to himself that he would soon see the girl again. A shudder swept through his body.

8. HONGKEW

The fiery, warm taste of the Glenlivet swept through his body and made him feel livelier. He had reached a dead end and needed time to think about how he would continue his investigation. He could not indulge in opium-induced visions to move on, even if one of these would have allowed him to discover Wang's killer. He wasn't sure if he had really visited hell, or at least the Chinese version of the underworld, but he still felt chills as he remembered his journey to the dark realm. He took another sip of the glass and, seeing that it had been emptied, he lifted it up to ask the waiter for another round.

Peter Hunt was in the huge and elegant dining room of the Astor House Hotel. The imposing building was five stories high, with an area of fifteen hundred square meters. It covered an entire block in the northern part of the International Settlement, beyond the Soochow Creek, a tributary of the Whangpoo River. The hotel was in an area called Hongkew, which had originally constituted the American Concession before it joined the British Settlement. Today it was rather a residential district, favored mostly by the large Japanese colony of the city.

Among its services, the Astor House had several private halls, a bar, billiard room, a library and more than two hundred rooms all equipped with their own bathroom. But its greatest attraction was undoubtedly the large dining room that occupied the first two floors of the building, forty-seven meters long, fifteen meters high and a capacity for five hundred guests. It was the most luxurious place to dine in the whole city.

"This morning I asked some questions among my contacts," said Chester Peng, who occupied a chair on the other side of the table. "Nobody seems to know that *Ko Zul*. Are you sure he is not a British citizen?"

"Yes, I'm sure. He spoke English with a slight accent, but I couldn't place it through the window."

Hunt received his new glass of whisky. He drank half before asking:

"What about those two gangsters?"

"Thugs of the Green Gang. Just as that girl, Meihua, feared, they were there to avenge Tony 'The Mountain' Lu."

Peng had already told Hunt the story of the recent death of the leader of the criminal organization. Although the death seemed to be attributed to a sudden heart attack, the suspicions of his associates had immediately fallen on the beautiful courtesan who accompanied him in his final moments.

Thinking of the girl, Hunt felt a lump in his throat. When she had touched him, in the vision of hell, he had felt an icy and unnatural cold. But the night before, catching her with his body in the doorframe, he had experienced the heat radiating from the girl. And not to mention the passion he had found in her crimson lips.

"... we will find her again," the antiques dealer was saying. Hunt looked at him with bewilderment and Peng repeated: "I say that I am sure that the woman will appear again. From what you heard last night, she and her accomplice still don't have the spell of the *red typhoon* complete."

"They are missing one of the elements of the formula," Hunt nodded, recalling the words of the conspirators. "Today they will meet again to fine-tune the details of their plan."

Whatever Peng was going to say was interrupted by a group of more than a dozen men and women who entered the dining room noisily. They laughed out loud and shouted at each other. In addition to being cheerful, they seemed to be quite drunk. They all wore fancy suits and party dresses. The members of the group traversed the entire extension of the dining room and went to one of the private rooms located in the side galleries of the establishment, followed by the glances of the other diners.

"Excuse the fuss, Captain," said the waiter

who attended them, as he arranged the cutlery on the table to bring them dinner.

"Who were these people?"

"Later there is a reception at the consulate across the street," the waiter explained. "It is common for some guests to come first to the bar and have dinner before attending those events."

Hunt stiffened on the chair.

"Which consulate is that?"

"The German one, sir."

The captain felt an electric shock running through his entire body. He stood with the glass of whisky in the air and gave Peng an exultant look.

"That's it, my friend! That man had a *German* accent. And the name given to him by the courtesans is due to his position! *Ko Zul*, the consul!

"Wow, the German consul in Shanghai," Peng mused. "Why would he want to attack Britain? The war ended five years ago."

"We'll find out soon, Chester." Hunt felt encouraged. "I was back in the race. Now, let's eat. Then I must attend a party."

On the other side of Whangpoo Road, in front of the hotel, four of the most important consulates in the entire city lined up in a single block. The first of these, counting from the western corner of the street, was the Russian consulate, occupied by a temporary legation because the Chinese government had not yet recognized the Soviet regime. Then there was the German consulate, reopened a couple of years ago once when peace was signed between China and Germany, after the Great War. In the middle of the block was the empty lot of the future American consulate, whose current offices were further down the street. The last of the legations was the Japanese one, very crowded by its nationals who lived right there in Hongkew.

Outside the German consulate were more than twenty cars parked along Whangpoo Road, next to a long line of guests waiting their turn to enter the huge but simple building that housed the legation. Among the attendees was Hunt, who had no difficulty sneaking into the reception. He simply mingled with the cheerful guests coming from the Astor House, crossed the street among them, waited in line next to the group, and finally everyone entered directly into the main hall on the first floor. No one asked for his invitation or verified his identity. Once inside, he found himself immersed in a human sea of Germans and couldn't help but feel restless.

Relations between Britain and Germany had been decreasing in tension since the end of the war. The British had made some attempts to reduce the amounts of reparations owed by Germany to the Allies in the wake of the conflict, such as the failed Genoa Conference, and opposed the occupation of the Ruhr that

France had begun last January because of delays in payments. However, for Hunt, as a former army officer, it was still strange to find himself surrounded by his former enemies.

However, he soon realized that in the small universe of Shanghai, it seemed as if the Great War had never taken place. The French drank alongside the Germans, the British smoked cigars with the Turks, and the Italians danced alongside the Austrian aristocrats. The Americans, as always, just looked from afar and were content to know that they were funding the businesses of all the other guests.

"If money go before, all ways do lie open," the captain murmured, recalling Shakespeare's *The Merry Wives of Windsor.*

He looked out at the crowded hall of the consulate and said to himself that there were 'the merry partners of Shanghai'. In that city, money was the driving force behind each of the decisions that were adopted. Every idea was approved or rejected based on the profits it would bring to the city's economy. Or what was the same, to the pockets of their owners. If there were assured gains for all, there were no differences in nationality, race or religion. Suddenly, Hunt felt dizzy and like leaving. Not only of the reception at the consulate, but from that false and hypocritical city.

He wandered around the hall for a few minutes until he spotted Meihua in the distance.

His apprehensions abruptly abandoned him. The killer looked more beautiful and radiant than ever, wearing a dress that blended Western fashion with Chinese traditions. For a moment, business ceased to be the center of all conversations and the eyes of the guests –men and women alike– turned to follow the girl as she swayed through the hall with her voluptuous body. The guests made their way for her as if she was a yacht separating the waters with its sharp bow. With the same fluidity of movements, the girl came to the group where the host was and greeted effusively the businessmen and diplomats who accompanied him.

A near flash alerted Hunt to the presence of a photographer who was portraying the various groups of guests. He was a young boy who wore a suit that fit him big. On the ribbon of the hat, he wore a Press card. Hunt waited for the magnesium smoke to dissipate to approach the boy, who was preparing the lamp for the next photograph.

"Do you work for any newspapers?" The captain asked.

"*North China Daily News,*" replied the photographer, with a strong Midwestern accent. "Johnny Burr, sir."

"Do you cover social events?"

"It's a way to practice with my camera." Burr lifted the Graflex Speed Graphic he was carrying. "My father has business in Shanghai and used to allow me to go with him to parties to portray the guests. Now that I'm 17, I got a position at the *Daily News* and I get paid for the photographs," he explained excitedly.

"So, I guess you know these people over there, huh, Johnny?" asked Hunt, showing the group that surrounded the consul and that the beautiful girl had joined.

Burr nodded. Hunt stuffed some bills into the top pocket of the boy's jacket.

"Tell me who they are."

Burr was pointing his finger as he identified them:

"The one who looks like the Kaiser is the host, Rudolph Kiel, consul-general of Germany. At his side, the fat guy is Monsieur Leclerc, administrator of the French Municipal Council. Then we have the richest man of all, Victor Sassoon, whose family business owns thousands of properties in the city. Finally, the taciturn Japanese is Watanabe. It is supposed he represent a Yokohama shipping company, but is suspected of belonging to the *Kenpeitai,* the secret police."

"Wow, you're a source of knowledge," Hunt laughed. He put another bill in his pocket and added: "And the girl?"

The photographer looked around before speaking in a low voice. Hunt barely heard him from the noise of the guests.

"She is Mei Ling, better known as *Meihua,* 'the cherry blossom'. She is one of the most important courtesans in Shanghai. More than half of the city's businessmen and diplomats are among its... *sponsors*."

Burr laughed on his euphemism. Hunt thanked him and let the boy continue with his portraits.

He spent some time circulating among the guests, while pondering the findings he had made that night. Kiel, the consul, moved in the circles of the powerful people of the city, including the British, who dominated trade in Shanghai. But he secretly conspired to attack his supposed allies. Hunt tried to devise a way to approach the consul without him suspecting his true intentions, but his thoughts kept drifting towards Mei Ling. She also featured two totally opposite faces: the sing-song girl who sold her sexual services to the rich and famous, on one hand, and the expert assassin, on the other. No one was who they claimed to be in Shanghai.

Hunt reached the bar, located in an adjoining lounge. He made his way among the dozens of patrons and ordered a whisky, which he drank with his back resting on the bar while contemplating his fellows. Men and women gossiped about business, politics and scandalous upper-class affairs.

"Wow, wow, the intrepid Captain Hunt."

Mei Ling was smiling at him from the other end of the bar. He hadn't seen her coming. He picked up his whisky and walked up to her. The girl drank *baijiu* in a small glass. She was radiant and smelled softly of jasmine. The captain immediately understood her success among the city's elite.

"I hope it doesn't get customary in our meetings," he said.

"What?"

"You, fleeing when I get very close."

The girl laughed sincerely, showing gleaming teeth like ivory.

"The first time, in *Diyu,* it was you who fled," Mei Ling replied. "If I remember correctly, my spirit was about to kill yours."

"*Touché!*"

For a few moments both drank from their glasses in silence, but without averting the eyes of the other. They were flirting, but at the same time they were also studying and evaluating their possibilities, like two felines that roam in the middle of a meadow. Soon one of them would attack the other, and it would be relentless. In the end, Hunt decided that he should avoid combat... for the time being. And he had to take the girl away from his presence.

"Last night you were able to kill me when I was busy with those thugs," he casually remarked. "And you didn't."

"It would have been dishonorable," she said, in a serious expression. "Also, you were helping me."

"With Wang Min you didn't have so many

considerations."

The girl glared at him.

"That man betrayed his oath," the girl said with gritted teeth. "He deserved the ending he had."

"So, are you some kind of executioner?"

Mei Ling sipped the translucent liquor and left the glass with a bang on the bar.

"The art of *xia* is governed by a strict code. Being a foreigner, you won't be able to understand it."

Hunt cracked out a sardonic smile.

"Even in China there is justice, my dear."

She shook her head, angry. Hunt was satisfied. His attempt to make her lose control was paying off.

"You're a cynic, Peter Hunt. Have you heard of the *mien shiang?*"

"A Taoist practice to 'read the face' of a person," said the captain, "and thus determine its personality."

She nodded.

"Your face is like an open book," she snapped. "It is evident that you have also killed, Captain. Remember, we are the yin and yang."

Much to his regret, it was now he who was beginning to get angry.

"Don't pretend that we are the same, Mei Ling. Although we both have the same skills, the difference is what we use them for."

"Typical of the British." Her tone was tinged

with fury. "Even when you are the invaders you believe you act like knights."

She made a gesture to leave, but Hunt needed to give her the coup de grace. Also, he wanted to say the last word. He grabbed the girl's arm and pulled her to him.

"Stay with me. I can pay you, 'cherry blossom'."

Mei Ling's pale cheeks flushed intensely. She took the captain's glass of whisky, which he had left on the bar, and threw the contents in his face. Then she launched an obscenity in Chinese and hurried away, followed by an intense flash. Hunt wiped his face with a handkerchief and saw Johnny Burr smiling at him with his camera up. Hunt called him with a gesture.

"I thought we were friends, Johnny."

"A scandal always sells newspapers, sir," explained the boy, smiling.

Hunt grabbed him by a lapel of the jacket and spoke in his ear.

"If you publish that photo, I will kill you."

Burr disappeared on the spot. The captain ordered another whisky and drank it in just two sips.

The reception was cheering up. A band of musicians played a foxtrot and several couples had taken to the dance floor. Hunt looked at the bankers, importers, hoteliers and diplomats around him and discovered something that made him smile. Many of them had come to the reception with their wives or girlfriends, but it was evident that Mei Ling was not the only courtesan present in the hall. Some of the girls were Chinese, but he also discovered French, Italian and a lot of Russians. The Soviet revolution had forced hundreds of thousands of opponents of the Bolsheviks to emigrate, especially the aristocrats and nobles who were considered the main enemies of the new regime. Several of the Russian girls who now sold their bodies in Shanghai had been until a few years ago the daughters of men as powerful as their current companions.

Hunt looked for Mei Ling and Kiel, but both had disappeared. After went down the main hall, Hunt ascended a staircase to an interior gallery that ran through the hall in all its extension. From there he observed the crowd and could not find the conspirators. He remembered the conversation he had heard furtively the night before, in the House of White Peony, and concluded that the girl and the consul had retreated to prepare the next stage of their plan. Hunt deduced that the consul's office must be on the top floor and headed to the next flight of stairs.

A sturdy man, dressed in a cheap suit, blocked the way. He looked like an ex-soldier and remained stiff in his post as only the Germans could achieve. Hunt approached him smiling and brought out his command of the German language.

"*Guten Abend, mein freund!* Good evening, my friend!"

"You can't pass," the guard replied dryly.

"I look for the bathroom," Hunt insisted, approaching the man so he could smell his face, which reeked of alcohol.

"*Verdammt Säufer!* Damn drunk!"

The guard put a hand on Hunt's chest to stop him. That was his mistake. Considering him a drunkard, he did not try to apply all his physical strength to control him. Hunt did use his. The first blow of the fist sank into the guard's stomach like a sledgehammer and left him breathless and voiceless. Hunt pushed him into a bend in the hallway and hit him again, this time on the back of his neck, with the edge of his hand. The man choked, and then fell to the ground, fainting. Hunt dragged the body into an empty room, closed the door, and went on his way.

The corridors of the second floor were deserted, illuminated only by lamps placed on some pier tables arranged at intervals of several meters. Hunt went through the corridors and soon the hubbub of the reception turned into a distant murmur. He pricked up his ears to discover if he heard any noise coming from any of the numerous rooms of that floor. He continued walking stealthy on the fluffy carpets, until behind a door he seemed to hear some voices. As he approached, he also perceived faint moans. He spied through the keyhole and discovered a man dressed in a dinner jacket, or at least with a part of it, who allowed himself to be attended on the carpet by a girl of exotic features, probably Siamese. The lady's dress was on a sideboard on the other side of the room. The captain's eyes widened as he observed the girl's skills.

Firm footsteps approached through the corridor. Hunt stood up and looked in all directions looking for a hiding place. Suddenly he heard Kiel's voice, and then a brief answer from Mei Ling. Both were coming in his direction. When they went around the corner of the corridor, they would run into him head-on. He tested the doorknob and found that the bolt was unlocked. He opened the door slowly, leaving enough space to pass the body, and snuck inside without making a sound. He stuck his back to the wall and stood motionless by the door. The couple frolicking on the carpet was two meters away from him, but none of them heard of his presence. Hunt closed his eyes so as not to see their stunts.

Hunt tried to concentrate on the consul's voice as he passed outside the room but could barely hear him from the moans of the Siamese girl. He begged for Kiel not to listen to them. He waited a full minute, almost an eternity in there, and then opened the door to check that the conspirators had walked away. As he left the room, he found that the girl was looking at him, smiling over his companion's shoulder. Hunt winked at her and closed the door behind him. He immediately rushed in following the direction Kiel and Mei Ling had come from.

At the end of the last corridor there were double doors of thick carved wood. Hunt deduced that behind them was the consul's office. He pushed the doors and found himself in a spacious room, covered with wood paneling, furnished with large armchairs, a gigantic table that probably weighed a ton, and several shelves loaded with books. On one wall opened a hearth, not lit, and on it hung the new German flag of horizontal stripes of black, red and gold. There were no official portraits on the other walls or any photographs on the furniture.

The office had a cold and impersonal appearance. Hunt could not deduce anything about the personality of his occupant, except that perhaps the man had no personality at all. After thinking for a few moments, Hunt went to a rolltop desk in a corner. He retracted the cover. Underneath he found letter paper, ink and pens arranged on a leather folder. He checked the compartments of the furniture and in one of these he found some handwritten notes, dated that same day, addressed to Herr Konsul, the "lord consul". They were signed by a certain Rheinhardt. Hunt read them with increasing trepidation.

Report time: 09:00
Together with my men we showed up at the Shantung Road Missionary Hospital and conducted a preliminary inquiry. During the three days he was interned there, the subject received no visitors. We will be back later to speak to the staff who attended him.

Report time: 11:15
New visit to the hospital. A couple of orderlies saw the subject wander the hallways before disappearing. According to one of the nurses, another of her colleagues would have been seen talking to the subject in the recovery room.

Report time: 13:30
Thanks to the funds allocated to persuasion (expenses will be reported at the end of the day) I was able to access the personnel files through an administrative secretary. The nurse who spoke with the subject is named Mary Ann Taylor and disappeared on the same day as him.

Report time: 16:00
I spoke to Fräulein Taylor's landlady at her old home (I applied interrogation method to ensure response). The young woman has not returned since her disappearance and left her

things abandoned. Despite the insistence, the landlady cannot provide more information.

Report time: 17:45
I showed up at the British Missionary Society. Obtaining information required heavy expenditure of operational funds. According to personnel interviewed, Chinkiang's mission recently received a guest from Shanghai. We will investigate if it is the woman and keep you informed.

Hunt deduced that Kiel had launched a thorough investigation to uncover the origin of the leak of his plans. Following Wang Min's lead, his men had easily reached the nurse who had helped him escape from the hospital. The consul's henchmen, through bribery and intimidation – method of interrogation, they called it – had even discovered the whereabouts of the missionary. That meant the girl was no longer safe. Hunt wondered where Chinkiang would be and how long it would take to get there.

He left the office immediately and left the consulate in a hurry.

9. THE YANGTZE RIVER

Very early in the morning, as the sun rose, Hunt stopped the Duesenberg tourer, with a squeak of the brakes, next to a large pier located at the southern end of the Bund. Moored on the jetty was a British warship, whose crew was making the final preparations to set sail. In an orderly manner, more than a dozen sailors loaded supplies, checked the hull and verified that all the men were present. Hunt watched the ship with admiration and smiled shaking his head.

"I can't believe it. How did you achieve it in such a short time?"

Chester Peng got out of the car with the captain and they both headed towards the ship.

"It turns out I know Rear Admiral Crawford, commander of the Yangtze Squadron," he explained, shrugging. "He is a great collector of Chinese antiquities."

"I see."

HMS Wasp was an Insect-class gunboat, seventy-two meters long and eleven meters wide. It had two decks, plus the bridge. Its classification was due to the fact that it was armed with two powerful six-inch guns, one at each end of the main deck. The hull was white, and the superstructure was painted gray. It was a small ship by the standards of the Royal Navy – a battleship reached two hundred meters long – but its small size and low-draft hull allowed it to perfectly fulfill its mission: patrolling the coasts and rivers. That gunboat, along with the other ships of the Yangtze Squadron, was part of the China Station, the British fleet that guarded the coasts of that region.

Peng spoke for a moment with the ship's chief petty officer, and he indicated that they could come aboard. They ascended the walkway that connected the ship to the dock and on the deck they found the captain of the gunboat.

"Captain McQueen," said the antiques dealer. "May I present you Captain Hunt."

The naval officer raised an eyebrow in a gesture of questioning.

"Army," Hunt explained. "Retired."

McQueen put his hand to his forehead in a brief military salute.

"Welcome on board, colleague."

Captain Terence McQueen was a tall, stocky Irishman in his thirties. He had reddish hair close-cropped and on his tanned face glowed blue eyes like the sea. The three rings of gold he wore in the cuff of his jacket identified him with the rank of commander of the Royal Navy but being in command of the ship he was called, simply, 'captain'. Hunt liked him immediately.

"We'll arrive in Chinkiang at sunset," McQueen said. "After Woosung we can advance at full throttle."

"Thank you, Captain."

The ship departed half hour later. Boat traffic on the Whangpoo River was plentiful. Dozens of cargo ships, tugboats, ferries, and military vessels shared the waters of the riverbed along with small barges, junks and sampans. The *Wasp* maneuvered easily through the center of the stream, slowly moving away from the Bund and the International Settlement. Soon after the coastal landscape became a succession of factory chimneys, mills and warehouses. There was the wealth of Shanghai, as all these industries belonged to foreign companies. Each factory had their own docks in the river, which were full of ships that also belonged to European and American shipping companies.

The gunboat continued its route north, downstream. Hunt settled on the deck and entertained himself for a while watching the crew as they performed their ordinary duties of coastal surveillance, checking the cannons and machine guns, and cleaning the deck. Each of the fifty sailors fulfilled a specific function and executed it quickly and accurately, under the watchful eye of the Chief Petty Officer and the officers. A ship was like a clockwork. For the mechanism operate properly, no piece could fail.

As the sun began to become unpleasant,

Hunt climbed the outer stairs to the second deck and made his way to the officers' mess. There he met Peng and drank a cup of tea that a steward brought him.

"I think I already know what Kiel lacks to prepare the spell," Hunt said. The antiques dealer looked at him with his Zen expression. "The blood of the dragon. Cinnabar crystals modified to be used in the compound. That must be what the Green Gang was going to get, until Wang Min betrayed them."

"Maybe he tried to sell the compound on his own," Peng said. "That's why they tried to kill him and then sent the killer after him."

"But they didn't count on him asking Miss Taylor for help in the hospital," Hunt continued. "Nor that he would reveal to her what he knew, before he died."

"It's possible," Peng nodded. He rested his elbows on the table and put his fingertips together. For an instant he stared at the pyramid that formed his hands. "So why kill Tony 'The Mountain'?"

Hunt's face suddenly lit up.

"Now I understand! According to what Kiel and the girl were talking about the other night, in the House of White Peony, the Green Gang was assigned to obtaining the spell. I guess they had to get the crystals too."

"But Wang Min stole them and handed them over to the nurse," Peng said.

Hunt shook his head.

"That's where we went wrong. Wang worked on his boss orders!"

The antiquarian's neutral expression disappeared, and his face lit up as he understood the truth.

"The betrayal of the triad was the work of Tony Lu himself," he said, nodding. "He commissioned his henchman to sell the crystals on his own but was discovered by the consul. Or the girl, which is the same."

"It is likely that the Mountain Lu also wanted to sell the spell to the highest bidder," Hunt added.

"That's it," the antiques dealer agreed. "And now the consul and Mei Ling must obtain the blood of the dragon by their own means."

"If they come to know that Miss Taylor has in her possession the vial with the crystals..."

Hunt left the sentence unfinished and moved his head in a gesture of sorrow. He finally understood that the key had been in the hands of the nurse from the beginning. He cursed himself for not having come to her sooner. Now, however, the young woman's life was in danger and the gangsters were already on her trail.

An hour after setting sail, the *Wasp* arrived in Woosung, a small town located at the confluence of the Whangpoo with the imposing Yangtze River. Dozens of steamboats and other larger vessels were anchored in the bay, surrounded by barges and boats unloading goods and passengers alike. That was the point of arrival in exotic Shanghai, whose port was so crowded that transatlantic ships preferred to stop at the mouth of the river to send their cargo in smaller ships to the city.

Hunt showed up on the deck and saw the flags of a dozen countries flying on ships, including the naval flags of several fleets imposing their presence in the free harbor, much to the chagrin of the local population. American patrol boats and Japanese cruisers were the most numerous. The British gunboat greeted with deep siren calls the other ships of the Royal Navy and continued along without stopping. The longer part of the trip was still waiting for the vessel.

The *Wasp* headed west, upstream through the channel that formed south of Chungming Island, which divided the Yangtze into two arms before it emptied into the East China Sea. The river delta was dotted with huge sandbars, but they were well mapped and easily dodged by the ship's helmsman. McQueen ordered full-throttle and soon the gunboat reached its maximum speed of fourteen knots. The Yangtze River was the longest in Asia and its course had a high traffic of boats. Throughout the journey, the *Wasp* crossed paths with fishing boats, passenger ferries, local junks and gunboats from other foreign powers.

On the riverbank were many small towns that lived off of the extensive rice, cotton, hemp and tea plantations. Hunt remained on deck for much of the trip, despite the hot and humid weather. Unlike his colleagues in the navy, he was not used to spending many hours locked between metal bulkheads with only tiny portholes to breath fresh air. Leaning on the board, he could watch on the riverbank the farmers who worked under the sun between the flooded farmland and the crab pickers, whose catch was highly prized in Shanghai cuisine.

After having lunch in the officers' mess and resting for a couple of hours in the captain's cabin, Hunt met Chester Peng on the ship's bridge. McQueen was also there with the officer of the watch and the helmsman.

"We are close to our destination," said the ship's captain.

Chinkiang was about five kilometers upstream from the ship's current position, but the Christian mission was further down, before reaching the city, one kilometer inland from the coast. The *Wasp* could moor at Chinkiang pier, but that meant Hunt and Peng would have to retrace the way back. Finally, they agreed that McQueen would disembark them directly in the area of the riverbank closest to the mission.

The officer of the watch inspected the coast with his binoculars and instructed the helmsman to approach the ship to the shore without running aground. The ship approached to a safe distance and then the two engines stopped. The captain ordered the anchor to be lowered and arranged for the sailors to prepare one of the auxiliary boats.

"Thank you," Hunt told McQueen. "We will be back tomorrow first thing in the morning."

"Wait a minute!" The Irishman exclaimed before his passengers withdrew from the bridge. "Do you expect to face any kind of difficulties during your raid?"

Hunt looked at Peng for a second, and then nodded.

"It's possible."

McQueen peered out onto the balcony of the bridge and uttered a stentorian yell:

"¡Davis! ¡Baker!"

Two sailors climbed the stairs that led to the bridge. Both were young and stocky.

"At your service, Captain!" They responded in unison.

"Look for three rifles in the armory," their captain ordered, "and prepare your equipment for a raid."

Ten minutes later, the men who were to disembark gathered on the port side, where a crew team was lowering the boat overboard. The two escort sailors were wearing equipment and helmets. McQueen took the third rifle and handed it to Hunt.

"I assume you know how to use this junk."

"Lee-Enfield Mk III bolt-action repeating rifle, .303 caliber, ten rounds," Hunt announced upon examining the weapon.

McQueen laughed.

"I'll be waiting for you with breakfast. Good luck, colleague."

The boat moved away from the gunboat with the last rays of the afternoon sun. Sailor Davis took the rudder and led it to the shore, a swampy terrain lined with reeds. Once they found solid ground, the members of the party got off the boat and hid it in the bushes. Then they started walking in the middle of a bamboo grove. A few minutes later, the sun set over the tall treetops. The group advanced silently and at a steady pace. They left the bamboos behind and continued along a gravel road that ran in the middle of some plantations. The moonlight guided them for almost an hour until they spotted a complex of Chinese-style buildings, but with obvious Western touches. The main construction was crowned by a large cross.

As they approached the complex, they saw that the main building was a chapel. Behind it stood a modest Western-style, two-story house. Chester Peng, who was at the head of the group, went to the house and knocked the door. A moment later, a middle-aged man with a suspicious face peeked out of the half-open door.

"Harry, it's me. Chester."

The man covered his mouth with a hand in a

gesture of surprise.

"Oh my God, Chester! What are you doing here? And at this hour?"

The man named Harry then noticed Hunt and, especially, the armed sailors. His countenance darkened.

"I'll explain everything to you," Peng said, succinctly. "Can we come in?"

The missionary's expression softened, and he motioned for them to enter. Hunt understood the apprehensions of that man. He knew that the presence of missionaries in the country's inland was not welcomed by all Chinese. Undoubtedly, night visits did not usually bring good news.

"Captain Hunt," Peng said, "Please meet Reverend Harry Gates."

"Welcome to the mission of Chinkiang, Captain."

Davis and Baker greeted with a bow of their heads. Gates smiled at them somewhat nervously, his eyes fixed on their rifles.

The Reverend invited them to come to his study. At that hour the place was almost deserted and silent. As he led them to the room, Gates explained that the mission was home to about fifty young Chinese men and women studying the Christian gospel, along with a dozen British missionaries. There they read the Bible, learned English and worked the land. It was a peaceful place, but from time to time they suffered some attack from nationalist groups or the troops of some warlord.

The sailors waited outside the studio as Peng and Hunt explained to the Reverend the reasons for their untimely presence on the mission. Gates listened to them with increasing unease.

"But no one knows that Miss Taylor is here!" exclaimed the Reverend at the end of the story.

"I didn't know either," Peng replied. "But that man Kiel managed to discover her, and we managed to discover him."

"The best thing will be that early tomorrow we take the girl with us," Hunt explained. "This way we can guarantee her safety."

"I can't believe anyone wants to hurt that young woman," Gates lamented. Then he looked up at the closed door of the studio. "Those sailors out there... Do you expect trouble?"

"We don't know, Reverend," Hunt replied, trying to sound confident. "But those men will protect us if something bad happens."

Reverend Gates arranged dinner in the dining room of his residence. There they met his wife Candice, a petite and quiet woman, and finally Hunt was able to meet Mary Ann Taylor.

The girl entered the dining room behind Mrs. Gates and the men got up to greet them. Hunt had not imagined that the missionary could be a beautiful young woman. He estimated that she would be about twenty-five years old. She was tall, thin, with long blond hair pulled back in a ponytail. She wore a simple white blouse and a long, wide black skirt. It almost seemed that she was trying to hide her beauty. Hunt stretched out his hand to her and for a few moments stared into her eyes, as blue as his. Mary Ann gave the hint of a polite smile and then sat quietly.

Hunt waited for them to finish dinner before explaining to the girl what had led them to the mission. Although he tried to say it tactfully, the nurse's eyes filled with tears.

"Oh, I'll never be safe!" She exclaimed between sobs.

"Now that we are here, you are no longer in danger, Miss Taylor," he tried to reassure her.

"What about the rest of the missionaries?" She wanted to know.

"If someone comes around looking for you, they will leave soon if they discover that you have left."

The girl opened her eyes to what that meant.

"I'm afraid you'll have to come with us first thing tomorrow, Miss Taylor," Hunt said. "There is a Royal Navy gunboat waiting for us on the river."

"How did those men find me? Do you say they are Germans? Why did they kill Wang Min?"

She threw the questions in a hurry, with an anxious expression on her face. Between Hunt and Peng, they summarized the story of what they had found out up to that point.

"Blood of the Dragon, you say? Surely it refers to the vial that Wang handed me before he was killed."

"That's right, Miss..."

"Oh, call me Mary Ann, captain."

"Peter, please."

She smiled, and her cheeks flushed slightly. Hunt held out a handkerchief to her and she wiped away her tears.

"So, without those crystals," the girl insisted, "wouldn't the spell work?"

"My dear," interrupted Reverend Gates. "You certainly won't believe in those superstitions, will you?"

"I wouldn't have believed it before, Reverend. But after what I saw that night in the garden..."

She left the sentence unfinished and shuddered. Hunt poured her a glass of sherry from the bottle left by the silent Mrs. Gates before retiring to sleep. Mary Ann drank it in one sip and felt better.

"That compound is essential for the realization of the *red typhoon,*" Peng said.

"So, we need to make sure it doesn't fall into the hands of those men," Mary Ann added.

"Do you still have it with you?" Hunt asked.

The girl nodded and said that she would go fetch it in her room.

Davis and Baker had eaten in the kitchen, while the Chinese servants looked with their eyes wide open their immense rifles. After dinner, Davis went back to watch the door of the dining room, but Baker went outside to smoke.

A covered gallery ran through the exterior of the reverend's residence. Baker leaned his back on one of the columns supporting the gallery and lit a hand-rolled cigarette. He hadn't taken two puffs when he heard a noise coming from across the yard.

He pricked his ear and heard the noise again. It was a very slight crunch, but in the stillness of the night he could heard it perfectly. The noise could have been produced by some loose animal, but anyway the sailor decided to check what it was. He crossed the dirt courtyard and approached some bushes that delimited the open space in front of the building. Now the noise was heard with more intensity. Baker pushed away a bush and suddenly encountered a young man who startled when he was discovered.

Baker's mind processed the information provided by his eyes in succession: the young man was white; he was wearing a kind of uniform; and was carrying a gun in his hand. Then the sailor remembered that he too was armed. He raised his rifle with one hand and took the barrel with the other, so he could point forward. At the same time, he opened his mouth to shout to the intruder to stop. However, the other man reacted more quickly, despite the surprise. He just raised his pistol and fired at point-blank range. The bullet hit Baker in the chest and threw him back but failed to knock him down. Baker finished aiming and shot in turn, but his hands were shaking. The bullet only grazed the intruder on the arm. Then Baker fell to the ground and stopped moving.

In the dining room, Hunt sprung up when he heard the first shot.

"Chester, look for the sailors. Reverend, take me to Mary Ann's room."

Davis opened the door after the second shot was heard.

"It's Baker, Captain! They are attacking him!"

"Go and help him, sailor, but do not expose yourself."

Gates and Hunt ran upstairs to the second floor of the residence. The missionary was white like paper. He pointed his finger at a door and Hunt opened it all at once. In the room, Mary Ann had shrunk in a corner. In her hands she held the vial with the crystals.

"It's them!" She cried out in despair. "They come to kill me!"

"Come with me." Hunt stretched out a hand. "We will be fine."

They ran downstairs. Hunt asked the Reverend to take all the occupants of the residence to a safe place and lock themselves in there. Peng was at the entrance of the building, hidden behind the door.

"Over there!" He indicated to Hunt, showing the gallery outside.

"Stay with the girl!"

Hunt picked up his rifle and went out on the

run. Davis was barricaded behind a column, with the rifle pointed to the yard.

"I see movement, Captain," the sailor whispered. "Behind the bushes."

"And Baker?"

"There, sir."

Hunt followed the sailor's gesture with his gaze and saw Baker knocked down on the edge of the courtyard, about twenty meters from the gallery. Beyond, he found that something was moving in the dark. He raised the rifle, pushed forward the bolt, and fired. He was immediately shot back. He threw himself to the ground and protected behind a column. Davis also exchanged fire with the intruders. Hunt deduced that there were several of them.

"Any estimate of the enemy force?" He asked Davis.

"I think there are three of them, sir."

"We can't let them get close. You cover the right of the yard and I cover the left. Now!"

The shooting intensified. The intruders fired handguns, but at that distance they were quite effective. Bullets pierced the columns of the gallery and several glasses of the residence were shattered. Hunt waited to see some shadow before firing. Each time he managed to detect any movement, he maintained a rapid rate of fire, actioning the bolt again and again to eject a cartridge and put a new one, as he had been taught during his basic training. He fired all the ammunition and reloaded the rifle with two clips of five bullets each.

"I'm going to move forward," he said. "Davis, cover me!"

The sailor fired to both sides of the yard. Hunt crouched down and advanced stealthily, protected by the shots of his escort. Reaching the middle of the field, he raised the rifle and fired. He used the muzzle flashes of his opponents to make a target. He heard a moan and one of the enemy shooters stopped firing.

"¡Davis, help Baker!"

The sailor ran in a zigzag through the courtyard until he reached his shot down companion.

"He's alive, Captain!"

Davis grabbed Baker from his clothes and dragged him back into the building. Hunt kept shooting and managed to advance to the line of bushes. He rummaged through the vegetation and found a white man lying on the ground, motionless. He put a pair of fingers on his neck and found that he had no pulse. In his dead hand he was still holding a Mauser pistol. That was enough to deduce that the intruders were men of the consul Kiel.

Hunt moved stealthily through the bushes, guided by the creaks produced by the other intruders when stepping on the fallen branches. Suddenly he heard whispers in German:

"*Wo bist du, Schmitt?* Where are you,

Schmitt?"

"Ich bin hier, Leutnant Rheinhardt! I'm here, Lieutenant Rheinhardt!"

Hunt was paralyzed for a moment. So, there was Kiel's henchman, Rheinhardt. Lieutenant? Surely he was a veteran of the war, like Hunt himself. He raised his rifle again and moved faster, eager to catch that man. But his anxiety betrayed him. Suddenly, he stepped on a fallen branch whose creak sounded like a shot in the stillness of the night. Two shadows turned to him and fired their pistols. Hunt lay on the ground as shots buzzed over his head.

He lay flat on his face, with the rifle in front of him, and he aimed at the flashes. He waited for the opportune moment and fired several times, bringing his fingers from the trigger to the bolt with the maximum possible speed to change the cartridges. A thump told him he had a hit. He sprung up and ran towards his target. A man with Germanic features was lying on the ground. Half of his face was gone. Hunt crouched over him and rummaged through the pockets of his jacket.

"¡Ahhhh!"

The attacker's scream alerted Hunt just in time. He half turned and saw a shadow falling on him. The blade of a bayonet flashed in the night. Hunt grabbed the enemy's wrist and they both rolled on the floor. His opponent would be about forty years old, stocky, and had his hair close-cropped. No doubt it was the damn Rheinhardt. Hunt struggled wildly to try to snatch the bayonet from the German, but the man held it with a grip like steel.

In the fray, the sharp blade was descending dangerously into the captain's throat. Hunt rolled again and tried to spot his rifle on the ground but couldn't find it. But he did look something that gave him hope back. He propelled himself by dragging his legs on the ground, carrying Rheinhardt's weight with him, until he approached the other man's body. The former lieutenant looked his dead companion for a second.

"Soon you will go to meet him, Rheinhardt."

The German was surprised to hear Hunt speaking in his language, but it wasn't enough to loosen the pressure of his weapon. Hunt kept him at bay with one hand and with the other he rummaged through the ground until he found the object he had seen. The tip of the bayonet was already a few centimeters from the captain's neck. Rheinhardt kept muttering expletives as he carried all his weight to stick the sharp blade.

"*Geh zur Hölle, du Bastard!* Go to hell, you bastard!"

"You first, damn *kraut!*"

The 7.63×25mm round, still fired at point-blank range, caused a rumble that flooded the night. Rheinhardt spit out blood, and his body suddenly loosened. Hunt pulled the Mauser C96 pistol away from his enemy's ribs and pushed the corpse aside. He got up snorting and wiped the sweat from his face with the sleeve of his jacket. A thread of blood ran down his neck where the bayonet had grazed him at the last moment.

He caught his breath and ran back to the mission. In the living room of the residence, Mary Ann tended to Baker with the help of Davis and Gates. The sailor was lying on a sofa and looked very badly injured. Hunt approached Peng.

"How is Baker?"

"He lost a lot of blood. We must take it to the ship immediately. What about the intruders?"

Hunt simply shook his head. The antiques dealer remained expressionless.

"How many they were?" He asked, finally.

"Three. Including Kiel's assistant, Rheinhardt."

For a few moments, both men stood by watching Mary Ann tend to the wounded sailor. With the experience of her craft, the girl cleaned and bandaged the wound. Soon the bandages were soaked in blood. She did not be daunted and continued to prepare the wounded so that they could transfer him to the ship.

Peng grabbed Hunt's arm and took him aside.

"Maybe I should talk to the British consul, Peter. This affair could become into an international incident."

"No, my friend. This is a *personal* incident."

10. SHIKUMEN

Herr Rudolph Kiel, Consul-General of Germany in Shanghai, descended from his Rolls-Royce 40/50 Silver Ghost limousine on Avenue Road and started walking lightly, as if he were taking a quiet stroll in the afternoon. A minute later, Peter Hunt descended from the Duesenberg Straight Eight tourer and began to follow him. He had been in the footsteps of the consul for three days, stuck to him like a shadow, stalking his boring routine. However, Hunt had a feeling that this time some important finding would occur. Something in his inside told him that the mysterious Kiel was about to start a new stage in his plans.

Immediately after returning from the Chinkiang mission, Hunt decided to concentrate his investigation on the consul. He seemed to be the leader of the conspiracy to attack Britain and, as far as Hunt knew by now, he did not yet possess all the elements to create the explosive weapon called *red typhoon* and be able to use it against Britain. Kiel needed the modified cinnabar crystals, the 'blood of the dragon', which Wang Min had stolen from him. That meant he had to replace the compound and Hunt decided he would be in the exact place and time when Kiel acquired it.

As a first step, the captain changed rooms at the hotel and got one that overlooked Whangpoo Road. From there he could easily spy on the German consulate. He settled down to guard the building from the window and every time he saw the driver prepare the official limousine to leave, he would rush down to get his own car that he kept parked in front of the hotel. Most of the consul's trips were concentrated in the diplomatic sector of the International Settlement and in the vicinity of municipal offices. Hunt also discovered that Kiel maintained a private apartment in the western sector of the French Concession, but rarely used it. Other times, Kiel would visit the German club, or the offices of some company from his country. However, this was the first time he had moved west of the city and abandoned his vehicle.

Hunt felt anxious and enraged at the same time. The return to the gunboat had been hard, in the middle of the night and with sailor Baker dying on a makeshift stretcher carried by Davis and Hunt. The doctor on board had managed to stabilize the wounded man with great difficulty and McQueen ordered to go full steam ahead to Chinkiang, where Baker was admitted to the local hospital. The Irishman was fuming from the attack on his crewman, but he calmed down quite a bit when he was informed that Hunt and

Davis had eliminated the three attackers.

On their return to Shanghai, near dawn on that long night, McQueen opened a bottle of Bushmills that he had hidden in his cabin and drank a glass with Hunt.

"To your health, my friend!"

Hunt drank the Irish whiskey in one sip and immediately felt exhausted. McQueen gave him the cabin and retreated to the bridge. A moment later there were slight knocks on the door. Hunt was about to fall asleep. He opened and met Mary Ann Taylor.

"Are you okay, Peter? The doctor should see that wound on your neck."

"It's superficial. Don't worry."

The girl stood in the doorframe, undecided. Hunt questioned her with his gaze. Finally, she decided to speak.

"Will there be another war? Will Germany attack our country?"

Hunt sat on the edge of McQueen's bunk and pointed the girl to the desk chair.

"I don't know, my dear," he replied. "Perhaps this issue of the *red typhoon* is just an initiative of a particular group of Germans."

"But the consul is a representative of his government!"

"It's weird, I know. However, the new German army, the *Reichswehr,* has only one hundred thousand men. The Treaty of Versailles prohibited them from heavy artillery and armored vehicles."

Mary Ann looked at him with a confused expression, because for her that data meant nothing. Hunt said:

"I want to say that, at present, Germany does not pose any danger to our country."

Once he said it, Hunt discovered that even himself did not feel calm with that statement.

The girl took her hand to a pocket of the skirt and from it extracted the vial with the crystals. She laid it out to Hunt, who watched admired the reddish blaze inside.

"So, what is this?" She asked.

Then she turned around and left. Hunt stared at the small container for a long time. Finally, he put it in one of his trouser pockets and fell asleep right away. However, he had an uneasy sleep that prevented him from recovering. The girl's question hovered in his head. He was tired of killing and avoid to being killed. Only five years had passed since the end of the war, and it seemed that the former enemies were rearming. He decided that when he returned to Shanghai, he would soon put an end to Kiel's plans.

But three days later he still hadn't discovered anything significant, and his patience was beginning to run out. However, the consul's mysterious walk to the western part of the concession was suspicious enough to harbor some hope. Hunt followed Kiel about a hundred meters away, with all his senses on his prey.

The consul wore an impeccable suit, was tall and wore a wide-brimmed hat, which made it very easy to distinguish him among the crowd.

Kiel walked aimlessly and unhurriedly, looking at the shop windows, stopping to look at the new concession buildings, and checking his pocket watch from time to time. After a few minutes he crossed the street sharply and retraced his steps on the opposite sidewalk. Soon after, Hunt discovered him looking through a stained-glass window reflecting the activity of the street. Then the captain understood that Kiel was trying to check if anyone was following him. Since that someone was himself, Hunt took due precautions and moved several meters away from his prey.

His heart beat hard. Kiel was going to meet a contact or go somewhere related to his secret plans. The conspiracy was in motion again. Hunt kept his head down and moved at the same pace as the consul, mixed in the crowd that filled the sidewalk. A few minutes later, Kiel took a side street and Hunt went after him. There the consul adopted the same security measures and only continued when he felt confident that no one was tracking his steps. Hunt saw him twist down Sinza Road and he also headed towards that street.

A couple of blocks later, Kiel went through a large stone arch that opened into a high wall. It was already dark and from afar Hunt couldn't make out what was on the other side of the wall. He waited for a few seconds and approached the entrance. The arch led to a long, narrow alley flanked on both sides by long rows of terraced houses. Hunt immediately identified it as a *lilong,* a residential complex of small dwellings accessed through the alley. Each of the units was known as *shikumen,* after the decorated stone porticoes that served as the entrance to the houses.

The main alley was more than a hundred meters long and from it branched other even narrower alleys that ran through the complex. As Hunt knew, there could be more than three hundred *shikumen* houses inside. He went into the *lilong* alley and after a moment he managed to distinguish the tall and upright figure of the German consul. On the way he came across some inhabitants of the complex, but overall, the place was quiet and uncrowded. On one of the sides there were porticos every four or five meters, made of stone and with decorative lintels. On the opposite wall were simpler iron gates that led to the back of the houses.

Further on the alley there was a man standing next to one of the porticoes. Kiel spoke to him in whispers. The man nodded a few times, and then opened the sturdy wooden door for him. Hunt stuck his back to another of the entrances and spied on them from there. Kiel disappeared into the *shikumen.* The man closed the door again and remained in the alley. Hunt waited for a moment and got back on his way. The *lilong* was deserted. The noise of the outside street was barely distinguished inside the complex.

As he approached the guard, Hunt found that the man was following him with his gaze as he approached him. The captain kept his eyes in front and stayed in the center of the alley. He was a simple passerby walking there. However, the man was suspicious and set off his alarms when he discovered a foreigner in that place. The Chinese said something in his language and blocked Hunt's way. The captain went on his way and shrugged, indicating that he did not understand that language. The man rebuked him again and tried to hold him to stop.

The edge of Hunt's outstretched hand slammed into the guard's throat, just above the thyroid cartilage. The man let out a choked moan and brought both hands to the sore larynx. He tried to scream for help but couldn't. The blow had left him voiceless. Hunt grabbed him by the shoulders and threw a firm knee in his stomach. The guard doubled in pain and fell to the ground on his knees. Hunt's attack was so sudden that the man could do nothing to defend himself. But that didn't mean he was defeated. He turned on his knees and crawled towards the portico. As he approached, he stretched out a hand and tried to knock on the door.

Hunt threw himself forward and caught up with the guard just as the man's fist was a few inches from the door. The captain gave him a certain kick in the ribs and knocked him down. The man looked at Hunt with the eyes wide open and again tried to scream, but the throat still did not respond. The captain pounced on the guard, but he rolled on the ground and managed to dodge him. He stood up in gasps and threw himself once again towards the door. Hunt jumped on top of him, and they both fell forward. Hunt grabbed the guard by the head and slammed it into the hard pavement of the alley.

The man was left lying unconscious. Hunt looked both ways into the alley and saw that no one was coming. He took the body by the legs and dragged it until it was stretched to the edge of the wall, where it was hidden in the shadows. Wasting no time, Hunt approached the portico that was now unguarded. The heavy wooden doors were closed, and no noise could be heard from the inside. The wall that flanked the alley served as the outer wall of the terraced houses. A couple of meters beyond the portico a window opened, but it was closed with thick shutters.

The stretch of wall between the portico and the window was just over two meters high. Hunt found that no one was hanging around the alley and then rested his foot on a ridge of the wall. He propelled himself upwards and reached just the edge of the wall with both hands. He held on as he could and for a moment he balanced and took a breath. Then he rose with the strength of his arms. He put his elbows on top of the parapet and pushed his feet against the rough wall covering, which helped him rise above the top edge.

On the other side of the wall was a small courtyard no more than two meters wide on each side. Hunt slowly pulled inward so as not to make noise. The small space was filled with flowers and shrubs in clay pots. At the other end of the courtyard opened doors that led to the main living room of the house, long and narrow. The room was in darkness, but the smoke of incense and a strong smell of spices floated in the air. From an adjoining room came the noise of voices and laughter.

The door leading to the room was ajar. Hunt spied through the opening and saw four men playing mahjong on a table full of chips. The guys looked like thugs, but they were absorbed in their game and in the jests they threw each other. Hunt went through the room undetected. On the opposite wall of the hall was another door leading to a hallway, which in turn led to the *shikumen* backyard. There was also the kitchen of the house, where a couple of women prepared several dishes of intense aromas.

In the space between the kitchen and the living room arose a staircase that led to the second floor. From above came Kiel's elegant and authoritative voice, alongside the wavering words of an older man. Both spoke in English. Hunt climbed the ladder surreptitiously, treading extremely carefully on the rickety rungs. What those men said became more intelligible as Hunt went up.

"... a lot of blood of the dragon, a lot. Big typhoon, huh?" said the old Chinese man.

"The quantities are required according to the specifications of the formula," Kiel said.

"Difficult preparation. Good master alchemist needs..."

"Don't worry about it, old man. Just prepare the cinnabar."

"Already, already. Delicate task, you know?"

Hunt continued his ascent, trying to prevent the old wood from creaking under his weight. The tension had bathed him in sweat and his heart was beating in a hurry. When he reached the top of the staircase, he could see that the consul was in a small room full of jars, flasks, bowls, bottles and vessels. The containers covered several shelves, a cabinet and the cover of a small table. The old man was sitting on a stool, leaning over the table, grinding cinnabar crystals and other elements that he deposited in a mortar where he mixed the compound. The only source of light came from a faint kerosene lamp arranged by the window.

A pungent smell flooded the entire second floor of the *shikumen,* and the air was saturated by a dense reddish dust. Kiel was standing behind the alchemist, holding a handkerchief over his nose, without looking away from the mortar. The twinkling light of the lamp made the consul's eyes shine with a crimson glow and cast shadows that danced on his face, giving him a delirious appearance. Hunt put a hand inside the jacket, ready to grab his revolver. With an accurate shot he could put an end to that man's plans. However, he assumed that those jars and bowls were full of chemicals that could blow up the *shikumen* or perhaps the entire complex of houses.

The smell of the substances emanating from the room was mixing with the aromas coming from the kitchen. Hunt felt his stomach churning and a burning nose. His fingers touched the butt of the revolver inside the holster, but he hesitated about drawing his gun. Rudolph Kiel was an official representative of his government. He had diplomatic immunity and the captain had no evidence even to report him to the City Council. He understood that all that remained was for him to continue to monitor the consul and thwart his plans when they were in the final stage of the attack. He let go of the revolver and decided to hide.

Before he could move, a scream startled him. A woman stood at the foot of the stairs, holding a tray with a steaming plate of food. The woman was screaming in a tone of surprise and fury. Hunt deduced that she was hurling strong insults at him in Shanghai dialect, although he did not understand a single word. Looking back at the old man's room, he was met with the dumbfounded gaze of Consul Kiel, who was standing in the doorframe.

"*Verdammt!* Damn!"

The hall on the first floor was filled with screams of men running towards the staircase, alerted by the woman. Hunt deduced that the gangsters were armed. He looked up and saw that the stairs continued after the second floor, towards an upper floor. Hunt ran down the next flight of stairs and sped up the rungs, which ended in a small attic. It had a narrow window located on the opposite wall. Hunt slammed it open and slipped outside, forcing his body through the opening. The roof of the house was gabled and covered with tiles. Hunt ascended the roof, trying not to slip, as the eave had nothing to handle.

When he reached the top of the roof he swayed on the ridge and ran with his arms stretched to the sides to maintain his balance. Behind him he heard the gangsters who were already coming outside through the attic window. Hunt tried to go faster. The line of houses stretched for tens of meters, with each division marked by a rime on the roof. Hunt jumped the dividing walls without difficulty and accelerated his race on the ridge of the roof, cracking dozens of tiles in his path. He looked over his shoulder, still running, and saw that three thugs were coming chasing him. The fourth man was very obese and was left screaming from the attic.

A gunshot thundered in the night. Hunt instinctively crouched down. He risked another look and saw that the man at the head of the pursuers wielded a gun. Another shot was heard. This time the captain felt the bullet pass near his head. He kept his balance with one arm and with his right hand he drew his revolver. Arriving at the next division, he barricaded himself crouched behind the edge of the wall, raised his gun, and fired. The gangster stopped abruptly, swung for a moment over the apex of the roof, and then rolled down the plane. His body jumped over the ledge and disappeared into the darkness.

There were two other thugs left. Hunt continued with his escape. Further over the roof he spotted the end of the line of houses. Then came a side alley and beyond stood another row of *shikumen.* Hunt did not slow down. When he reached the end of the building, he pushed himself with all his strength and landed on the other side of the alley. The tiles of the ridge were loose and jumped in all directions upon receiving the impact of the captain. For a few seconds his body leaned dangerously towards the plane of the roof, but he managed to regain stability and kept running.

His pursuer was not so lucky. He managed to jump over the alley and fell at the ridge of the roof, but the weak wooden frame broke under the loose tiles. The man's foot sank sharply into the hole, and the ankle broke with a piercing creak. The gangster gave a cry of pain and lost his balance. He went headlong into the plane of the roof and slipped into the void. The third man didn't even try to jump from one roof to another. He crouched down at the end of the row of houses, drew a gun and began shooting.

Bullets buzzed as they passed Hunt and crashed into the tiles around him. He tried to put more distance with the shooter, but he knew that the gun still had enough range. When he reached the next dividing wall, he threw himself face down and hid behind the rim. He still had his Webley in his hand. He passed the gun over the parapet and returned fire blindly. Unable to aim, the bullets were lost in the air. With his body stuck to the roof, he turned upside down and adopted a shooting position from behind the wall edge. He had only two bullets left. He poked out part of his head so that he could observe the target and carefully pointed at the crouching figure on the other roof. He waited for the precise moment and shot. He saw a tile burst into pieces and understood that he had failed.

He calculated that his opponent's pistol must have at least seven shots. The gangster was firing incessantly from his position, so he would soon exhaust the magazine. Hunt waited lying flat until the shooting stopped. He spied on the wall and saw that the man was reloading his gun. Hunt burst out, picked up the revolver with both hands, and shot into the center of the silhouette that formed his target. The gangster groaned in pain and tried to get up. He immediately lost his foot and rolled across the roof beyond the ledge.

Hunt didn't have time to enjoy his feat. Through the main alley came several men running in his direction. They could advance faster than he did, but they would only be able to stop him if they climbed to the roof. Hunt continued his escape by advancing through the ridge, while keeping an eye on his pursuers. Some yelled at him, and others fired their guns, but they didn't have a good shooting angle. Hunt crouched as he kept running. He had to jump over two other side alleys before spotting the end of the *shikumen* complex.

The line of the last houses ended in the perimeter wall. Hunt carefully pulled down to the eaves of the roof and there he clung to a drainpipe. Then he went down it until he reached the sidewalk of a secondary street. For a few moments he leaned against the wall and caught his breath. On the other side of the wall came the cries of the men who were looking for him. They would soon discover that he had left the complex. He took a breath and ran again. When he reached a main street, he stopped to orient himself, until he managed to determine where his car was. He made a long detour, which served to regain his composure, and finally reached the site where he had parked the Duesenberg.

He imagined that by now Kiel must have returned to the consulate. Maybe he was eager to speed up his plans now that he knew he had been blown out. Hunt started the engine and accelerated the car, taking advantage of the fact that traffic had decreased at that time of night. For a few moments he drove back to his hotel, but suddenly he had another idea. He turned sharply on the next street and headed towards the western sector of the French Concession. Half an hour later he stopped in front of a modern, luxurious-looking building.

He got out of the car and circled the building, while keeping an eye on the windows on the top floor. The apartment was dark. Although unknowingly, he followed the same route that Mei Ling had used a few days ago. Hunt rushed up the back escape and snuck into the apartment through the living room window. He moved stealthily to the next office and closed the curtains before turning on the lamp on the desk. He inspected the books lining the wall shelves and searched the desk drawers. In one of these he found a diary bound in fine suede covers.

He opened it by the most recent annotations, and several sheets of thin paper fell to the ground. He unfolded the documents on the desk and read them under the lamp light. He discovered that the sheets were letters that the consul had recently received. For his part, in the diary there were transcripts of the answers that Kiel himself had dispatched. Between the pages of the notebook, he also found sketches, maps and even a couple of old photographs. His heart ran amok almost as much as he fled the *shikumen,* although no one was chasing him there. After a few minutes he returned the papers and the diary to their place, turned off the light, and sneaked out of the apartment.

While driving the Duesenberg back to his hotel, this time calmer and enjoying the trip, he went over the history he had been able to build from those documents. The plan of his enemies was on a much larger scale than he had been able to imagine. That story was both fascinating and perverse.

11. POTSDAM

When the Audi Type K convertible coupe rushed across the Glienicke Bridge heading west, its driver was relieved to leave the decaying German capital behind. Until five years ago, Berlin had been the center of an empire, but now it was nothing more than a shadow. Hundreds of beggars roamed its streets, on every corner there were long lines of unemployed people and at night the gangs gave free rein to their crimes. Where before order and culture reigned, now brothels, decadent bars, and drug dealers prevailed. Furthermore, hundreds of degenerate artists dared to show their obscene art in theaters, galleries and cabarets. All respect for authority had been lost since leftists had taken control of local and national institutions. The 'republic' was a cancer in the heart of Germany that had to be removed as soon as possible.

Count Albrecht von Dahlen felt revitalized arriving in Potsdam, a beautiful and quiet city where magnificent palaces, extensive gardens, beautiful churches and various museums stood. With his renewed enthusiasm, the count pressed the accelerator thoroughly. The 3,600 cubic centimeter engine propelled the car at more than ninety kilometers per hour. He kept the Audi on the right side of the road, moved away from the Havel River and continued towards Jungfern Lake. Shortly afterwards he passed by the newly built Cecilienhof Palace, intended as the residence of the Crown Prince, whose occupant had left it in a hurry at the end of the war. Before reaching the New Garden, the immense park designed by King Frederick William II of Prussia, the Audi entered a secondary road that crossed a small grove and led to an elegant English Tudor-style villa.

The count stopped the car near the entrance of the house and jumped out. While taking off his protective helmet and goggles, a servant ran to receive him. After greeting him with a bow, the servant handed him a tunic that he was carrying folded over his arm.

"They are about to begin, *Herr Graf*."

Dahlen muttered a few words and picked up the tunic as he made his way to the house. A butler allowed him access through the front door. From the spacious and elegant lobby, the count went to a small adjoining room where he could change his clothes. He took off the jacket from his suit and over the shirt he wore the tunic, a white surcoat with a large black cross embroidered on the chest. He adjusted the tunic with a decorated leather belt and returned to the lobby. From somewhere in the house came the sound of music, which he soon recognized as *Ride of the Valkyries,* from Wagner's opera *The Valkyrie.*

The count oriented himself through the corridors of the mansion following the origin of the music. This came from horn loudspeakers installed above the entrance of a large room arranged in the same shape as a Christian chapel. In the background stood an altar and in front of it were lined up several rows of wooden benches. On the walls hung pictures with scenes of medieval battles and pennants with black crosses. The altar was dominated by a huge banner with the coat of arms of the German Empire: a black eagle with the crown of the Holy Roman Empire.

More than fifty attendees, dressed in identical white surcoats, occupied several of the benches. There were only men present. They were all middle-aged, haughty, and kept a solemn appearance. Dahlen advanced down the central aisle of the chapel to the first row of pews, where he was enthusiastically received by the attendees. Almost immediately the music increased in intensity and there was silence among the crowd. When the piece finished playing, an elderly man stood behind the altar. He had a robust appearance, despite his years, and in his eyes a restrained fury was reflected. His robe was black with the cross embroidered in the center of a white shield located on the chest.

"Good afternoon, dear brothers," he greeted,

in a stentorian voice. "The Germanic Noble Society begins its session."

At the turn of the century, at a time of the height of the Empire, esoteric German nationalism was in vogue in the country's intellectual and mystical circles. On the eve of these ideals, several secret societies were founded to debate and disseminate the principles of the *Völkisch* movement: the superiority of the Nordic race, anti-Semitism and the virtue of monarchical rule. The goal of those men was to lead the empire along the path of traditional 'Germanic' values, inspired by the ancient medieval orders of chivalry, from which they took their symbols, such as the black cross pattée, as well as their pre-Christian esoteric beliefs and an organizational structure like Freemasonry.

Before and during the Great War, the Germanic Noble Society had attracted several important members of imperial and Prussian society, managing to influence important military and political decisions. However, the resounding defeat in the conflict had plunged most of its members into deep disappointment and their ranks had been drastically reduced. At present, the power of society was greatly diminished and only the most loyal members remained active, who were completely committed to recovering the lost values of imperial society and, to no lesser extent, to destroying those who caused that disaster.

Meetings like the one that took place that afternoon were becoming less frequent and only a handful of fanatics attended. Anyway, the discussions were still intense and the feeling of revenge of the members was increasing. Knowing the anger and frustration of his brothers, the great master of the society focused his speech on criticism of the current situation in Germany. His darts were directed at the government of the republic (a word the speaker uttered with real disgust), the Treaty of Versailles, the former enemies in the Great War, the Jews and the Communists. In his eyes, only loyal aristocrats, monarchists and conservatives could save the country from the debacle in which it was plunged. His diatribes were greeted with jubilation by the attendees and several times his speech was interrupted by spontaneous ovations.

Then the speaker changed the tone of his words, and from hatred he went on to ecstasy. He praised the Kaiser and the military, reminding those present that the army had not been the cause of defeat in the war, but had been stabbed in the back by the traitors who conspired in Berlin and who had signed the armistice of November 1918. Republicans, leftists and Jews were the real causes of the defeat; the 'November criminals', as they were called in right-wing circles. With furious passion, he called on his brothers to regain the greatness of the empire, the glory of its armed forces, and the supremacy of German industry. Even by the force of arms, he reminded them. Members of the society erupted in cheers and more than one of them had to wipe away the tears that rolled down their cheeks.

After the speech, the brothers went to the hall to drink champagne, smoke cigars and dream of the great future of the Reich. Count Dahlen shared the evening with big businessmen (several of them bankrupt), conservative politicians (who no longer held popularly elected positions), former military officers (who lived on modest pensions) and several members of the nobility like him (whose titles no longer had any value in the new republic).

As the bottles of liquor were emptied, the anecdotes of the war became more epic, the missed imperial past seemed even more splendid and were heard the plans of some political parties to carry out a coup d'état before the end of that same year. Dahlen, who barely tasted the champagne, sighed and wished those braggarts would leave soon. They did nothing but speak and lament, but they would be unable to take the initiative and give their lives for the cause if necessary.

It was late at night when the ethyl nostalgia ended and most of those nationalists finally left, back to their routine lives. Only three men remained in the hall. The host and grand master of the Germanic Noble Society, Friedrich Gerber, was a 75-year-old steel industrialist. He was sitting by the fire that burned in a large marble hearth, with a thick blanket over his legs. Emil Kemnitz, former general of the Supreme Command of the Army, tall and athletic at 68 years old, drank *Schnapps* with his eyes lost, no doubt recalling some battle. The youngest of the three was Count Albrecht von Dahlen, 55 years old, with aristocratic demeanor. As the other members of the society left, he had stripped of his robe and dressed again in his elegant jacket. He cleared his throat to get the attention of his brothers.

"Gentlemen, I believe that the time has come to put an end to the degrading situation of our beloved Reich. I will not allow Germany to fall apart."

"Well said, my friend!" Gerber exclaimed.

"I just arrived from the Netherlands," Dahlen said, "where I visited His Majesty."

Gerber rose like a spring and together with Kemnitz approached the count. Wilhelm II of Hohenzollern, German Emperor and King of Prussia, had been forced to abdicate his two crowns in November 1918, at the end of the Great War. He had then gone into exile in the Netherlands, where Queen Wilhelmina granted him asylum. The former Kaiser had been living for three years in Huis Doorn, a manor house in the province of Utrecht.

"How is our Kaiser? What did he tell you about the situation in the country? Do you think he can come back soon?"

The industrialist and the former general harassed the count with their questions. Dahlen raised a hand to ask them to calm down.

"His state of health is splendid," he informed them. "He is dedicated to hunting and chopping firewood. In addition, he is very concerned about the situation of his beloved Germany."

"We must bring him back as soon as possible!" Gerber exclaimed. "People will welcome him with open arms!"

For those men, the 'people' comprised the nobles and *junkers,* the landed aristocracy of Prussia who dominated the upper echelons of government, the armed forces, and the diplomacy of the empire. The other inhabitants of the Reich were not important and should only submit to what their leaders told them. Apparently, none of them remembered the period of chaos that had ravaged Germany at the end of the war, the so-called November Revolution, whose objective had been, precisely, to end the monarchical regime. Five years after the end of the war, revolutionary and paramilitary groups were still engaged in a subversive war that included political assassinations and coup attempts.

"I guess you have a plan," Kemnitz said, touching his nose in a gesture of complicity.

"That's right," Dahlen said. "I intend to restore the Kaiser, denounce the Treaty of Versailles, and rebuild the army to return Germany to its privileged place in the world."

His companions had their eyes bright with excitement.

"You can count on us," the industrialist announced, with a solemn tone.

The retired general nodded in turn with his head. The count then laid out his plan for them.

"As you may recall, my father, the former Count, traveled extensively in China and was well versed in the history and culture of that country."

Both men looked at each other somewhat surprised by the reference to the Asian nation, but made gestures of assent, since the former count's fondness for sinology was well known.

"I myself accompanied my father during my youth on some of his visits to China," the count recalled. "There I learned the language, at least the Mandarin dialect, and got to know the local customs. One of the issues that most caught my attention was the technological and military development achieved by Ancient China. For its time, it was a very advanced people, whose inventions are still valid today."

"Now I have re-read some texts that my father had in his library, and I came across an interesting reference. During the 11th and 12th centuries AD, the Chinese alchemists of Taoism invented an explosive weapon they called *red typhoon.* It is a kind of special gunpowder capable of destroying everything in its path, like a firestorm."

Former General Kemnitz looked at the count with an engrossed gesture as he imagined what he could have done on the front lines if he had had such a weapon.

"That *red typhoon...* does it still exist?" Gerber asked with bright eyes.

"It is said that the formula for creating the compound was lost centuries ago," Dahlen replied. Faced with the disappointed faces of his teammates, he added with a triumphant smile: "But I know where to find it! That was precisely the data I found in my father's library."

The three men shook hands and patted their backs. On their faces there was great joy.

"It's splendid news, Dahlen," said the industrialist, sitting by the fire again. "I am already old, and I don't want to die without seeing our beloved empire restored."

"Can we produce this weapon?" Asked the former general, who looked as excited as the great master of the society. "We will need large amounts of the compound."

"I own some industries overseas," Gerber said. "We must avoid the limitations of Versailles from preventing us from manufacturing this *roter Taifun*."

The terms of the treaty not only significantly reduced the size of the German army, but also prohibited Germany from trading arms and the manufacture and storage of chemical weapons, armored vehicles, tanks, and military aircraft. The navy had been reduced to a symbolic force of obsolete ships and the air force had been disbanded.

"Wait a minute, gentlemen," said the Count. "We must go slowly to achieve our goals."

"You have it all laid out in your mind, huh, Dhalen?" Kemnitz commented, his eyes clouded by the excess of *Schnapps*.

Or maybe he was crying with emotion. The count was not sure. He looked at his brothers with a triumphant smile and after a gimmicky pause, he added:

"We will create a small amount of the explosive and throw it on a foreign capital. The city will be reduced to ashes."

Gerber and Kemnitz were blown away by the surprise. Both looked at each other silently, and then the industrialist asked in a trembling voice:

"Which capital are you referring to, Dahlen?"

"London, obviously. The British are our most powerful enemies."

The retired general poured himself another glass of the strong liqueur and looked at the count with an anxious gesture.

"Do you intend to start another war, my

friend?" He asked in a jovial tone, as if it were the most natural thing in the world.

"Quite the opposite, *Herr General.* I wish to avoid it at all costs."

Kemnitz questioned him with his gaze.

"Our current army is a shadow," Dahlen explained. "We need to rebuild it, under the leadership of the Kaiser, to get along on an equal footing with the other powers. But at the slightest violation of the Treaty of Versailles, the Allies would pounce on us. Particularly the British. However, with their capital destroyed, they will be too busy and demoralized to oppose our rearmament."

"And what about the French?" Gerber recalled. "If we destroyed Paris, we would get them to leave the Ruhr."

In January of that year, France had occupied Germany's coal and iron rich region of Ruhr, where the large steel factories were located. By the end of the war, Germany had pledged to pay substantial reparations to the Allies, but it was increasingly difficult for it to meet its obligations as a result of the hyperinflation of its economy and political instability. Finally, the French had had enough of the large German debts and had decided to go get the money themselves. Industrialists like Gerber were losing great fortunes due to the seizure of their factories by the invaders.

"France is a weak country," Kemnitz said.

"Britain, on the other hand, is a much more formidable enemy. The French will not go to war if they do not have the support of the British."

"We agree, then," Dhalen said. "We will get the *red typhoon* formula, manufacture it in secret, and launch it over London."

"Once the city is destroyed," Gerber added, "we will bring back His Majesty and rearm the army."

"Will we have Ludendorff's support?" The count asked.

Kemnitz nodded his head sharply.

"Of course," said the retired soldier. "And old Hindenburg's too."

Field Marshal Paul von Hindenburg and Infantry General Erich Ludendorff had been the supreme commanders of the German Army during the war. The marshal had retired at the end of the conflict, but he was still a figure much admired by those nostalgic for the empire. Ludendorff, for his part, was active in politics and was a well-known leader of the right-wing sectors of the country. The military, both active and in retirement, would flock to the call of those two men.

"We must proceed immediately," said Count Dahlen. "You, Kemnitz, must secure the support of the army to draw up a rearmament and recruitment plan."

"*Jawohl!* At your service!" exclaimed the former general, giving a military salute.

"And you, Gerber," the Count continued, "must finance the operation and provide your facilities for the manufacture of the weapon."

"It will be a pleasure, *Herr Graf.*"

"I will return immediately to my country house to gather all the background on the *red typhoon* and prepare the search for the secret formula."

For several weeks, the three conspirators kept in touch through letters and telegrams. Kemnitz spoke to his contacts in the *Reichswehr,* the republic's diminished army, and warned them of an imminent call to arms. Several retired officers met secretly in manor houses and military clubs to draw up operational plans for troops and war materiel. Gerber instructed his trusted managers to look for a factory suited to the count's requirements, located outside the scope of the Treaty of Versailles, and asked his accountants to divert money to certain bank accounts registered on Swiss banks.

Dahlen, for his part, read dozens of his father's occult books and studied diaries, maps and scrolls to find the mysterious Taoist formula. He wrote to his contacts in China and consulted experts in Berlin and other cities in Germany and Europe about the ancient alchemists of the Song dynasty. Finally, after three months, he asked his collaborators to meet again at the villa in Potsdam.

This time there were no brothers dressed

in tunics with black crosses nor did Wagner's majestic chords sound. The three men discreetly went to the host's office and there finalized the details of the next stages of the plan.

"Very well gentlemen," said Dahlen, "now I can finally go in search of our weapon of hope."

"Will you travel personally to China?" Kemnitz asked.

The count nodded with a gesture.

"Through a friend in the Ministry of Foreign Affairs, a man loyal to the cause, I have managed to get sent to China," the count said.

Gerber raised his eyebrows in surprise.

"Will you go in an *official* capacity?"

All three men were recognized opponents of the government of the republic. Dahlen let out a sardonic laugh.

"Albrecht Graf von Dahlen would never represent this damn republic," he announced, in a deep voice. "But this man would."

He extracted a passport from his jacket pocket and laid it out to his companions. They reviewed the document, which had the official seals of Foreign Affairs, with increasing amazement.

"Now I understand your new beard and mustache," said the industrialist, returning the passport to the count. "The truth is that you are unrecognizable."

"Congratulations on your appointment, *mein Herr,*" laughed Kemnitz.

Count Dahlen opened the diplomatic passport and observed the photograph on the document next to the name and position of its holder: Rudolph Kiel, Consul General of Germany in Shanghai, China.

12. PUDONG

Hunt was able to reconstruct in detail the origin of the conspiracy based solely on the documents he had found in the apartment. The letters and diary entries were so detailed that he could almost see those men as they dreamed of the past glories of their defunct empire. He had not even had difficulty imagining what they thought or said during their meetings in the village of Potsdam, for it was well known that the German nobility and leaders were authoritarian and anti-Semitic. Moreover, in his own notes and messages, Kiel – Hunt was not accustomed to thinking of him as 'Count von Dahlen' – did not hide his feelings and openly mentioned his disdain for the current government of his country, as well as his contempt for the Jews, even if they were his compatriots.

As the ferry rocked gently across the waters of the Whangpoo River, Hunt mentally went over what he had found out the night before. The conspirators were powerful men who together could control German industry, army, and nobility. If they managed to manufacture the *red typhoon,* they would have absolute power that they would unleash not only on their nation, but throughout Europe. Or maybe in the whole world. And the first to suffer that new power would be the British. Hunt imagined London razed to the ground and shuddered. At least now he knew what and who he was up against. He had to do everything possible he could to stop them. And the impossible too.

The air was loaded with moisture and a warm breeze was blowing over the water. The rickety ferry approached the eastern bank of the river, where the Pudong area extended. There was the true wealth of Shanghai. Dozens of factories, cotton mills, warehouses and docks crowded on the shore opposite foreign concessions. Tall chimneys spewed their toxic fumes into the sky and thick ducts threw waste into the water, which was then dragged downstream into the Yangtze.

Those crude and scruffy constructions belonged to the same companies whose magnificent and sturdy buildings lined the Bund, on the west bank. Seen both banks from the center of the river, they formed a notorious contrast that was nothing more than a reflection of the situation of Shanghai. On one side were luxury and modernity, and on the other, the effort to produce the wealth enjoyed by a few. Hunt had heard isolated, but reliable, comments about the miserable working conditions of those industries, of their workforce made up of women and children residing in slums precariously built behind the factories.

Pudong showed the true face of Shanghai and that's why not even the owners of the companies went out there. On the ferry were only Chinese passengers, who kept their eyes down when Hunt looked around on the boat. Although the crossing of the Whangpoo only took a few minutes from the docks of the Bund, at the end of the voyage Hunt felt that he was disembarking in another world. Stepping on the eastern shore he was enveloped in a gray cloud of coal dust and could only make out the shadows of the factories and warehouses.

A few hours earlier, Hunt had met with Mary Ann and Chester at the latter's office on Honan Road. However, now it seemed to him that an eternity had passed since that encounter. As always, the antiques dealer maintained a neutral expression on his face and had joined the tips of his extended fingers, forming a pyramid with both hands. The girl, on the other hand, walked nervously through the office. Finally, she had ended up exasperating the stoic Chinese, who offered her a cup of ginseng tea and assured her that she was safe there.

"The *shikumen* alchemist is called Kao Fang," Peng said. "He is a former Taoist monk who makes a living as a healer and potion maker. He is rumored to also work for the Green Gang and other criminal groups, crafting poisons and explosives."

"What a change," Hunt said. "From religion to crime."

"What an aberration!" Mary Ann exclaimed. "How can anyone abandon their beliefs and betray them in this way?"

"I guess the latter is more lucrative than the former, my dear," the captain said.

The girl lowered her gaze and blushed. Hunt was certain that she would never be able to sacrifice her religious or moral convictions in exchange for personal gain. Welcome to Shanghai, he thought.

"My contacts in occult circles were very helpful," Peng continued. "Kao Fang has been acquiring large quantities of cinnabar and other alchemist substances on the black market."

"Is it possible that he has already the formula of the *red typhoon*?"

"I guess it's possible," the antiques dealer admitted. "However, gunpowder must be stored elsewhere. The compound cannot be made in the small space of the *shikumen.*"

"We should keep an eye on that alchemist," Hunt said. "He will finally lead us to the secret weapon."

Peng raised both eyebrows and smiled at the corner of his lips. Hunt looked at him exultantly.

"You already arranged he has been followed, didn't you?"

"Let's say I have my 'Honan Road irregulars'," Peng said, amusingly. "Although they are not little beggars, they know the streets perfectly."

Hunt nodded, admired. The 'Baker Street Irregulars' were a group of wandering children who helped Sherlock Holmes in his cases.

"These are rickshaw drivers, right?" Hunt smiled at his friend. "I would say that I have seen the same coolies several times outside your premises."

"Elementary, my dear Watson. In fact, one of the coolies should be about to give me his report."

Peng got up and poured a glass of Glenlivet for himself and another for Hunt. Mary Ann sternly looked at the alcohol as she continued to drink her ginseng infusion. The captain winked at the girl and hurried his drink.

"How much longer will I have to stay hidden?" She asked.

Her eyes were tired, and his hands trembled slightly when she held the cup.

"Soon we will be able to go home, Mary Ann. I will take you myself."

"England? I don't remember what it's like anymore," she said, sighing. "It seems to me that I have been in Shanghai all my life."

"Yes, that's what this city produces," Hunt agreed. He sat next to the girl and took one of her hands between his. "As soon as we discover the hiding place of our enemies, we will leave here. I promise you."

"What if they discover us first?" She asked back, raising her voice. "I believed myself safe in the mission and they found me anyway."

"Chester and I will protect you, my dear. Just as we did in Chinkiang."

Mary Ann drank her tea silently. Hunt assumed that the mission did not bring back good memories. Especially for the sudden and violent departure.

After a few minutes, Peng went to the showroom and returned with a young Chinese man, with a tanned face and sweaty skin. Seeing the foreigners, the rickshaw driver hesitated, but then the girl spoke to him in the Shanghai dialect and the young man calmed down. Mary Ann offered him a cup of ginseng infusion and soon the coolie was enthralled with her. Hunt admired the girl's temperance and empathy. She was certainly an excellent missionary.

The young coolie and Peng engaged in a quick conversation in the local dialect of Chinese. Mary Ann nodded at times, but other times she struggled to follow what both men said. Hunt, for his part, poured himself another glass of whisky and set out to wait for the report to conclude. Finally, the driver put the cup on the table, bowed to those present, and retreated. Hunt couldn't hide his impatience.

"Well?"

"Kao Fang frequently visits the Pudong area on the other side of the Whangpoo River," Peng said. "The coolies followed him there and saw him enter a construction site. A steel factory, it seems."

Hunt tightened like a violin string.

"Did your informant mention whether this steel mill had a name?"

"'Gebeng', or something like that," Peng said, shrugging his shoulders. "Many coolies are illiterate, my friend."

To Chester and the girl's surprise, Hunt laughed. The others looked at him dumbfounded.

"It's 'Gerber'. Gerber Steel Mill. We have found the *red typhoon!*"

Hunt told them everything he had found out about the plot during his clandestine visit to the consul's apartment the night before. The true identity of Kiel, the financing of the steel industrialist and the military preparations of the former general. Peng maintained his Zen expression during the story, but Mary Ann listened to it with increasing horror.

Less than an hour later, the captain was sitting behind the wheel of the Duesenberg tourer. The girl and the antiques dealer were watching him from the sidewalk, outside the antiques shop on Honan Road.

"I will take the first available ferry on the Bund," Hunt said.

"I should go with you, Peter," Peng said, somewhat distressed.

Hunt shook his head.

"You better stay with Mary Ann, Chester.

Things will get tough in the factory."

"I'm sorry to be a burden," the girl lamented. The antiques dealer assured her that it would be a pleasure to accompany her. She approached the car window. "Take care of yourself, Peter. Remember you have to take me to England."

"That's how it will be, my dear. We will travel on a luxury steamer, you will see."

The Pudong area was crisscrossed with canals that snaked between the factories on the coast into the inland farmland. Hunt got off the ferry and set off along a gravel road that ran along one of the canals, following the guidance provided by Peng. He left behind the large factories and warehouses and then passed by several groups of modest Chinese dwellings where the workers resided. He continued about fifteen minutes along the road and finally spotted the steel factory under construction, located inland, away from the river.

The development of the complex was in its initial stages. There was hardly a low office building, some worker sheds, a few material depots, and a central concrete structure that would no doubt house the main foundry when it was in operation. The factory was surrounded by bamboo scaffolding, the typical material used in local constructions. Hunt observed the complex in the distance and found that there were few workers on the site. He waited for almost an hour, wandering by the surroundings.

As the sun set, he saw the workers leaving the compound walking in an orderly line. Crossing the perimeter fence, they passed under a sign written in English, German and Chinese characters: "Gerber Industries".

It was the dead of the night when Hunt climbed the wire fence and jumped into the compound. The site presented a gloomy landscape, only illuminated by moonlight. In the air still floated the black fumes that the nearby chimneys expelled throughout the day. Hunt crouched forward, barricading himself behind the machinery and steel bars used for construction. He assumed that there might be some guard, but no noise could be heard outside. Arriving next to the foundry, he stuck his back to the wall and stopped to listen. It seemed to him that a thud was arising from the inside.

He slowly climbed the scaffolding, formed by a dense web of interlocking reeds tied at intersections. The bamboos were very resistant, although flexible at the same time. They warped and creaked under Hunt's weight, but he was able to ascend without problems. Once he gained confidence in the structure, Hunt began to climb faster and soon reached the top of the scaffolding. From there he passed to the upper edge of the outer wall of the building. The roof of the foundry was not yet finished. Several planks crossed from one side to the other as a temporary cover, leaving large gaps between them. Hunt lay flat on one of the planks, leaning towards the opening, and from above he spied inside the factory.

About ten meters below, at ground level, there were several machines and supplies for the manufacture of steel, distributed in a wide and cavernous foundry. There were large industrial furnaces, coke tanks for fuel, conveyor belts, chimneys that rose to protrude through the roof, pipes that ran through the thick walls and electrical cables that fed energy to the engines. However, all the equipment looked new and unused. The machinery was not completely interconnected and there were some empty areas where it was evident that other equipment needed to be installed.

A group of about eight men was busy inside the vast foundry. They were all dressed in work overalls and covered their eyes with thick goggles, except for an old Chinese man next to them. He wore a long jacket and baggy pants, in the style of his people. Hunt immediately recognized Kao Fang. He gave instructions and a couple of men approached an industrial furnace that was on. From above, Hunt could see the burning metal gushing inside.

The men held a clay crucible, the size of a football, with long tongs that they held between them. They handled the tongs from a safe distance to the oven and placed the container above the melted metal. Hunt calculated that the furnace was burning at more than a thousand degrees Celsius in temperature. Even where he was, he could feel the heat coming from the foundry. Within a few minutes, the crucible turned reddish from the intense heat. The men then took it to a stone base where they placed it on a pedestal so that it would stand upright.

Kao Fang began to pour various compounds into the burning receptacle. The substances crackled and melted, releasing vapors of different colors, in addition to strong acre and acidic odors. The alchemist stirred the mixture with a long rod while singing a litany in a language that Hunt failed to distinguish. Soon after, Kao Fang poured the contents of the crucible into a smaller container and put it in water to cool it. At the bottom of the container had formed a reddish compound of intense brilliance. Finally, the alchemist mixed the crystals with black granules and macerated the substance in a mortar. There was the *red typhoon.*

Despite the distance he was at, Hunt felt a strange force emanating from the compound. It was a mixture of heat and energy waves, as if the power of the weapon was tangible even before it was used. The feeling ran through his whole body. For a moment, he forgot the reason why he was there. Until his gaze caught a detail that abruptly returned him to reality. On a worktable, next to the utensils and substances of the alchemist, there was a roll of antique-looking paper, about thirty centimeters high, which was kept open with a pair of paperweights. Hunt felt a shudder when he realized that there was the Taoist spell that allowed the creation of the powerful weapon.

He slid down the planks until he managed to hold on to one of the pipes that ran vertically through the wall. Kao Fang's minions, like his master, were engrossed in the creation of the compound and stood with their backs to the wall. Hunt went down the pipe until he reached the ground and once there, he hid behind the conveyor belt that ran through the foundry nave. The noise of the metal burning in the furnace concealed his steps as he approached the table. He reached the end of the belt and watched the table from there. He calculated that he was no more than five meters away from his target.

He mentally counted to three and rushed to the table. He pushed away the paperweights, picked up the old scroll and hid again behind the conveyor belt. His heart was beating wildly. He rolled the delicate paper back on the wooden roller on the far left, tied it with the rope attached to the other end, and put it in the inner pocket of his jacket. He kept the body crouched and hurriedly returned to the wall pipe. He ascended quickly, propelling himself with hands and feet. Before going up to the ceiling planks he looked down. Neither the alchemist nor his minions had taken their eyes off the vessel where they were creating the *red typhoon.*

Hunt climbed onto the planks and paused for a moment to catch his breath. He felt the roll burning next to his chest. There he had a secret that had been lost for nine hundred years.

"Fascinating, right?"

Hunt got startled and leaned back. Mei Ling was standing about twenty meters from him, right on the edge of the wall. She wore a black robe, fitted to the body, with a long cloak of the same color. At the waist protruded the hilt of her *jian* sword. The heat and reddish glow that came from the foundry made her silhouette twinkle as if it were a mirage. Hunt got up slowly.

"Aberrant, rather," the captain said. "I can't let this continue, Mei Ling."

"You can't help it, Peter Hunt. The *red typhoon* is indispensable to our plan."

"Your plan is to destroy my country!"

"I don't mean Kiel's intentions, but the plans of my people."

Hunt was shocked. From the beginning he had found it curious that an experienced warrior like that girl had allied with a foreigner to obtain a valuable treasure of her own culture, but now he understood it. It was just a marriage of convenience.

"Hand me the roll, Peter. I don't want to kill you."

Involuntarily, Hunt put his hand to his chest, as if trying to protect the valuable document underneath.

"Maybe I should hand it over to the consul," he replied. "Does he know that you have your own agenda?" he asked, in a defiant tone.

The girl raised her chin and let out a sardonic laugh.

"I guess he suspect it. But he knows that without me he would not be able to reach his goal."

"Then help me to stop him," the captain asked. "Once the threat to England disappears, I will leave here, and you can do as you please with the weapon."

Mei Ling looked at him silently for a few moments. Her face, illuminated only by the glow that came from inside the factory, had a melancholic air. Hunt tried to smile, but the adrenaline running through his body paralyzed all his muscles. Finally, the girl looked down and shook her head.

"Sorry, Peter. I also need Kiel to achieve my goals."

"I assumed you would say that."

He said it in a disappointed voice, but at the same time pulled his revolver from the cover under the jacket.

"You love your country," said the girl. "And I love mine."

Mei Ling took a step towards Hunt. He shot. The girl quickly stepped aside and dodged the shot. Hunt blinked, incredulously, and fired again. Mei Ling tilted her body in a dizzying gesture and avoided the bullet again. At the same time, she grabbed the hilt of the *jian* sword and drew the weapon at lightning speed. The captain couldn't believe what he had seen, but he also didn't plan to stop and analyze it. Mei Ling threw herself to a charge towards Hunt and he fired twice in quick succession. The girl brandished her sword and deflected the projectiles with two graceful blows from the sharp blade.

Hunt ran while cursing himself for underestimating the girl. Her abilities were superior to what he had imagined. Besides, she was extremely agile. As Hunt advanced along the edge of the outer wall, guarding his steps, and jumped on the planks holding the ceiling, Mei Ling seemed to glide smoothly, as if flying from one place to another. Hunt was cornered up there and he knew it. He had gotten into the wolf's lair and had no escape. Upon reaching the opposite end of the roof he encountered the scaffolding that asserted the other wall of the building. There he saw a long bamboo cane that had been released from the moorings. He grabbed hold of it and used it as a pole to propel himself over a large opening where a chimney appeared above the burning furnace.

"If you give me the roll now, I will let you go!" The girl shouted from the other side of the opening. "Otherwise, I promise to kill you slowly!"

She let out a sinister laugh that froze the captain's veins. Hunt stepped back, tripped over a flange, and fell sitting on the planks. A crystal jingle diverted his gaze. The small vial with the crystals, which Mary Ann had given him at the *Wasp,* had escaped from his trouser pocket and rolled down the planks towards the opening. Hunt had been carrying it since then, but he didn't even remember it. In an instinctive gesture, he stretched forward and picked it up.

"Now I have the crystals and the spell!" He shouted.

Hunt held the vial and slowly got up. He looked at the girl with a bold smile on his face. He felt that he had regained the initiative.

"We can make an agreement, Peter."

The girl's voice had softened, but her eyes betrayed her fury.

"If you want it..." He threw the glass vial into the air, in a perfect arc towards the furnace below, in the middle of the foundry. "Go for it!"

"¡Noooo!"

Mei Ling's scream tore the night apart. Hunt didn't get to see her face of fury and frustration, but he could imagine it as he threw himself into the scaffolding and jumped down the reeds, hanging almost blindly down the bamboos.

He was at half the height when the furnace exploded and destroyed the foundry. The entire building shuddered and suddenly a hole opened in the wall where the scaffolding rested. A flare made its way through the opening and ejected concrete, metal and a wave of red fire. Hunt was thrown away violently and for an eternal instant he turned through the air, shrouded in a cloud of heat and dust. Then he hit the ground and rolled several meters, uttering groans of pain.

He got up carefully, half dizzy and in the middle of a coughing fit. After a moment he regained his balance and controlled the spasms. He then put a hand on the inside of the jacket and breathed a sigh of relief as he checked that the roll was still in his pocket. Finally, he looked up and found that the building was engulfed in flames and its walls were rapidly crumbling. The gigantic pyre of debris and fire had an intense red glow.

13. WOOSUNG

From the window of the teahouse located above the pier, you could see the fleet of steamers, junks, barges and freighters that came and went from Shanghai. Merchants, missionaries, spies and simple tourists intermingled at the port of entry to the big city, at the confluence where the Whangpoo River flowed into the majestic Yangtze. However, the ancient town of Woosung was nothing more than an unattractive place of transit in which there were some old forts of the Qing dynasty that had been bombed, and easily captured, by the British in 1842, during the First Opium War.

Mary Ann approached Hunt, who was looking out the window, and took him by the arm.

"Are you okay?" She asked.

When they met that morning on the Bund, Hunt had his face bruised and his clothes scorched. But now he was wearing a new suit that he had put on after washing and shaving in the back room of the teahouse.

"I feel like new," he assured her. "I'm just hungry."

"Soon they will bring us *yum cha.* Tea and

snacks."

"Splendid."

The girl rested her head on the captain's shoulder. He smelled her soft perfume and felt comforted.

"¿Will we be leaving soon, Peter?"

"Chester is looking for passage right now," he explained. "We will leave this afternoon."

The three of them had arrived early that morning at the port, on a smelly fishing barge that took them from Shanghai. Peng asked his companions to stay hidden in the teahouse, which belonged to a friend of his. The antiques dealer left them settled there and then went out to arrange the departure of the two English nationals. He only returned for a moment to leave new clothes for the captain and left immediately.

Hunt, for his part, had no problem staying in the shadows. Now that he had got the scroll of the *red typhoon,* he didn't want to take any risks until he left that damn place. His enemies had him identified and he knew that they would not rest until they recovered the valuable document. In addition, he was to protect Mary Ann. The girl was courageous, but she had no chance in the face of Kiel's heartless minions.

An old Chinese woman called them with a gesture. On a table she had arranged several round bamboo steamers and an iron teapot with porcelain cups. Hunt hadn't eaten anything since the day before and his mouth watered. He sat at the table and with some difficulty he tried the *dim sum* with a couple of chopsticks. Mary Ann poured him the tea and explained the names and ingredients of the snacks as he devoured them. There were steamed buns stuffed with pork, dough *dumplings* stuffed with vegetables, rice noodles, cooked shrimp, pieces of meat, rice balls, and pieces of fried fish. Hunt drank several cups of *oolong* tea to accompany the meal.

"That consul or duke or whatever, why does he hate us?" Mary Ann asked when they finished eating. "Because his country was defeated in the war?"

"He's a count," Hunt said. "He just pretends to be a consul."

"Whatever. But the war was started by them. And it ended five years ago."

"For people like von Dahlen, or 'Kiel' as we know him," the captain explained, "the German defeat meant the end of their lives. I mean, their way of life."

"I know. In Germany, titles of nobility were abolished."

"Not only did they lose the titles, but also their rank and, most importantly, their power. You see, in Germany the nobility and landowners, or *Junkers,* controlled the entire empire."

Hunt explained that, according to what he had read in the count's diary, he had fought in the war in command of a cavalry regiment on the Eastern Front. After the conflict, Dahlen returned to the family business and became involved in politics, supporting the monarchical and nationalist movements. Like his father, the previous count, Dahlen was also a member of the occult group Noble Germanic Society. However, the new republic did not have a place for them. Along with the other members of the brotherhood, they had been longing for revenge for years and planning the reconquest of power.

"To achieve this, they need to have a very powerful weapon," he concluded. "Therefore, Dahlen adopted the identity of 'Rudolph Kiel' and came to Shanghai as consul. His diplomatic status conferred on him immunity and allowed him to create a network of high-level contacts in the city."

"What about that Chinese woman, Mei Ling?"

"She allied himself with Kiel just for convenience. She belongs to some secret Chinese organization, perhaps nationalist, and desires the weapon for her cause. Either they pretend to share the find or Mei Ling will betray Kiel at some point."

"Do you think she is still alive?" Mary Ann asked, surprised. "You told me that the factory was left in ruins."

"That girl is amazing," he said, not without some admiration. "I wouldn't be surprised if she managed to escape before the collapse."

"I guess she's beautiful too," she murmured, with a note of suspicion in her voice.

Hunt was about to say that Mei Ling was *very* beautiful, but then he noticed the gesture that showed the girl's face and held back.

"I'm glad I took the vial with the crystals with me," Hunt said, changing the subject. "I thank you for handing it to me."

Hunt smiled at her, but Mary Ann kept her brow frowning.

"Aren't the crystals supposed to be mixed with gunpowder to create the *red typhoon*?"

"That's right. But the blood of the dragon is also a mixture of cinnabar crystals with other toxic substances," the captain said. "I guess the explosion of the industrial furnace came into contact with the compound that Kao Fang was creating and that caused the destruction of the factory."

"The scroll you took from the alchemist contains a very great danger, Peter. What will you do with it?"

"I will give it to the British Museum for analysis and storage. My boss, Sir John Connelly, heads a department dedicated to the study of these objects."

"They should destroy it!" The girl exclaimed, with an angry gesture. "That spell is an abomination, Peter."

"I know, my dear. But it will be in a safe

place."

Once we arrived in London, he refrained from adding. And that was several weeks away. He wondered where Chester Peng would be. The antiques dealer had left more than two hours ago in search of passage on some ship. Hunt looked out the window, towards the fleet of boats, and wished to know if any of them would soon set sail taking him and the girl.

A few minutes later a boy entered the teahouse. Hunt followed him with his gaze as he made his way to the old lady tending the place. Hunt wouldn't have noticed the boy – with Chinese features and modest appearance – if it weren't for the fact that he hadn't taken his eye off him and Mary Ann since entering the teahouse. They were not the only foreigners present, there were also some European and American sailors, but the missionary was the only woman. The captain deduced that the boy was looking for a couple. Still looking at the boy, he took one hand to the holster of the gun under his jacket.

The old lady pointed her chin at Hunt and Mary Ann and the boy approached them. Hunt grabbed the butt of the revolver but held the gun in place. The boy spoke in Chinese and Mary Ann responded in the same language. The boy nodded and ran out. Hunt exhaled hard and let go of his gun.

"What was that?"

"The boy was carrying a message from Chester!" She announced, excited. "It only said: *'Queen of Java, 5:00 p.m.'*"

"I guess it's a ship," he said. "But there's something that doesn't go well."

The girl shuddered and looked at him inquisitively.

"Chester would have come in person," the captain explained. "Something bad has happened."

Hunt asked the girl to stay there and not talk to anyone. He checked his gun and rushed out of the teahouse.

Woosung's docks were bustling with activity. Hundreds of longshoremen, coolies and sailors crowded into the jetties, taking care of drawers, containers and passengers at the same time. The noise of the sirens of the ships was joined by the cacophony of a dozen different languages, all struggling to make themselves heard amid the intense hustle and bustle. The air smelled of fish and smoke expelled by the chimneys of the steamers. Hunt questioned several foreign stevedores about the ship he was looking for, obtaining everything from head shakes to insults, including some indications that finally directed him towards the oldest part of the port.

The ancient forts cast their shadow on a few rickety and small draft ships. They were mostly sampans and junks trading in the

Yangtze Delta or upstream, but there were also some deep-sea vessels, mostly former freighters unable to navigate the more extensive routes of international trade. The crew members who roamed the docks also seemed to have known better times. Some of those men looked more like pirates than sailors. Anyway, Hunt came over to talk to them, although in response he received sullen looks or suspicious grunts. He had to resort to insistence, and a good sum of money, for some longshoremen to point out a ramshackle jetty located at the end of the old pier.

There he encountered a mixed steamship, of passage and cargo, which bore the name painted on the side of the bow: Queen of Java. The ship measured almost seventy meters in length and about nine in beam. It had a single deck, in the center of which stood a passenger cabin. Above it was the bridge and, further back, emerged the only chimney of the ship. The hull paint was chipped off, but the structure looked solid and able to cope with the inclemency of the sea. Hunt calculated that the ship was about fifty years old.

Several crew members wandered around the pier near the walkway that connected to the deck. Hunt described Chester Peng as best he could, but the men just looked at him indifferently. For foreigners, moreover, all Chinese looked the same. The captain tried again showing some bills, but not even the money caught their attention. Hunt was going to give up when a middle-aged sailor with tanned skin called him with a gesture.

"His friend was here earlier," he said in English, with a strong Portuguese accent. "He secured a couple of tickets for this afternoon."

"Yes, it's him. Do you know where he went?"

The man shrugged. Hunt put some bills in his hand that quickly disappeared under the worn shirt.

"I think he left there." The sailor indicated a path that ran up a promontory, towards the ancient forts. Hunt nodded, ready to leave, but the sailor put a hand on his shoulder. "You are not the first to ask about that man. Another Chinese guy was also looking for him."

Hunt muttered a thank you. As he walked away, the man shouted at him:

"If you are one of the passengers, remember to be here at five o'clock in the afternoon! This boat leaves on time, and the captain waits for no one!"

Hunt nodded vaguely and ran to the promontory. Surely the Chinese gangster had been there more than an hour ago, but Hunt had a hunch that he hadn't gone far. He followed the upward path, moving away from the coast about a hundred meters until he reached the base of the forts. Arriving at the structure, he discovered a blood stain on the ground. He drew his weapon and stealthily surrounded the defensive wall.

Behind them were some rusty cannons mounted on wooden gun carriages, between which grew wild bushes. Chester's body poked out among the branches.

Hunt ran to his side. The antiques dealer lay flat on his face between two carriages, next to a bush parched by the sun. A blood stain was spreading down his back. Hunt turned him. His friend made a faint moan.

"Chester, for God's sake! What happened?"

"Peter... is it you? The boy... did he manage to give you... the message?"

Hunt nodded sharply. Chester coughed and a trickle of blood flowed through the corner of his lips.

"One of Kiel's men... he discovered me on the docks. I tried to dodge him, but he caught up with me when I went up the promontory..."

Hunt shuddered with rage and helplessness. His friend had been stabbed in the back. He tried to hold Peng in his arms, but the antiquarian shook his head.

"There is no remedy, my friend." He tried to smile, but he only grimaced in pain. "My *hun* soul is about to leave my body."

"I thought you were a Christian," Hunt said, laughing forcefully.

"I guess my Chinese side is bigger than the English one," replied the antiques dealer in a whisper. "I'm sorry... not having been able to... stop..."

"Don't worry, Chester. I know how to take care of myself."

"The gangster... knows about you and... Mary Ann."

Hunt wanted to tell him that there was no problem, that he would take care of that man, but he could not speak. Chester had died. The captain's lips tightened to form a thin white line of relentless fury. He slowly stood up and took one last look at his friend's body. Someone was going to pay for that. He exhaled air forcefully and ran back to the teahouse.

He went back through the docks, pushing people away. He received several rebukes back and more than a grumpy man tried to stop him, but he managed to advance through the crowd. The teahouse was at the beginning of the port area, close to customs and travel agency offices. Hunt yelled at a group of tourists, but seeing that they were not moving, he raised his gun and brandished it in plain sight.

"Move aside, damn it!"

He crossed the boardwalk and went to the teahouse. Before he arrived, he could clearly hear a woman's cry of terror. It was Mary Ann, he was sure. Without stopping to think, he kicked open the door of the establishment and planted himself at the entrance. The few customers who were there when he had left, along with the old lady who tended the place, had disappeared. In the hall there was an overturned table and behind the furniture there was a scuffle. Hunt pushed aside chairs and tables and saw a thug trying to catch Mary Ann, who was struggling on the floor.

The girl spotted Hunt and screamed in relief. But at the same time, she tried to get up and dodge the thug to go to meet the captain. The man grabbed her by the waist when she passed by him and hid behind her, pointing the tip of his dagger into her throat. He was a big, sweaty Chinese man who smiled with a disgusting grimace. Hunt assumed that the bastard had stabbed Chester. The gangster said something threatening and stepped back. Hunt did not speak the language of that guy, but he knew the international language of the murderers: If he did not let go of his weapon, the man would kill the girl.

Hunt pointed the Webley Mk VI revolver right between the thug's eyes. The man was barricaded behind the girl but kept his head away so he could look at the captain. However, he did not stop moving to offer as little target as possible. Hunt calculated that he was less than ten meters away from his target, but he had no margin for error in the shot. Mary Ann tried to remain calm, but she trembled uncontrollably. Hunt kept his pulse steady but felt the sweat bathing his face. He put his finger on the trigger and waited for an opportunity.

The Chinese man cast a string of curses and

inadvertently separated the tip of the dagger a few millimeters from the girl's neck. With the other hand he grabbed her throat and squeezed the girl towards him. Mary Ann lowered her head, caught the man's hand with her teeth, and bit with all her strength. The thug screamed and set aside from the girl. At the same time, Hunt fired. The .455 caliber bullet hit between the gangster's eyebrows and killed him instantly. Mary Ann got rid of the corpse and ran into the captain's arms. She was crying and laughing at the same time. Before she could suffer a fit of hysteria, Hunt took her by the hand and forced her to run.

"We must leave now," he said.

Outside, a car stopped with a squeak of the brakes next to the customs building. Three Chinese gangsters got off from the car. This time they were armed with guns. Hunt quickened his pace, dragging the girl with him. The thugs discovered them and ran after them. Hunt and Mary Ann made their way to the boardwalk, but the crowd prevented them from advancing faster. The captain looked over his shoulder and saw the thugs approaching them quickly.

Further on the dock there were a couple of Chinese sailors unloading a fishing speedboat, about seven meters long, with an inboard engine. Hunt changed course and approached the boat. The men looked at him in surprise, but he didn't give them time to react. He just jumped on board and then helped the girl board. Only then did the sailors begin to protest and curse Hunt. He raised the revolver and with a gesture ordered them to move away. When he lost sight of them, he started the engine full out. The boat jumped away from the dock.

"Keep your head down!" Hunt shouted at Mary Ann.

The gangsters arrived at the edge of the pier and from there shot at the boat. The bullets pierced the wooden hull but did not reach the fugitives. Hunt steered the vessel to place it behind a big freighter and managed to get them out of reach of the thugs.

Mary Ann was sitting in the cabin with her arms folded over her chest. She was still shaking. Hunt left the engine in neutral and approached her. He took off his jacket and put it on the girl's shoulders.

"Soon we will be safe. On the other side of the harbor there is a ship waiting for us."

"I can't stand it anymore, Peter. This place... It's cursed!"

"I won't miss it either," he murmured.

The noise of an outboard motor reached them. Hunt looked up and found that the gangsters were coming in another fishing boat. He muttered a curse and threw himself at the controls. He restarted the engine and went into the waters of the great river.

Dozens of ships of all types and sizes

sailed the waters. Huge steamships were held still as flotillas of cargo and passenger barges surrounded them. Other boats simply advertised Shanghai's travel agencies and hotels. Tugboats came and went in search of the larger draught vessels and small fishing boats went to sea. European and American gunboats were anchored forming a separate group of warships. Not far from these, some junks of the Chinese navy patrolled the access to the Yangtze River.

Hunt navigated the boat among the other ships, dodging the smaller ones and trying to hide in the shadow of the larger ones. Some skippers shouted indignantly at him as they saw him passing near their boats and the passengers of the steamers looked at him with expectation from the height of their decks. The gangsters' boat gave him no respite. Its occupants were as much or riskier than Hunt himself and had no respect for ships or the lives of others.

Reaching them, the thugs fired again at the fugitives. Hunt performed evasive maneuvers, but there were too many boats in the vicinity. Mary Ann threw herself to the floor of the cabin and began screaming in terror. Hunt felt his heart run amok. The engine was at full power, but he could not increase the distance with his pursuers. After a few minutes the boat surrounded a steamer that had been entering the port and finally went out to the open waters of the Yangtze.

"Mary Ann! Can you steer the boat?"

The girl got up laboriously and stumbled to the helm. The boat made great leaps as it sailed the water at high speed. Hunt gave the girl the pilot's seat, and she held the steering wheel.

"Just keep the course," he asked.

The captain stood in the stern of the boat and from there he returned the fire. The shots were lost in the air due to the wobble of the ship. The gangsters didn't even notice. Hunt cast curses and looked around for any ideas. Then he saw some metal barrels that were attached with a rope to the board rail. There were three containers of about ten liters of capacity each. Hunt laughed like a madman as he untied them and checked that they were full of gasoline. He then lifted them overboard and threw them one by one into the water.

"Don't turn around!" He shouted at Mary Ann.

The three barrels floated away towards the boat that was chasing them, which was on the same course as the fugitive ship. Hunt rested his arm on the stern rail, to avoid sudden movements, and waited for the other boat to pass near the barrels. He aimed carefully and fired. The shot just hit the water. Hunt wiped the sweat from his eyes and pointed again. The barrels looked smaller and smaller and were already beginning to move away from the boat.

The gangsters fired incessantly on the

fleeing ship. Some bullets hit the cabin and Mary Ann gave an involuntary turn as she crouched. Hunt waited for her to catch her course, controlled his breathing, and fired his last shot. One of the barrels burst out with a bang. The enemy boat tried to divert, but then the fire reached the other barrels, and the fireball engulfed the vessel. The boat made a sharp turn and then its own fuel tank also exploded. The three men were thrown out of the ship, amid screams and engulfed in flames. The boat was quickly consumed, and its remains disappeared underwater.

"Mary Ann, are you okay?"

She nodded without taking her eyes off the course they were taking. Her hands held on to the steering wheel so tightly that her knuckles had turned white. Hunt gently pushed her away and regained control of the boat. For a few minutes he simply put distance to the shipwreck, his eyes fixed on the horizon. Then Mary Ann sat next to him and rested her head on his shoulder, saying nothing. He ran an arm over her waist and navigated with one hand. He made a wide turn back into the waters of the harbor and headed towards the rickety freighter that would take them away from there.

14. QUEEN OF JAVA

The ship's passenger deck was divided into two halves by a central aisle. On each side of it three doors opened. Peter Hunt stopped in front of one of these and called softly with the knuckles of his left hand. On the right he carried a tray covered with a piece of cloth.

"Mary Ann, it's me," he whispered.

The girl immediately pulled out the bolt and opened the door. As soon as Hunt entered, she closed again and threw the bolt back. The compartment was small, about two meters long on each side. Two bunks hung of a bulkhead, one on top of the other. There was a central table accompanied by two folding chairs. A round, tiny porthole, located on the outside wall of the cabin, allowed some natural light to enter during the day. At that time, however, only a few stars were visible in the dark sky.

"Where are we?" Mary Ann asked.

She had not left the cabin since they had embarked earlier that afternoon.

"In the Yangtze Delta."

Hunt put the tray on the table and removed the piece of cloth. Mary Ann's face lit up when she saw the peaches, plums, apricots and lychees on the tray. The smell of ripe fruit flooded the air in the compartment. Mary Ann and Hunt sat on the chairs and the captain peeled the fruits with a knife that he had get in the kitchen. The girl ate with pleasure, smiling as she felt the sweet flavors in her mouth.

"The ship will take us to Hong Kong," Hunt explained. "We'll be there in four days."

The girl's beautiful face darkened.

"Do you think those men discovered which ship we boarded?"

Hunt knew that Chester Peng had been attacked next to the old forts, near the pier where the *Queen of Java* was docked, shortly after booking the tickets on the ship. However, the captain didn't want to scare the poor girl more than necessary. While chewing on a piece of lychee, he shrugged. With his mouth full, he murmured that it was not very likely that they had been discovered. However, to himself, he did not have many illusions. Although he had eliminated his pursuers in the bay, it was possible that there were other gangsters hanging around on the pier.

"Tomorrow you will be able to go out on deck," he promised, trying to cheer her up. "We will already be far from Shanghai, and it will be safer."

"Oh, Peter!" The girl was excited. "I don't know how to thank you for everything you've done for me."

She leaned over to him and hugged him tightly as each of them remained in their chairs. Hunt let out a groan of pain. She got up on the spot.

"Peter, you are injured."

Hunt tried to downplay it, but his bumpy visit to the factory had been just the night before. The explosion and the heavy blow to the ground had left him quite stunned. After the impact he stood up with difficulty and took him more than an hour to be able to return to the pier, from where he crossed the Whangpoo River back to the Bund. Then he had traveled to Woosung with Chester and the girl and there he had been in a shooting with the gangsters who were chasing them. The truth was that he felt his whole body aching. The sleep was about to overcome him.

"Take off your shirt to check on you," Mary Ann ordered.

Hunt snorted, but she insisted and finally he had to obey her. Without getting up, and with difficulty, he took off his garment. She put a hand to her mouth, and her eyes widened. Hunt looked at his chest and saw that it was covered with large reddish bruises and some superficial burns. Mary Ann looked at his back and her face paled.

"Oh my God!" She exclaimed, without taking her hand out of her mouth. "You must have internal wounds and more than one broken bone."

"Don't worry, my dear. I've been worse," he replied, with a smile.

She put her arms akimbo and looked at him disapprovingly.

"This is serious, Peter. Take off the rest of your clothes and lie on the bunk."

He stared at her with a puzzled gesture.

"Do you mean *all* the clothes?"

"I'm a nurse, Peter. I have seen many naked men. It means nothing."

Hunt stood up and gave her a crooked grin. She blushed.

"I mean I'm used to it. That's all."

The captain stripped off his clothes and found that he had bruises and lacerations also on his legs and even on his buttocks. He lay on the bunk and his eyes began to close immediately.

"Where are you going?" He asked, in a pasty voice. Mary Ann was opening the cabin door. "It's too early for you to go out."

"I must get bandages and some ointment." To Hunt's questioning gaze, she added: "The crew spends most of their time aboard the ship. Surely they have first aid implements."

When Mary Ann returned, a few minutes later, Hunt was soundly asleep.

He woke up a long time later. It was already daylight. A ray of light entered through the porthole and illuminated his face. He blinked several times and was suddenly startled. He searched for his trench watch and found that he had slept more than twelve hours. His body was covered with bandages, and he felt the skin oily from the ointment. He did not remember the treatments that the girl had applied to him. No doubt, exhaustion had quickly overcome him. Making a little effort, he pulled the sheets away from the bunk and took a couple of unsafe steps, not caring about his nakedness.

Turning back, he saw Mary Ann watching him from the top bunk. She was blushing and held the sheet tightly to her chin.

"Ehhh... good morning," he said.

She avoided looking at him as he put on his pants.

"What happens?" Hunt asked.

"I have no clothes other than that," replied the girl, pointing to the dress hanging from a chair.

Hunt understood that she was naked under the covers. He felt a twinge of desire, but immediately handed the dress to the girl and turned.

"I'll go looking for breakfast."

A couple of hours later, they both went out to the main deck. Mary Ann smiled as she felt the warm rays of sun on her face. Hunt guided her through a loading area, then surrounded the main mast, and continued to the forecastle, higher than the rest of the deck. Below them, the sharp tip of the ship cut the sea forming long contrails on both sides of the hull.

"Good job with the bandages," Hunt said. "Today I feel much better. Thank you, Mary Ann."

"A doctor in Hong Kong should see you anyway," she said. "You have bruises even in... Uh, I'm glad you're better."

Hunt suppressed a smile. They leaned on the board and gazed at the distant coastline, dotted with small islands. Hunt explained that they were sailing in front of Chekiang province.

"Despite what has happened in recent days," said the girl, "I think I will miss China. It's a fascinating place."

"Yes, and dangerous," Hunt added. "How long have you been here?"

"Three years. But I only know Shanghai and its surroundings."

"Why did you decide to come to a place like this?"

She folded her arms and looked at Hunt with a defiant gesture.

"Don't you think a girl like me can be a missionary?"

"Er, of course," he said, raising his hands in a conciliatory gesture. "But China is a distant and tough country for a young... and pretty girl."

Mary Ann blushed. He liked to see her like this, a little embarrassed and smiling.

"Wasn't there a boyfriend who begged you to stay in England?" The captain asked, after a while.

"There was no one," she replied, looking

down. "My life was divided between the hospital where I worked in London and the church in my neighborhood. When I learned of the work of the missionaries, I thought it would be more valuable if I could do the same here in China."

"Healing bodies and souls," Hunt said. "It's a hard work, but important."

She stared at him to see if he was joking. When she became convinced that he was not trying to tease her, she stretched out one hand and stroked his cheek.

"And you, what do you believe in, Peter Hunt?"

"Interesting question," he replied. For quite a while, he looked towards the coast silently, as if it were the first time he thought about it. "I believe in freedom and in the intelligence of men. Well, some of them, at least," he added, laughing.

"But you don't believe in God, do you?"

"After the Great War?" He shook his head. "Also, I want to forge my own destiny instead of thinking that some higher being is plotting it for me."

"All adventurers are the same. I met some men like you in Shanghai." Mary Ann looked at him again. "They long for freedom, but it seems they were always running away from something."

"In my case, I just run away from boredom. Well, and men armed to the teeth."

"Isn't it tormenting you to have killed,

Peter?"

"Of course," he replied. His replica was too fast and dry. The girl looked away. "I don't do this for fun, my dear. Nor for living an adventure. This is the real world, where there are people willing to do anything to achieve their goals. I saw it in the war, and I see it now."

"You're carrying a revolver," she insisted. "You are also willing to do anything to achieve your goals."

"*Behold, the righteous shall be recompensed in the earth; much more the wicked and the sinner!*" Quoted Hunt.

Mary Ann looked at him harshly.

"*Proverbs, 11:31,*" she recalled. "You're a cynic, Peter."

The girl looked down and said nothing more. Shortly later the sky became cloudy, and the air was full of moist. Just as Hunt thought it would rain soon, an intense downpour began to fall. He took Mary Ann by the arm, and they returned to the cabin. As they passed through the deck, several crew members stared at Mary Ann. She was the only woman on board and her beauty was evident, even clad in her simple dress and her hair tied back in a ponytail.

Arriving at the compartment, Hunt saw that the water had made translucent the girl's dress. She wasn't wearing any underwear. He instructed her to take it off while he looked for some food. He immediately went to the kitchen, his pulse racing. When he returned, she was sitting on one of the folding chairs, wrapped in the bunk sheets. The captain carried two steaming clay bowls that gave off a strong smell of sea and spices. According to what Hunt had understood the cook, the dish consisted of a perch soup with pieces of ham, bamboo shoots, mushrooms and eggs.

Hunt left the bowls on the table and pulled a glass flask from the back pocket of his pants. It was filled with a viscous, reddish liquid.

"I bought this from the cook with my last money," the captain explained. The girl questioned him with her eyes. "It's something called "Shaohsing wine."

"It's *huangjiu,*" Mary Ann said. "Fermented rice liqueur. I understand that this variety is highly appreciated."

"Excellent. Have you tried it?"

Hunt took a sip, avoided a grimace from the bitter taste, and held out the flask to Mary Ann.

"No, thank you. I don't drink alcohol."

He nodded and ate from his plate silently. When he finished, he drank a few sips of the rice wine to wash down the meal. He was starting to feel more relaxed. His clothes had already dried and now he felt a pleasant warmth running through his body. He decided to enjoy the boat trip and the girl's company. He even told to himself that perhaps they had left the dangers behind and that their mission was over. He had thwarted Kiel's plans to manufacture the *red typhoon* and got the spell scroll to deliver it to Department X, where it would be kept safely in the vault under the British Museum. He smiled unconsciously.

Mary Ann was looking at him with a funny twinkle in her eyes.

"Wow, I think I must try this."

The girl picked up the flask and drank a long sip. Immediately she suffered a strong fit of cough. She paled sharply. Hunt was alarmed for a moment, but they both stared at each other and finally laughed. Mary Ann drank another sip of the wine and this time she enjoyed it.

"Take it easy," Hunt warned. "This *huangjiu* is quite strong."

"I know how to take care of myself, Peter Hunt."

The girl's voice was already sounding drunk. Hunt, who was also somewhat inebriated, just smiled. She gave another drink to the flask and shuddered.

"Oh, God, I'm dizzy." The girl got up laboriously from the chair and went towards the bunk, trying to prevent the sheet that covered her body from slipping. "I just need to rest a little..."

She fell lying on the bunk and fainted.

At some point, Hunt also fell into a heavy sleep and lost track of time. He woke up suddenly and for a moment forgot where he was. The cabin was dark, and he was still in the chair. He had fallen asleep with his head down. His neck hurt and his legs were numb. Several minutes passed until he managed to situate himself in time and space. Then he understood why he had woken up so abruptly. The ship had pitched hard and was rocking back and forth. Outside it was raining torrentially and the sea was raging.

Were it not for the storm, Hunt and the girl would have died without ever waking up. The cabin door opened slowly, and although it creaked, the noise of the wind and waves crashing into the ship's hull drowned out any other noise on board. Perhaps that is why the killer had waited until that moment to go against the two English passengers. Under the scarce light that slipped through the porthole, Hunt distinguished the outstretched arm, finished in a hand holding a docker's hook, which was introduced through the crack of the door, in the direction of the bunks.

Hunt blinked several times until he understood the danger lurking. Then his instinct took over and ordered his body to charge against the door. The killer growled in pain as he was hit. He tried to pull his arm back, but Hunt had it trapped with all his weight. Desperate and sore, the intruder pushed the door into the compartment and struggled with Hunt, each making force in the opposite direction.

The captain cursed in a whisper and moved

away sharply. The door slammed open, and the intruder went headlong in. He tripped over the table and flipped the two chairs. However, he managed to balance himself and remained on his feet. He was a young man, with Chinese features, who wore worn garments that gave off a strong smell of the sea and fish. He was certainly one of the ship's crew. Hunt immediately attacked him with punches and kicks.

The sailor shouted imprecations in a furious tone and brandished the hook towards Hunt. He pulled away as best he could, but in the small space it was difficult to dodge an opponent. The sharp hook whistled in the air, and its thin tip flashed near Hunt's face. He stepped back to the table and his fingers found the empty flask. He grabbed it by the neck and crashed it onto the intruder's head. The glass shattered, and the sailor staggered in a daze. A trickle of blood descended from the hair to the eyebrows.

So much fuss ended up waking Mary Ann. She sat on the bunk and took a moment to focus with her eyes on the two fighters. She looked for the sheets to cover her body and gave a scream of dread. The sailor was distracted for a moment and gawked at the half-naked girl who looked at him with exorbitant eyes. Hunt immediately caught him with a hold and ran an arm around his neck. The sailor struggled furiously, but his movements only managed to choke him more quickly. Hunt squeezed his arm until the man's face flushed and his legs stopped moving.

Hunt released the intruder, who fell unconscious to the ground.

"Put your clothes on," the captain ordered the girl.

Mary Ann jumped off the bunk and put the dress over her head. Hunt didn't take his eyes off the sailor and didn't even notice the girl's nakedness. When she was dressed, they took the intruder between them and sat him in one of the chairs.

"Go to the kitchen and find a rope to tie him up," Hunt asked the girl.

"Oh my God, Peter! We are in the middle of a storm!"

"Don't be afraid, Mary Ann. The ship is steady, and it will be able to weather the waves. Go carefully and take your time."

Hunt closed the door when the girl came out. He looked at the unconscious sailor and assumed that he had been bribed in port, when Kiel's men discovered that he and Mary Ann would board the *Queen of Java* to flee Shanghai. Surely, he had been offered a good amount of money for discreetly eliminating the two passengers on the high seas. Then, for the murderer it would be as easy as throwing the bodies overboard and returning to his work. The next day, when the other crew members noticed the disappearance of the English passengers, they would attribute it to an accidental fall into the water in the middle of the storm.

The crew consisted of about twenty men from the Dutch East Indies: Malays, Javanese and Sundanese. There were also some Chinese, like that man, a couple of Cambodians, a Vietnamese and a Portuguese cook. All were under the command of Captain Verbeek, a grumpy Dutchman who traded throughout Southeast Asia from his homeport in Batavia. Hunt wondered if there would be any other sailors bribed, but in the end, he deduced that the gangsters would only trust one of their own countrymen. Anyway, he decided that for the rest of the trip he would stay away from the other Chinese crew members.

Mary Ann was taking quite a while. The ship ascended the crests of the waves and then fell sharply into the valleys, only to climb again a moment later. The sailor began to regain consciousness and shook his head to wake up. Hunt picked up his revolver and pointed it at the failed killer. He didn't have any bullets left in the gun, but that guy didn't know it. A moment later, the Chinese focused his eyes on the barrel of the Webley and opened his eyes widely.

"Do you speak English?" Hunt asked. The sailor kept his eyes fixed on the revolver and said nothing. "Of course, you speak it. There is no other way to communicate with the other crewmembers."

The sailor raised his head and looked at Hunt

with a hateful rictus on his face.

"Who ordered you to attack us? What should you do after killing us?"

The man blurted out a series of insults in his language. Hunt wished the girl would arrive at once so she could translate his words to that damn man. Hunt repeated his questions and raised the revolver until it was pointed right between the sailor's eyebrows.

"You had to meet with someone in Hong Kong to report our death, right? And pick up your money," Hunt said. "I don't think those men paid you in advance."

A glow in the Chinese's gaze indicated to Hunt that he had been right in his assumptions. If he managed to figure out the name of the contact in Hong Kong, he could track down the killers and thwart their plans. But this time he would go with the entire Police Force behind him.

"If you tell me the truth," Hunt insisted, "I promise not to kill you."

The sailor looked at the revolver again, almost as if guessing that it was not loaded. Hunt was getting impatient.

"Talk, damn it!"

He approached the sailor with the gun in front. The ship suddenly ascended a wave and then fell immediately. Hunt bounced off the ground and lost his balance for a moment. The Chinese stood up from the chair like a spring and lunged at the captain. He took the revolver with both hands and tried to get hold of it. Hunt held it tightly, but a new pitch from the ship knocked the two opponents down. The Webley was thrown away and slid on the floor. The ship oscillated more and more wildly, and it was almost impossible to stand up.

Hunt hit the sailor as best he could, but he was a tough man, and he withstood the blows well. He waited for a new jump from the ship and dragged away from Hunt. He pushed his feet against a bulkhead and propelled himself facing the floor into the corner where the revolver was. He grabbed the gun with one hand and turned until he was on his back. Hunt crawled towards the sailor, who was already pointing the Webley at him. Hunt ignored the futile gesture and pounced on the Chinese, who pulled the trigger. Nothing happened. The killer's face was petrified for a second, but then he kept pulling the trigger as Hunt fell on him. The captain pushed the gun away in one fell swoop, and then smashed his two fists like maces on the sailor's head.

The Chinese scrambled like a madman until he managed to slip under Hunt. The man got up, quite stunned, and he left the cabin stumbling. Hunt cast a curse and went after him. The sailor came to the end of the cabin aisle and went out to the deck. Hunt followed him and the strength of the elements fell on him. The wind was blowing with a severe whistle and the rain was so dense that it prevented seeing beyond a couple of meters. Hunt barely distinguished the shadow of the killer crossing the bow loading area.

The captain advanced between large packages tied to the deck that threatened to be loose at any time. His body was soaked, and his hands slipped as he tried to grab hold of the ropes. The ship was swaying dangerously, threatening to keel over. Hunt could hear the desperate cries of some crew members working on the deck to hold the cargo and prepare the lifeboats if needed. Although Hunt was frightened by the storm, he did not relent in his efforts to reach the killer.

The sailor-turned-murderer looked over his shoulder and found that the Englishman was coming after him. He looked in all directions and understood that he was trapped. He could only continue to the forecastle, whose clear deck was exposed to the storm. In desperation, he grabbed the railing of the board and climbed up the staircase to the deck of the castle. Hunt followed him in the same way and yelled at him to stop.

"Listen, damn you!" He shouted at the top of his lungs to make himself heard about the storm. "I will pay you if you guide me to your contact in Hong Kong!"

The sailor turned to confront Hunt. He shouted more expletives and raised a fist in the direction of the Englishman. That was his mistake. Hunt spotted what was coming from the sailor's back, directly towards the ship, and only managed to hold himself with all his strength from the railing of the board and shrink the body. A second later, the *Queen of Java* pointed bow cut a wave as high as a wall and pitched wildly, rising like a whale emerging from the sea.

A thick curtain of water furiously whipped the forecastle and swayed the ship towards the opposite band. Hunt felt the blow of the wave and was out of breath. He kept his arms tense and clung desperately to the board as the water pushed him back. A moment later, the ship descended in free fall and the deck of the castle was cleared. There were no traces of the killer. Hunt cursed the loss of valuable information, though not the fate of the greedy man. He laboriously returned to the main deck and from there he retraced his steps to the passenger cabin. The way back seemed eternal.

Mary Ann stood in front of her compartment door. She was soaked and had a red face from the effort and frustration.

"I didn't find any ropes," the girl announced. "I searched everywhere. I fell to the ground a couple of times and..."

She was shaking uncontrollably. Hunt hugged her and whispered that everything had passed.

"And that man?"

"He won't bother us anymore," was his

laconic reply.

They entered the cabin and took off their wet clothes, not caring that they were both naked. Hunt wrapped the girl in some sheets and laid her on the bunk. She took him by the hand.

"Do you think we will both fit here? I don't want to sleep alone."

Hunt lay on the sheets. The bunk was narrow, and he had to squeeze against the girl.

"Get under the covers or you're going to get sick," Mary Ann said.

She covered him and their bodies came together. The girl fell asleep almost immediately, despite the intense movement of the boat. Her exhaustion was greater than the threat of the storm. Sometime in the night, Mary Ann woke up to find that Hunt was staring at her intensely. The storm had passed. She smiled in the dark and noticed his desire as she brushed her body against his. She squeezed even tighter against the captain and asked him between gasps:

"Do you want to?"

He nodded in the dark but understood that she had not noticed his gesture. He cleared his throat and asked:

"Are you sure?"

"It's not my first time, Peter," she explained, in an embarrassed voice.

"Oh, I'm sorry."

"But I haven't been with anyone since I came from England," he added.

"Three years!" Hunt exclaimed, surprised. "Come here right now."

They melted into a hug and forgot everything.

15. EAST CHINA SEA

The compartment was as hot as a Turkish bath. The sun poured in through the porthole, projecting a concentrated beam of light onto the bunks. The enclosed air inside had become dry and heavy. Hunt had set aside the sheets in the middle of the night, but the two bodies that shared the narrow bunk were still covered in sweat. It was impossible to sleep. He absentmindedly stroked the girl's bare back.

"Can we stay like this for the rest of the trip?" Mary Ann asked, in a numb voice.

They had been aboard the *Queen of Java* for two days. The storm had dissipated before dawn and the ship was sailing back in calm waters. Since they spent the night together, Hunt and the girl had hardly left the compartment, except to go to the bathroom or in search of food. When Hunt came out, he was barely wearing his pants. Inside the compartment, they didn't even bother to get dressed. The temperature was rising at every moment.

It seemed as if the whole ship had fallen into a state of drowsiness. Crew and other passengers were also fleeing the heat and the deck was permanently deserted. The Portuguese cook prepared cold dishes, and the water was served rationed. The journey was becoming slow and boring. Only the English couple seemed to be comfortable with the forced confinement. Several sailors smiled undisguised at Hunt as they saw him in the hallways and more than one had winked at him.

For his part, Hunt himself felt calm and relaxed. The attacks and persecutions began to fall into oblivion. Perhaps from now on the journey could be transformed into a real pleasure trip. Thinking about it, he felt encouraged and eager to take a breath. He jumped up and put on his pants. Mary Ann was left lying flat on her face in the bunk. He admired her beautiful body for an instant. Then he leaned back on her and kissed her on the cheek. At the same time, he slapped her butt.

"Hey!" She complained.

"Come on, my dear. It's a splendid day."

Hunt went to the bathroom at the end of the hallway. He groomed himself as best he could and while getting dressed, he regretted having to wear again the same clothes he had worn throughout the trip. He promised to himself that in Hong Kong he would go to the best tailor in the colony and that he would take Mary Ann to buy a dozen dresses before they embarked for England. He would go to the offices of the P&O shipping company and buy tickets in the luxury suite of the first steamer that sailed back home. That idea comforted him as he stepped out on deck and waited for Mary Ann looking out to sea by the passenger cabin.

Outside the heat was inclement and there was almost no breeze, but Hunt was pleased to enjoy the sun on his face. That feeling made him feel alive. He closed his eyes for a while. When he opened them, the girl was next to him. She wore clothes as worn as his, but somehow managed to look fresh and beautiful as if she were aboard an elegant transatlantic steamer. Hunt smiled at her, and she grabbed his arm.

"You were right," Mary Ann said. "The day is splendid."

"*The Sun came up upon the left, / Out of the sea came he! / And he shone bright, and on the right / Went down into the sea.*" Hunt recited.

Mary Ann laughed and nodded with a cheerful expression.

"Did you rise today as a sadder and wiser man?" She joked. "I like Coleridge too. Although I prefer Wordsworth."

"If we were on the shore of a lake," he replied, "I would have chosen *Daffodils.* But at sea, I found *The Rime of the Ancient Mariner* more appropriate."

"I didn't imagine you were a romantic, Peter."

Hunt leaned over to her and kissed her. Mary Ann rested her head on his shoulder. They stayed like this for a long time, enjoying the scenery. The ship was entering a large bay surrounded by islands and soon the coast was in sight. The girl drew apart from Hunt and looked at him with a gesture of disappointment.

"Will we make *another* stop?" she complained. "I feel that we will never reach our destination."

"We went to Foochow," Hunt explained. "We will be there for a couple of hours before setting sail again. It is necessary to replenish coal and food."

Every day of travel, the ship made a call. It was the only way to have fresh food and enough coal for the boilers. The day before they had stopped at Wenchou, shortly before the storm broke out, and the next day they would make a stop in Amoy. From there they would sail directly to their destination in Hong Kong. In each port, besides, some passengers boarded and disembarked, mostly small merchants of tea, rice and textiles who offered their products in the nearby provinces.

Foochow was located on the north bank of the Min River, where it flowed into the East China Sea. The *Queen of Java* entered the estuary of the river and docked at one of the quays in the international zone. Foochow was one of the ports open to trade after the Opium War and the signing of the Treaty of Nanjing between China and Britain. The jetty, used by ships of different nationalities, was bustling with activity, although everything was smaller and less convulsed compared to Shanghai.

Three passengers were waiting for the arrival of the old steamer. They were middle-aged, taciturn-looking Chinese men. They didn't look like merchants at all, but they didn't attract attention, and no one was interested in them. Simply, they just went up the walkway in silence and with their eyes down. Hunt, who had approached the boarding area to catch a glimpse of the port, also did not notice the new passengers. If he had paid more attention to them, he would have discovered that the guys did observe him and, in addition, that they searched with a disguised look for the whereabouts of the girl.

Stocking up took less than two hours. The sailors, aided by the port coolies, loaded the ship quickly and efficiently. The ship could not afford to be stopped for too long. The storm had already delayed it from its original itinerary. Hunt watched the preparations for a while, until the inclement sun made him take refuge in the shade, on the other side of the cabin. Mary Ann had settled right there. Hunt found her sitting on a chair on the deck, protected from the sun by a paper umbrella she had somehow gotten.

"One of the Chinese sailors gave it to me," she explained, before the captain's interrogating gaze. "He is a very nice man."

"Hmm," hunt murmured, still suspicious of the crew.

He wished the girl had no contact with anyone on board, but he didn't want to scare her. On the other hand, the crew were quite reserved and did not relate to the passengers. When Captain Verbeek ordered to search for the missing man, after the storm, his crewmates obeyed silently, and then shrugged at finding no trace of the sailor. Verbeek merely cursed and Hunt heard that he would replace the crew member once the ship arrived in Hong Kong.

The ship set sail soon after. After leaving the estuary, it turned south and approached the island of Pingtan, where the Strait of Formosa, which connected to the South China Sea, began. The strait, one hundred and eighty kilometers wide, separated the mainland of China from Formosa. The island had been ceded to the Japanese almost thirty years ago, after the crushing defeat they had inflicted on the Qing Dynasty in the war for influence over the Korean peninsula. As Hunt had read, this conflict, with its humiliating outcome, had been the germ of the revolution that overthrew the Chinese monarchy in 1911.

Several small islands, some no more than islets, dotted the waters surrounding Pingtan, the larger of its sisters. They formed an archipelago of calm waters where dozens of fishing sampans were busy, along with some larger boats, but of little draft. One of the latter, a Chinese junk, left the protected coasts of the archipelago and went out into the deeper waters of the strait. Upon arriving there it changed course and sailed in the direction of the *Queen of Java.*

Hunt, who was still watching from the deck, saw the approaching ship, but it didn't seem strange to him. The space of the sea passage was more than enough for numerous vessels to share. Although several of these remained close to the coast, their helmsmen knew the area perfectly and each followed a separate route from the others. Besides, a sailing ship, like the junk, would never reach a steamboat.

Mary Ann was dozing in her chair, the umbrella held in such a way as to protect her face. Hunt looked for another chair and tried to nod off next to the girl, but something in a corner of his mind prevented him from relaxing. Without even sitting down, he looked back at the approaching junk. The Chinese ship maintained an oblique trajectory that carried it straight towards the steamer. If both vessels had moved at the same speed, the junk would have been able to intercept the *Queen of Java.* Hunt felt restless. He peered overboard and, as the distance narrowed, he was able to contemplate the other ship in detail.

The hull of the junk was made of wood and had dimensions somewhat smaller than those of the *Queen of Java.* Hunt calculated that its length measured about sixty meters. Distributed throughout the vessel, three long masts carried large rigid trapezoidal sails, supported by long horizontal bamboo reeds. On the wide and clear deck, there were more than twenty crew members, led by the captain from the quarterdeck.

Hunt assumed that one of the two ships would deviate at any time, as they were already quite close. Since the *Queen of Java* was faster and more maneuverable, a small change of course would be enough for the helmsman to dodge the Chinese vessel. Hunt stared at the deck of the approaching ship and realized that all the crew of the junk were looking in the direction of the steamship. None of them showed any concern. Then, an alarm went off in his mind. Just then he heard one shot, immediately followed by another one. Hunt shuddered. The shots came from *his* ship.

"Oh, God!" Mary Ann exclaimed, opening her eyes. "What was that?"

Hunt grabbed her hand and lifted her from the chair. They approached the passenger cabin and Hunt asked Mary Ann to crouch in a corner.

"Stay here and don't move," he ordered.

According to what Hunt could estimate, the shots came from the bridge above the passenger cabin. Both decks were connected by an internal spiral staircase, but that access was ruled out if there was anyone armed on the bridge. Hunt circled the cabin from the outside and found a metal ladder leading to the back of the bridge, where the lifeboats were kept. There were two boats on each side of the steam engine chimney.

Hunt quickly climbed the ladder, jumping on the steps, and advanced crouched over the roof of the cabin. He barricaded himself for a moment next to one of the boats and then hid behind the chimney. From there he was able to spy through the windows what was happening inside the bridge. In a corner of the room, he spotted Captain Verbeek and the helmsman. They were both half shrunk and kept their hands up. A man pointed a gun at them and shouted inaudible orders at them from where Hunt was. From the dashboard emanated a wisp of smoke where the attacker's two warning shots had hit.

The kidnapper approached a window, still gesticulating. Hunt was able to see him better and immediately recognized him as one of the passengers that had boarded in Foochow. He cursed himself for not paying more attention to them, but at least he thought he remembered their faces. He assumed that the other two guys were accomplices of the intruder and wondered where they would be. A moment later, the ship sharply slowed down, and the engine stopped. The ship was left adrift. Hunt understood that at least one of the assailants had to be in the engine room. Probably, the third intruder would be tasked of disabling the radio telegraph, located in a room under the bridge.

Those guys weren't ordinary pirates, Hunt guessed. He was sure that it was not a coincidence that they decided to attack *that* ship and precisely during *that* journey. The *Queen of Java* was a small ship, and its cargo was not very valuable. Maybe it wasn't even listed in the official records. It was evident that the three intruders were on board because of *him.* And their accomplices were in the approaching junk. Hunt told to himself that he must neutralize the pirates before the crew of the junk could board the *Queen of Java.* He remained crouched and quickly descended the ladder, back to the main deck.

Some passengers had gone out on the deck and wandered with an expression of strangeness at the sudden stop of the ship. Some murmured among themselves, and others demanded to speak to Captain Verbeek. The crew on the deck looked as surprised as the passengers. Hunt approached one of the sailors, who was looking up at the bridge to try to find out what was going on. Hunt took him aside and asked if he spoke English. The man, probably Javanese, nodded with a gesture.

"Listen to me," Hunt said. "There are armed men on board."

The sailor opened his eyes very wide and stepped back.

"Are you sure?" he asked in barely intelligible English.

"They have taken over the bridge and the engine room. That's why the ship stopped."

The sailor looked at him dumbfounded. Hunt grabbed his arm and shook him to liven him up.

"Are there weapons on board?" He asked. "Firearms?"

The crew member hesitated. Hunt looked at him harshly and then the man babbled:

"Eeehh... I think captain have rifle in cabin."

Hunt looked overboard and noticed that the junk was almost on the side of the steamer.

"Take me there. Quickly!"

The sailor guided him through the corridor that ran under the deck to the bow of the ship, where the captain's cabin was located. The compartment was even smaller than Hunt's. On one side there was a narrow bunk and on the other a sideboard with drawers, made of wood, which also served as a desk. In between there was hardly any room to walk. Hunt glanced through the small space and then it occurred to him to search under the bunk. He crouched down and stretched out his hand until his fingers touched the unmistakable shape of a long weapon.

Hunt extracted the rifle, an old Mauser Model 1895. It weighed four kilos, measured one hundred and twenty centimeters long, and carried a five-round clip inserted into the magazine. Hunt rummaged through the drawers of the sideboard but found no more bullets. That was better than nothing. He would have to take care of every shot he made.

"Look for your crewmates," Hunt told the sailor, "and stay in the hold. We are likely to be boarded."

Hunt went out onto the deck near the stern to avoid being seen from the junk, which was almost next to the steamer. The passengers and crew were already aware of the assault on the ship and had gathered in the ship's cargo area. They looked nervous and abandoned to their fate. Mary Ann was not among them. Hunt went to the place where he had left her and found her still crouching and with her back stuck to the cabin.

"They're pirates, Peter!" The girl exclaimed as soon as she saw Hunt.

"They come for us, Mary Ann."

The girl's eyes reflected the fear that gripped her.

"You mean they work for Kiel? But how..."

"I'm afraid they saw us board this ship and they advanced overland. They have many resources at their disposal."

"What will we do now?"

He showed her the rifle.

"I will try to stop the intruders before we are approached by their comrades in the junk."

She looked at him speechlessly.

"Go to the compartment and lock the door," he said. "Don't open unless I tell you."

He directed her towards the entrance of the cabin, and he went to the opposite end. He climbed the back ladder again and took position next to one of the lifeboats. He pointed the rifle at the bridge, his elbow resting on the boat, and ran the bolt to put a cartridge in the gun's chamber. He could still see the crew members held hostage, stopped at gunpoint by the assailant. However, the man was partially hidden by a bulkhead. Hunt waited patiently for his chance, but sweat slipped down his cheeks and his heart beat fast. Beyond the bridge, the shadow of the junk was cast on the steamer.

The assailant moved and was silhouetted against the window. Hunt aligned the sight with the rifle's crosshairs and fired. The window glass shattered, and the man's head burst out. Hunt ran to the bridge and peeked in the broken window. The crew looked dumbfounded at the pirate's corpse.

"Verbeek, I'm Hunt! Be prepared to depart when I tell you."

The Dutchman looked at Hunt in surprise, armed with his own rifle, but after a second, he nodded and uttered an exclamation in his language. The helmsman jumped behind the ship's controls. Hunt took it as an acceptance of his instructions and ran away.

He jumped down back to the deck. He recalled that at the end of the cabin aisle there was a hatch that communicated with the cargo area. He deduced that from there he could reach the engine room. He went running through the corridor, but before reaching the hatch a door slammed open. Another of the pirates came out of the radio room, no doubt alerted by the sound of the rifle. The man saw Hunt and raised his pistol. The captain threw himself to the floor just as the pirate fired. The bullet passed over him.

At close range, the rifle was useless. Before he could action the bolt and point the gun, the pirate would have already fired his pistol. But the solid piece of wood had other uses. Hunt jumped up and took the rifle by the barrel, brandishing it in an upward bow, like a club. The pirate's jaw broke with a horrendous crackle, and the man burst out backwards. He didn't move again. Hunt took away the man's pistol, a Mauser C96 with a wooden grip, and hung the rifle on his shoulder with the strap. He then opened the hatch and descended a vertical staircase to the main hold. In front of it, in the central part of the ship, was the engine room.

He passed between large wooden crates, bales of fabric, bamboo baskets and various types of containers, until he reached the watertight door of the room. He turned the central steering wheel that removed the locks and slammed open the metal gate. The heat of the room hit him hard and took his breath away. The boilers were still on, and the interior of the enclosure was full of steam, like a fog bank. Hunt adjusted his breathing but sweated copiously as he entered the room. He advanced crouched and with the gun pointed at the front. Visibility was poor. Beside him, the machines were grinding due to the high temperature they produced.

A shadow moved forward. Hunt fired, but the shot bounced off the iron bulkheads. He took another couple of steps and stopped to listen. A sound coming from the side alerted him to the proximity of the pirate. He squatted down instinctively. The assailant's shot was lost between the machines. Hunt turned to the noise but couldn't see anything from the cloud of steam flooding the room. Forward he spotted a large coal pit, overflowing with dark rocks. He circled the reservoir, advancing stealthily, but the soot from the coal flooded his throat and made him cough.

The pirate suddenly appeared next to him. Hunt raised his gun and pulled the trigger, but a sudden cough deflected the shot. He put his free hand in the coal pit and threw dust and rocks towards his opponent. A black cloud enveloped the pirate's face and made him convulse. In desperation, the Chinese pounced on Hunt. They debated furiously, both coughing and with irritated eyes. The two enemies intertwined their arms and stretched their legs so as not to fall. They turned in the steam, panting for the heat and effort, both determined to fight to the death.

Hunt felt the heat increase, almost to the point of burning him. With great effort he turned his head and saw something shining to the side, like the open jaws of a dragon about to launch a flame. While still struggling with the pirate, he managed to get close to the huge boiler furnace. He felt his skin burning and no air reached his lungs. With supreme effort, he grabbed his opponent's clothes and pushed him back with all his strength. The pirate tripped over the rim of a metal fastening bolted to the floor and came out projected backwards. During an instant of horror, the body swayed over the opening of the furnace, and then fell inward. The howl of pain drilled into Hunt's brain, and the smell of burnt flesh almost made him sick.

The pirate managed to throw himself out of the furnace and twisted on the ground, engulfed in flames. Hunt pointed the gun at what was once the man's head and fired twice. The charred body stopped moving. Suppressing his nausea, Hunt searched a bulkhead for the speaking tube that communicated with the bridge.

"Verbeek, I'm in control of the engine room!" He announced through the brass mouthpiece. "Now tell me how to activate the turbines!"

There was no response. A chill ran down his back.

"Answer me, damn it!"

A familiar female voice came through the tube after a moment:

"We're in control of the ship, Peter. Get out of there and surrender."

Hunt imagined Mei Ling on the bridge, speaking through the tube with a satisfied smile. He cursed to himself and ran away. However, he did not go to the bridge, but to his compartment in the passenger cabin. When he reached the deck, he saw that the junk was tied to the board of the *Queen of Java* and that the pirates had boarded the steamer. Several intruders spotted him and ran after him. Hunt fired back with the Mauser, without even looking. He knew he was outnumbered, but at least he was trying to delay his capture.

He threw himself down the aisle of the cabin, but it was late. The pirates had already located the compartment and were pounding on the door. Seeing the captain appear, they threw themselves on him. Hunt tried to back off, but the other intruders coming from the deck had blocked the hallway. For a moment, Hunt was caught between the two groups. The pirates were armed with daggers, hooks and clubs. They raised their weapons and smiled mercilessly, inviting him to give them an excuse to beat him. Hunt calculated that he had a couple of shots left in the Mauser but trying to use it was suicide. Maybe he would manage to hurt some of the pirates, even kill one or two, but the others would massacre him.

He dropped the gun and raised his hands.

Several men caught him and pushed him to the door of the compartment. One of the intruders waved his head to the compartment. Hunt understood that he had to play along if he wanted to survive.

"Mary Ann, it's me," he said out loud.

"Oh, Peter!" The girl shouted from the other side of the door. "Are you ok?"

"Yes, I'm fine. I'm sorry, my dear. This time they won the game."

On the other side of the door there was silence. Hunt imagined Mary Ann shrunk in terror. He hated himself for failing her, but now all that remained was to buy time.

"You'd better open the door."

A moment later she pulled out the bolt and the door opened. The pirates threw themselves into the compartment and pushed the girl out. Mary Ann watched Hunt with her face disjointed with fear. The captain smiled and winked at her. He wanted to convey to her that at least they were alive and that they had to survive to fight another day. She didn't understand the sign and lowered her face in a gesture of resignation. Both prisoners were taken to the deck.

Mei Ling was waiting under the bridge. She was dressed in a tight black robe and a long cloak of the same color, under which her fearsome *jian* sword loomed. On her face she kept a radiant smile of superiority. Hunt hated her, but at the same time he thought the warrior looked rapturous. One of the pirates came forward and laid out to his boss the spell scroll, which Hunt had kept hidden under his bunk. The girl's eyes flashed with excitement. Then she put away the manuscript between her clothes, and her gaze became hard.

"You've caused a lot of trouble, Peter Hunt."

"And yet, I'm still here," he challenged her.

"Not for long."

"Are you finally going to kill me, *Meihua?*"

Hearing her sing-song girl name, Mei Ling paled.

"What will it be like?" Hunt insisted, before she replied. "A beheading, like Wang Min, or will you make me walk the plank, pirate style?"

The girl stepped forward and looked at him closely.

"You are not afraid of death. The *mien shiang* tells me."

Hunt recalled that the girl mastered the Taoist technique for 'reading faces'. He tried to maintain a neutral expression, but fury invaded him hopelessly.

"You're lucky that Kiel wants you alive," Mei Ling said, looking at the two prisoners.

She then approached Mary Ann and grabbed her by the chin.

"However, he didn't tell me anything about your girlfriend."

Mary Ann gave a muffled scream. Hunt struggled, but his captors managed to immobilize him. Mei Ling let out a sinister laugh.

"Yes, you fear for her, right?" The warrior let the girl go and came back to Hunt. "Then listen to me very well, Peter. This woman's life is in your hands."

16. THE PIRATE JUNK

Under his feet, Peter Hunt felt the rhythmic wobble of the junk as the flat hull of the ship sailed the gentle waves that formed in the direction of the coast. He wondered how long it would take to reach their destination and where they would disembark. He assumed that they were entering one of the large bays that opened south of Pingtan Island, in the remote province of Fukien. The rugged coastline was dotted with islands, an ideal refuge for pirates. The junk had been sailing for several hours and was already beginning to get dark. Hunt guessed that they would soon have to call at some port or at least anchor for the night. At that moment he would try to escape.

The pirates only captured him and the girl, just as Hunt had assumed. For a fateful moment Hunt feared that the pirates would sink the *Queen of Java* with the crew and passengers left to their fate, but Mei Ling had given the order to lock them all in the hold. With the command bridge deserted and the radio telegraph destroyed, the steamer would be left adrift for several hours, perhaps until the next day, before another ship passed by and its crew was surprised to see the ship apparently abandoned. From that moment it would be quite a while before some curious captain sent someone to investigate the ship and discover its prisoners. By then, there would be no traces of the junk.

Once aboard the pirate ship, Mary Ann and Hunt were separated. The girl was taken under the deck, amid screams and vain attempts to free herself, while the captain was pushed into a cabin located under the poop deck, at the stern of the junk. The cabin covered the entire width of the ship and was provided with a large bed recessed in the inner part of the hull. At the center of the room stood a table of sturdy wood, with two chairs arranged on both sides. Small portholes located at the back of the chamber allowed a scarce light to illuminate the interior.

Hunt was tied to the chair in front of the table, which was fastened with firm nails to the wooden floor. No one disturbed him for hours. All that time he remained in the same position, thirsty and numbed by tiredness. At some point in the night, he felt the curtain that covered the entrance threshold to the cabin was drawing. He shook his head to push away the tiredness and saw Mei Ling walk past him. The girl came to the table and lit an engraved bronze lamp. The flame flooded the interior of the cabin with a faint yellowish glow. The warrior leaned her hips against the edge of the table and looked at Hunt with a serious expression.

"You have no escape, Peter Hunt. Are you aware of it?"

"Yes, I know," he replied, lowering his head so that she could not guess his true intentions through the *mien shiang*.

Mei Ling stood on Hunt's back and cut his lashings with a sharp dagger. Hunt rubbed his sore wrists. The girl shouted an order and a crew member brought food and drink on ceramic plates of different shapes and colors. The cups were not matched either. Hunt assumed that the pirates had obtained the tableware in various lootings. If anything, he cared little when he could account for the food. The fish was fresh, probably recently caught, and the *baijiu* liquor was burning in his throat.

The girl sat in the other chair and ate with Hunt. She skillfully handled the chopsticks, with which she tasted small bites of each dish. She held her alcohol, drinking occasional sips of the cup. Hunt was complicated using the chopsticks but managed not to look like a barbarian in the eyes of the young Chinese woman. Anyway, she avoided laughing on the occasions when he missed a piece of food from the utensils. When they finished, the same crew member brought them a bowl with water to wash their hands.

"It was splendid," Hunt said, with a fake smile. "Was this the last supper of the condemned?"

"Only if you force me to do so," the girl replied immediately.

"Kiel would be upset if something happened to me," he reminded her.

"Kiel is far away," replied the girl. "An accident can always happen. To you... *or her.*"

"Leave Mary Ann out of this matter. She is innocent."

"Innocent? She helped Wang escape from the hospital and hid the cinnabar crystals. And she involved *you* in this matter."

"Don't dare hurt her," Hunt muttered, leaning over in his chair.

Mei Ling stood still in place, feeling secure with the table between them. After a moment, she asked:

"Do you love her?"

The question caught Hunt by surprise. He thought about the answer for a few moments and decided to answer honestly:

"I like her very much. I don't want anything bad to happen to her."

Mei Ling stared at him for a few moments, no doubt 'reading' the expression on his face. But Hunt was tired of pretending and just let her draw the conclusions she wanted. The girl got up from the chair and leaned over the table.

"Love is the downfall of the warrior, Peter Hunt."

"I doubt that a sing-song girl knows what love is."

The slap was quick and surprisingly painful. His cheek was left burning, but Hunt was relieved that at least the girl hadn't attacked him with a *dim mak* punch. Or, worse, with her sword.

"You insist on provoking me." Her eyes glowed in a mixture of fury and pride. "You want to humiliate me for have been a courtesan."

"I assumed you still were." Hunt looked back at her harshly. "You are the one who must decide, Mei Ling. Warrior... or prostitute?"

"I am much more than that. But an Englishman wouldn't understand it."

"Try me. After all, I have nowhere else to go."

Mei Ling looked at him for a few moments to make sure he was serious. Then she sat on the edge of the bed and told him her story.

"I was born in the north of Kiangsu province, in a poor village ravaged by monsoons. My parents were small farmers, or so I think remember. They already had several children when I was born. At the age of five I was taken to a village larger than ours, located several kilometers away. There I was left in the care of a quiet and stern woman who lived in a large house painted in bright colors. At first, I thought she was an aunt, but then I discovered that there were several girls in my same situation."

"The girls had to clean, cook and take care of the animals on the adjoining farm, but they fed us well and taught us to read, sing and dance.

Many men visited the house and spent a long time with the older girls. It didn't take long for me to discover that the woman was the *amah* of the local brothel. My parents had sold me to her."

Mei Ling related the story of her early years in a dispassionate tone and kept her countenance firm. However, at no time did she look directly at Hunt. Her eyes were lost somewhere and at a distant time. After a few moments, she continued.

"Soon I too would have to hand over my body to those men, who were mostly wealthy farmers, imperial government officers, or soldiers on leave. However, my beauty and talent offered me another destiny. When the *amah* saw that I excelled in all the arts of seduction, she understood that she could gain an even greater advantage than by offering my services in her brothel."

"One day we made a long journey south, first on foot and then by train. After several hours we arrived in Shanghai. For a ten-year-old girl, the city was something exotic and fascinating. I never imagined that there could be a place like that. Although I stayed there, I was still a prisoner. The *amah* had sold me to another brothel.

"The House of White Peony?" Hunt asked.

The girl nodded vaguely, as if she had barely heard him. With a distracted gesture she rubbed the tattoo on her right hand.

"There I was marked as a luxury courtesan and my training continued. The female teachers were even more severe than the previous *amah* and the arts were difficult to learn. But again, I stood out and was finally ready to transform into a sing-song girl. At the age of fifteen I began to receive my first clients."

Hunt shuddered at the thought of a girl transformed into a prostitute against her will. Maybe in China they tried to disguise that abuse as if it were an art, teaching the little girls to sing and dance, but in his eyes that made it even more disgusting.

"I learned to let go of my feelings, Peter," she said, as if she had read his thoughts. "Having been with hundreds of men of all classes, I had no choice."

"Despite that, I still strived to be the best. If I was going to live that life, I had to take advantage of all its benefits. I got powerful sponsors and they gave me many valuable gifts. Unlike the other girls, who accumulated dresses and jewelry to wear on any occasion, I sold the objects I received and collected the money. I didn't plan to be in that house forever."

Hunt poured himself more *baijiu* and looked admiringly at the beautiful warrior.

"In less than three years I already had a small fortune hidden in my room. Some girls can buy their freedom," she explained, "or marry their benefactors and escape from that world. But I had other plans. One fine day, I just walked away."

"And they didn't look for you? I imagine you were a great investment for the owners of the house."

The captain assumed that this brothel belonged to the triads or one of Shanghai's dozens of secret criminal organizations.

"Of course they looked for me," Mei Ling replied. "They issued an alert to all their contacts and offered a reward to the other criminal organizations to find me. But I had left Shanghai that same night and was heading to the eastern mountains."

Hunt recalled that Chinese martial arts were studied in distant temples that were hidden in several mountains that were considered sacred to Buddhism and Taoism.

"There you learned to fight," he said.

"It took me weeks to arrive and as many weeks to be accepted into a temple. Studies are reserved for men and monks are jealous of their knowledge."

"I guess your beauty cleared your entrance."

Mei Ling let out a fierce laugh that must have been heard throughout the ship.

"Those monks are immune to earthly pleasures. I could have walked naked in front of them, and they wouldn't have moved a single muscle."

The girl explained that she had to earn

her place in the temple. The masters shaved her hair, beat her, treated her like scum, and forced her to be their servant. But she resisted all the humiliations and slowly left to earn their admiration. After all, an old monk saw something in her and decided to train her. For five years she practiced every day, from dawn to dusk, until she was able to defeat all the other monks in individual combat. The old master told her she was ready and true to his principles, forced her to leave the temple.

"In spite of everything," said the girl, in a resigned voice, "I was still a *yínfù,* a licentious woman."

"So why become a warrior?" Hunt asked.

He was captivated by the story, but still didn't understand the girl's motivation to achieve her goal.

"Because I was going to fight a war." The girl's voice was broken by emotion. "A long and bloody war that I needed to win. That *I'm going* to win," she added, her throat clenched.

She walked over to the table, filled a glass with *baijiu,* and drank it in one sip.

"During my years in the House of White Peony I was with many men," Mei Ling explained. "Powerful and influential men, but at the same time corrupt and ruthless. Most were foreigners, although there were also several Chinese. But they all had one thing in common: they liked to talk after making love."

"I listened to dozens of stories, speeches, complaints and even whining, until I understood that everyone was looking out for their own interests. They only cared about money and power. European businessmen, American industrialists, diplomats, Kuomintang leaders, warlords... They are all the same. They just want to squeeze China until there is nothing left."

"Do you think you can change the situation, Mei Ling?" Hunt shook his head in disbelief. "With your gifts and your sword?"

The girl had blushing cheeks and bright eyes.

"I'm not the only one who believes it! While in the temple I met several warriors who thought like me. They wanted a new China, great and powerful, at the service of their people."

Hunt scratched his chin and nodded slowly.

"You're going to use the *red typhoon* for your purposes. What will it be like? An explosion in Beijing? Razing several cities, perhaps?"

"There will be a sacrifice, it's true. But we will get rid of oppressors and foreigners who steal our wealth!"

Hunt told to himself that the girl was not crazy, but she was a fanatic.

"Together with the other warriors we formed a secret society and drew up our plans," Mei Ling continued. "Each of us had a function and a place to go. In my case, I had to go back to the sing-song house to spy on our enemies and get information."

"It was bold to return after five years," the captain said.

"I knew what I was exposing myself to. When I showed up at the door, the *amah* was slow to recognize me, but when I asked if I could come back, she told me that I was still her property."

"That same afternoon she took me to the courtyard and gathered all the girls there. Two guards tied me face to a pole and stripped me from the waist down. Then the *amah* whipped my butt with a bamboo cane. Although she could not leave permanent wounds, it still took several days for the marks to disappear. When I was cured, she took me back to the yard and repeated the process. She waited for me to recover again and punished me for the third time. Then she handed me over to her most depraved and grotesque clients. In the end, she assumed that I had learned my lesson and became her most successful girl again."

Hunt couldn't help but feel infected by the girl's confidence. At that moment he came to think that somehow, she would achieve her goals. He wondered if China would not be better off under her command. However, there was something that didn't fit.

"Why did you ally yourself with Rudolph Kiel? Isn't he one of the foreigners you despise so much?"

"Oh, I despise him, make no mistake!" Mei

Ling pointed an accusing finger at him. "But I need him. He and his partners have contacts at the highest levels of our government that I need to approach. And, of course, he has a lot of money to finance the operation."

"Too bad," he murmured. "At the end of the day, you are nothing more than a cynic."

This time, Hunt was prepared for the slap. However, although the girl raised her hand, she left it suspended in the air and just looked furiously at the captain.

"I am willing to do anything for my country and my people."

"Me too, Mei Ling." Hunt got up from the chair and approached the girl. He found that she was trembling with excitement. "Kiel intends to use the *red typhoon* against England and I cannot allow it."

"Sorry, Peter. I promised Kiel that he could copy the spell formula and take the items to prepare the compound."

"China's future will be stained with blood," he insisted.

"It will be a better future anyway," replied the girl. "China was a great nation, Peter. Our ancestors invented paper, gunpowder, the compass and the printing press. While in the West the Dark Ages were lived, in China progress was being made in all fields of knowledge. From astronomy to metallurgy, through art and military techniques."

"Today, on the other hand, we are nothing. A few years ago, we overthrew the monarchy, but we transformed ourselves into a weak, fragmented republic ravaged by warlords. Our ports are in the hands of Europeans and Japanese, while millions of Chinese live in poverty and mired in disease. But soon, all of that will end. China will re-emerge!"

Mei Ling walked over to the recessed bed, removed the belt holding the *jian* sword, and left the weapon on the mattress. She then stood in the center of the cabin and removed the cloak, which he dropped to the ground.

"You asked me if I was a warrior or a prostitute. Actually, this is who I am."

With quick gestures she took off the robe that wrapped her and stood completely naked in front of Hunt. He swallowed as he admired the firm breasts, the rounded hips and the dark triangle between her legs. Then the girl turned around and he was speechless. A huge brightly colored tattoo was spreading all over Mei Ling's back.

"This is *Fenghuang,* the Chinese phoenix," she said, speaking over her shoulder.

The drawing of the mythological bird ranged from the base of the neck, with its wings extended and a tail of long feathers that reached up to the turgid buttocks. The creature's body, a mixture of other birds and real animals, was painted black, white, red, yellow and green. Mei

Ling stretched out her muscles, and the phoenix seemed to fly over her naked body. The effect was almost hypnotic.

"*Fenghuang* represents virtue and grace," the girl explained. "It symbolizes the union of yin and yang and remain hidden when problems are coming. But then, it reappears in times of peace and prosperity."

Mei Ling faced Hunt again. Her face had an exalted expression and a mystical aura that did not come from the light of the lamp.

"I'm the phoenix, Peter. I was hidden, but now I will come out into the light." She took his hand and placed it between her soft breasts. Her heart was beating wildly. "My heart and body belong to China."

There was nothing more to say. Mei Ling dressed promptly and led Hunt outside. The junk had stopped in a cove protected by two rocky promontories of a small island. The ship was completely dark, illuminated only by the light of the full moon whose splendor was reflected in the calm waters of the cove. At the other end of the deck, a group of crew members quietly performed the maneuvers to anchor. Hunt saw that behind them was Mary Ann.

Not caring about the stealth of operations, Hunt ran to the girl and hugged her tightly. She sank her face into his chest. Hunt felt the warm tears wetting his shirt.

"Oh, Peter, I thought something bad had

happened to you!"

"I'm fine, my dear. And you?"

He pushed her away to see her better and suddenly felt his blood boiling. Mary Ann had a dark bruise under her eye and her cheek swollen. Then the captain noticed that her dress was torn on the back.

"Oh my God! What did they do to you?" Hunt asked, in a voice full of bile. "Did they..."

"No, no. One of them went too far with me, but I managed to push him away."

Hunt followed the girl's fearful gaze and saw a sinister-looking, dirty pirate watching her resentfully. The man rubbed one hand with the other involuntarily. Hunt saw the marks of a bite on his calloused skin. Without thinking, Hunt pounced on the man.

"No!" Mei Ling shouted.

The warrior grabbed Hunt by the arm and prevented him from advancing. Then she pushed him away sharply and stepped forward to stand between the two opponents. The pirate smiled and made a mocking face at the English prisoner. He still had that rictus on his face when the sword flashed under the moonlight, as fleeting as lightning. A second later the pirate's head separated from the body and rolled down the deck, smiling eternally. The other pirates moved away to dodge that leftover. The rest of the body stood as his companions watched in horror, but then it fell backwards, with a dry noise. A pool of blood formed around it.

Mei Ling issued some orders in Chinese. Hunt didn't understand her words, but he could guess the threat implied by her ice-cold tone. The men hurried back to their duties, their eyes down and their throats dry. The warrior turned to her prisoners.

"I'm sorry," he said. "No one will disobey my orders again."

17. THE ISLAND OF THE PHOENIX

A barge took them to the beach covering the short trip from the junk, which had anchored near the coast thanks to its low and flat hull. A couple of burly sailors propelled the small boat paddling at a steady pace and within a few minutes Mei Ling, Hunt and Mary Ann jumped ashore. While the pirates dragged the barge through the sand, out of the water, the warrior led her prisoners into the interior of the island.

"The pirates told me that this site didn't even have a name," Mei Ling said. "For them it is simply a remote place that serves as a hiding place."

She paused for a moment and gazed at the darkened landscape that silhouetted against the moonlight.

"For me, on the other hand, it will be the place of the rebirth of my country. So I called it *Fenghuang dǎo,* the island of the Phoenix."

The terrain, covered with vegetation, ascended towards a central hill. A path of pebbles led from the beach to the forest. There seemed to be no permanent settlements or other inhabitants other than pirates. Hunt took

Mary Ann by the arm and together they moved forward guided by the moonlight. They left behind the rockeries that delimited the coast, furrowed with shrubs inclined by the constant wind, and shortly later they entered among the trees. Soon its thick tops hid the moon, and the group was shrouded in darkness. Hunt felt Mary Ann shudder.

"Follow that light," said Mei Ling, who was moving forward without hesitation.

Hunt saw that the warrior pointed her hand, in the middle of the gloom, towards a point located at the other end of the forest. The captain stepped forward and discovered a twinkling light coming from a distant torch. Using the tiny beacon as a guide, he continued to move forward carefully, keeping an eye on his steps so as not to stumble. He pointed the way to Mary Ann and every so often he was checking that he was heading in the right direction towards the faint light that called them into the darkness. Hunt said to himself that this place was an ideal hideout for pirates. The forest was close to the coast, but it was dense enough to make impossible to see what was happening beyond the tree line.

The road crossed the thicket and ended at the foot of the central hill. There a narrow cavern opened, whose entrance was marked by the torch that had served as their guide. The rock wall protected the flame from the wind and prevented its faint glow from being seen beyond the forest. A fierce-looking sentinel stood guard sitting on a tree stump. Mei Ling made a gesture of recognition and went into the cavern, followed by the two English captives.

A narrow passage covered with stalactites led to a large interior opening. Hunt immediately understood that this chamber was not natural but had been carved into the rock. The walls were quite smooth, though not totally straight, and the irregular ceiling was fastened with timber made from tree trunks that had been cut down in the nearby forest. From the other end of the chamber emerged a tunnel, also built by man, which disappeared to the interior of the hill.

The cavern showed all the signs of being the main lair of the pirates. There were lounge chairs leaning against the walls, large trunks filled with the spoils of robberies, trestle tables to eat, shelves made of bamboo and ropes extended between the woods that were used to hang freshly washed clothes. Several torches lit up the cavern and a strong smell of food flooded the air, coming from a campfire that pirates used for cooking.

At a glance, Hunt calculated that there were more than fifty pirates inside the cavern. Some slept or chatted in small groups, but most were busy with the organization's supplies, food, or its impressive collection of weapons. Hunt assumed that the hideout was temporary. The pirates would arrive there after a looting, wait for the waters to calm down, and then go out to sell the stolen goods and return to their homes. And so on until the next job. As they had obtained nothing from the assault on the *Queen of Java,* the captain deduced that this time they had acted in pay with the sole purpose of catching him and the girl.

A guard instructed them to sit in a corner and another man brought them food. Hunt handed his ration to Mary Ann.

"I'm not hungry," he whispered.

He did not wish to tell Mary Ann that he had eaten abundantly with their captor.

"What will they do to us?" Mary Ann asked, her mouth full.

She was hungry and ate quickly.

"For the time being, nothing. They are waiting for Kiel to arrive."

"And what do he want from us? They have already recovered the spell."

"I think he's going to question us." He should have said 'torture us', but he would have only managed to terrorize the girl. "He would like to know whether I was able to alert the English authorities of his plans."

Mary Ann's eyes lit up.

"Did you do it? Were you able to talk to the English consul in Shanghai?"

Hunt shook his head.

"It would have been useless, my dear. Just

like it happened to you when you fled from Yuyuan Garden, I also know that the authorities would never have believed me."

Mary Ann lowered her gaze and nodded with a resigned gesture.

"At least I could tell Chester Peng what happened. He believed me... and now he's dead."

Her eyes filled with tears. Hunt hugged her and for a while she ate quietly. Until she suddenly raised her head and looked at Hunt with eyes wide open.

"When Kiel knows that we haven't talked to anyone about this matter... He's going to kill us!"

That's how it was, Hunt thought, but he banished that idea from his mind. He had to plan how to flee the island before the consul arrived.

Soon after, they were approached by Mei Ling. She carried the scroll in her hand. She was accompanied by two burly pirates.

"Come," the warrior ordered them.

"Will we go to meet with Kiel?" Hunt wanted to know.

Mei Ling hesitated for a second, but then shook her head.

"The consul is waiting for us somewhere else. There is something we must do before we go to meet him."

They went to the tunnel coming out of the cavern. Each of the pirates picked up a torch. One of them opened the march and the other stood behind the prisoners. The tunnel resembled the corridor of a mine. It was less than two meters high and just over a meter wide. At short intervals, wooden arches supported the walls and the rock ceiling. The ground was slippery from moisture and the air became thinner as they went under the hill.

The tunnel had a steep slope that was going downhill. After advancing about fifty meters, Hunt deduced that they were below sea level. A dense, brackish smell invaded the environment. At each moment the tunnel became narrower, and everyone had to walk with their hands stretched out to the sides to grope for the walls and thus avoid crashing into a ledge or a sharp edge. The passageway concluded on stairs crudely carved into the rock. Hunt descended slowly, treading carefully so as not to slip. Mary Ann was holding firmly to him by her hand.

The staircase led to a large arch that opened into a natural cavern, much larger than the chamber that served as a lair for the pirates. This grotto, located in the heart of the hill, was the size of the nave of a church. From the high ceiling hung long stalactites, shiny with moisture, and the floor was covered with the corresponding stalagmites. At the center of the chamber was an underground lagoon, a dozen meters in diameter. On the edge of it were several burning bonfires that illuminated the inside of the vault and provided some warmth.

One of the campfires was larger than the

others and was fed by large amounts of firewood. Above the fire, hanging from a metal crossbar, was an iron crucible. Form its inside shone a reddish substance. On one side, on a trestle table, were arranged the implements of a primitive alchemy laboratory. Mei Ling stood behind the table and spread the roll on it.

"What the hell!" Hunt exclaimed.

Mary Ann looked at him with a gesture of questioning.

"She's going to prepare the formula," he whispered to his partner. "Damn, Mei Ling intends to create the *red typhoon* right here!"

The guards fastened the torches to rings embedded in the wall of the cavern and then approached a lump deposited on the ground, between some rocks. When it was picked up, Hunt saw that it was a person wrapped in blankets. It must have been someone old or sick, because he did not move of his own and emitted some harsh moans. The pirates carried him and left him carefully at Mei Ling's feet.

The warrior crouched down and whispered a few words in Chinese. Then she removed the blankets, and the body was exposed. From where he was, Hunt could see that it was a man, but his features were disfigured, and the skin was blackened. A grim hunch settled in his mind and forced him to approach the body involuntarily. Then he saw that the man had a horribly burned body and, on his face, only a single reddened eye was distinguished.

"Don't you recognize him, do you?" Mei Ling asked. Hunt was startled. "He, on the other hand, remembers you very well. Isn't it, Kao Fang?"

The old alchemist's only eye was focused on Hunt. Despite being surrounded by a jumble of destroyed meat, the eye still conveyed a feeling of unbridled fury. Hunt swallowed and stepped back.

"Kao Fang could not escape the explosion at the Pudong factory," the girl explained, as she prepared the bowls, mortars and jars on the table. "He only came out alive thanks to the protection of a metal plate."

What was once that man's mouth made guttural sounds that only Mei Ling understood.

"He says he hopes to see you in hell," the warrior translated.

Hunt maintained a neutral expression, but Mary Ann turned her head and covered her mouth with one hand.

"What do you intend to do, Mei Ling?" The captain asked. "That substance is extremely dangerous."

"You won't believe that I'm going to deliver the formula to Kiel without first trying it, right? China's future depends on this."

"You want Kao Fang to guide you through the process," Hunt said, avoiding looking at the dying man.

"He's the only one who knows how to do it,"

she confirmed. "He must teach me *now.*"

The alchemist was about to die, and with him would go the secrets of his art. Hunt wished to have his revolver to put an end immediately to the macabre plans of the warrior and her partner, the German consul. He looked around and wondered if there was anything he could use as a weapon.

The warrior had stopped paying attention to her prisoners and was focused on studying the roll and arranging the elements to make the explosive weapon. From the crucible of the campfire emanated a smell like sulfur and the smoke made the eyes burn. Mary Ann started coughing. Hunt looked around and wondered if he would make it to the tunnel before the guards reacted. But immediately his intentions were cut short. More than a dozen pirates broke through the entrance arch and approached the table. Their faces, illuminated by the bonfire, showed surprise and disbelief.

One of the men, apparently the chief of the pirates, spoke in a dry tone to the warrior. She responded in an angry and firm voice. The pirates retreated.

"What happens?" Hunt asked Mary Ann in a low voice.

"Pirates are afraid. They say that this is witchcraft."

"They are not wrong," he murmured.

"Mei Ling threatened to kill them all," Mary

Ann added. "Somehow, they believed her."

Hunt nodded silently. It was incredible the power that the warrior exercised over other people. Her mere presence and a small demonstration of her skills were enough to frighten anyone. Even hardened men like those. The girl's features had hardened, and her eyes were emitting an evil glow. The pirates looked at each other and then contemplated the preparation of the spell. Their bodies were stiff with fear, and their gazes did not depart from the table, as if they were hypnotized.

The alchemist babbled a few words, surely instructions, which Mei Ling followed with quick and precise gestures. She ground crystals in a bowl, mixed other substances in a jar, and poured foamy liquids over the resulting compounds. At the end, the warrior pointed a finger at the two guards. They hurried to take the crucible of the campfire with some improvised tongs. The contents of the metal container were bubbling and spewing a cloud of reddish smoke.

Kao Fang sang a litany between coughs and spasms. Hunt understood that the man was about to die. Mei Ling imitated his chant and repeated it loudly, while still manipulating the elements of the formula. The compound seemed about to boil and released sparks and large bubbles on the surface. A strong smell of gas flooded the grotto. Mei Ling almost shouted the words of the spell, totally oblivious to her surroundings.

Hunt could no longer bear the frenzy that was dominating the warrior.

"Mei Ling, listen to me! This is madness!"

For a moment it seemed as if she hadn't heard him, but suddenly she stopped reciting the spell and looked at Hunt with a furious gesture.

"Soon I will have the *red typhoon* at my service! No one will be able to oppose its strength!"

Hunt had irritated eyes and felt his throat dry. Mary Ann kept coughing and the pirates had stepped back away from the compound. The only one who seemed not to be affected by the emanations was Mei Ling, whose voice had resumed the chant while her hands scrambled the substances. Hunt covered his mouth with one hand and advanced towards the warrior. A guard intercepted him and hit his face with the back of his hand. Hunt stumbled and felt the bitter taste of blood on his lips.

"Oh, Peter, we're going to die!" Mary Ann exclaimed.

He looked with exorbitant eyes at the crucible, located on a rock base, which was bubbling loudly on the table.

Hunt grabbed Mary Ann's arm and slowly backed away, guiding the girl to stay by his side. No one noticed them. The warrior did not stop mixing brightly colored substances with toxic aromas. The air had become unbreathable, and an increasingly dense haze enveloped the grotto. The pirates had moved quite far from the table, which vibrated with the boiling of the compound.

Kao Fang's voice became an almost inaudible whisper, and suddenly ceased altogether. Hunt realized that the alchemist had died. He looked at Mei Ling with a relieved gesture but deduced that the warrior had not noticed that the alchemist was no longer guiding her. Her hands were raised on the crucible, holding some black grains. Hunt followed Mei Ling's gaze and understood that she was using the directions of the paper roll to continue the process. The warrior stopped chanting the spell and separated her hands.

Hunt watched in despair as the black grains of gunpowder fell on the fiery, bubbling mixture.

"To the water!" The captain shouted to Mary Ann.

No one heard or noticed them. Hunt pushed the girl into the lagoon and threw himself behind her. They dove into the water and were enveloped by blackness. Hunt propelled himself down and dragged Mary Ann with him. Then he turned face up and looked to the surface, illuminated by the glow of the campfires. An instant later the glow grew in intensity and turned red. Even underwater Hunt could feel the severe rumble of the explosion, the howl of the shock wave, and the air burning.

The water stirred, and the temperature rose

sharply. Hunt hugged Mary Ann and together they curled up, struggling to hold their breath. The stalactites on the roof of the grotto cracked and fell like spears on the lagoon. Hunt kicked hard and managed to sink to dodge the sharp rocks. Then the reddish flare disappeared, and the lagoon plunged back into darkness. Hunt grabbed the girl by the waist and swam to the surface.

They crawled out to shore, panting and coughing. When the captain's eyes adjusted to the gloom, he felt as if he had emerged in a different place from the one he had left. The rock in the cavern was blackened by the heat and most of the stalagmites peeking out of the ground had turned into scattered pebbles. The trestle table had vanished, and the body of the alchemist was a formless, scorched and steaming mass. The pirates had been thrown several meters from their original position and their bodies were dismembered and twisted.

Hunt stood up laboriously and watched the destruction around him. Some logs from the campfires remained lit, making dark shadows dance over the walls of burning rock. Mary Ann seemed about to faint. Hunt dragged her towards the arch that communicated with the staircase.

"Peter!" A voice whispered.

Hunt shuddered. Mei Ling was lying next to some rocks, near the exit. Her body was twisted into an unnatural way. Her clothes were nothing more than steaming shreds and half of her face had simply disappeared. Hunt approached her, trying not to vomit from the repulsive smell of burnt flesh. The warrior stretched out one arm and he bent down to hold her hand.

"I did... it for... China", she explained in a barely audible tone.

"Don't talk. I will try to help you."

Despite the extreme pain that engulfed her, she managed to smile.

"You are a... gentleman... Peter Hunt."

He looked at her not knowing what to say. His eyes filled with tears.

"I was wrong," she said, in a raspy voice. "Now... I know."

Mei Ling squeezed his hand tightly.

"Find Kiel... You can still... stop him."

Hunt brought his ear to the warrior's mouth, and she whispered her last words. Then she exhaled a long sigh and stopped moving. Hunt looked away, unable to continue observing what was left of that beautiful young woman. He wanted to curse her for her stupidity and fanaticism, but he felt exhausted and preferred to remember in his mind the image of the real Mei Ling. He sat on his knees next to the body until Mary Ann's sobs brought him out of his trance. When he got up, he saw the *jian* sword thrown next to its former owner. He took the weapon with one hand and with the other he guided the girl out of the grotto.

The walls of the tunnel were burning. Several of the timbers that held the roof had been consumed and there were rocks falling off all the way. Walking the fifty meters of the passage was a torture. The girl tripped several times and Hunt filled his hands with blisters as he groped for the dark walls. Toxic fumes floating in the small space nearly choked them. Upon reaching the exit, Hunt gathered the few forces he had left, raised the sword and burst out into the chamber. He immediately understood that his caution was futile.

The *red typhoon* had wiped out everything. The tunnel had undoubtedly acted like the barrel of a weapon, ejecting a wild flare that scorched the furniture, shredded the rock walls and burned the bodies of the pirates in the chamber. The place was blackened and steaming. Hunt led Mary Ann through the fog, trying to prevent her from seeing the mutilated and broken bodies scattered on the ground.

Going outside the cavern, they both swallowed puffs of air like two drowned people and stopped for a moment to replenish their energies. Hunt noticed that the guard sitting on the tree stump had disappeared. After a minute, the captain took the girl by the hand, and they went into the forest. This time they carried no torches and only had the faint moonlight to guide them. Hunt was pushing the branches away with his hands and groping the ground with his feet. Progress was slow and difficult. He had the feeling that it took forever to leave the forest and reach the bush area.

He found the pebble path and immediately headed towards the beach. They were almost running when they suddenly met five pirates who had remained on the beach. The men looked confused and kept looking up at the hill. No doubt they had seen the storm of red fire emerging from the cavern and dissipating among the trees. When the men saw the two prisoners, they surrounded them and began yelling at them.

"They ask what happened in the cavern," Mary Ann explained.

"I don't have time for explanations. Stand behind me."

Hunt held tightly the sword and raised it with one hand. He tried to take a step forward. The pirates wielded their own weapons – clubs and daggers – and gestured to him to let go of the *jian*. Hunt cracked out a demonic smile and threw himself on the attack.

He lunged left and right, keeping his body behind his weapon. The pirates brandished their clubs, but they were shorter than the sword. Hunt felt the sharp steel cleanly cut the bodies of his opponents. He heard screams and curses, but at no time did he stop making feints and throwing slashes. Out of the corner of his eye he saw a couple of pirates flanking him to attack from the side. Hunt turned, always keeping the girl behind him, and attacked swiftly, in a state of frenzy brought on by an adrenaline rush.

The *jian* sword was light and very maneuverable. Although Hunt had never used it before, it didn't take him long to get used to its weight and design. No doubt Mei Ling would have been horrified to see him wield it like a madman, but the important thing was to survive and quickly eliminate his enemies. Especially if there were five of them. The thin blade kept flashing at the moonlight and ripped out more screams from the pirates, until no one was left standing. Hunt was breathing heavily, and his arm was numb. As he looked around, he found that his opponents were all dead or incapacitated.

He wiped the sword on the leg of his pants and slid it down the belt. Mary Ann took him by the hand, and they ran to the seashore. The barge was stranded in the sand, further on. Between them they pushed it to the edge of the water and jumped inside. Hunt picked up the oars.

"Where will we go?" The girl asked.

Hunt looked in all directions as he began to row.

"Far from this damn island."

18. MOGANSHAN

It had taken him more than a week to get there, but Peter Hunt was finally at the place where his enemies intended to gather. While drinking *oolong* tea from a porcelain *chawan* bowl, sitting at the bar of the busy inn, he mentally reviewed the journey he had begun the day after his escape from the island of the Phoenix.

The barge was drifting when it was found by the sampan of some fishermen from Putien shortly after dawn. The sun was already rising high, warming the air and burning mercilessly with its rays. Mary Ann had fallen asleep almost immediately after they left the island. Hunt had rowed for several hours, watching the sky slowly clear, until the forces abandoned him, and he also fell, exhausted. When the hull of the sampan hit the barge, as both boats came together, Hunt woke up suddenly and wondered where he was.

The fishermen gave them water and food and conical *dǒulì* bamboo hats to protect themselves from the inclement heat. Mary Ann told their rescuers a simplified version of their adventures: that they had been attacked by pirates, kidnapped as the only foreigners on board, taken to an island to hide them while the captors asked for ransom, and their miraculous escape during the night. The fishermen were simple people and they believed what the girl told them. Then they made wild gestures and many comments among themselves, complaining about the pirates. At Hunt's insistence, translated by the missionary, the fishermen agreed to take them back to the site of the attack.

The sampan was propelled by a long oar located at the stern, called *yuloh,* but had sails for when it was necessary to navigate quickly. The crew deployed them, and the boat soon picked up the wind and advanced following the instructions of the castaways. The sampan was a small ship compared to a junk, so the return journey took much longer than it had taken the pirates to get away from the steamer. Only in the afternoon Hunt spotted on the horizon the silhouette of the *Queen of Java* rocking in the gentle waves of the Strait of Formosa.

The crew and passengers lay on the floor of the hold under the deck, bathed in sweat and with dry and sore throats. Some had fainted from the lack of air and excessive heat. Captain Verbeek cried with excitement at the sight of Hunt on the other side of the upper hatch of the hold. However, he immediately recovered and began to give orders to his men to immediately set the ship in motion. They sailed all night and arrived at Amoy at dawn. Hunt and Mary Ann returned to their compartment, exhausted, and slept throughout the journey. Before disembarking, Hunt recovered his Webley revolver, which he had concealed after the fight with the crew member who tried to kill them.

At the port, Verbeek reported the pirates' attack to the authorities, but Hunt and the girl disappeared before they could be questioned. Through the local British consulate, they got help to return to Shanghai by train and once there, Hunt sent a telegram to Sir John Connelly with the news. The director of Department X responded to him the next day with new instructions and informed him that he had transferred a new remittance of funds to the branch of the Hongkong and Shanghai Banking Corporation located on the Bund. Then, at last, Hunt was able to prepare his final assault on the plans of the false consul Rudolph Kiel.

Mount Mogan, or *Moganshan* in Chinese, an oasis of freshness and hot springs, was discovered by Westerners in the late nineteenth century. First the missionaries, and then the wealthy citizens of Shanghai, began to flock there to escape the crippling coastal summer. Soon a village was established, at the foot of the mountain, provided with shops, inns, a church and a tennis club. The richest, on the other hand, built elegant villas on the slopes of the mountain covered with bamboo forests.

The two-hundred-kilometer journey from Shanghai was strenuous and expensive, even thirty years after the resort's founding. The journey took between ten and fifteen hours, first by train or barge from Shanghai to Hangchow, and from there by bus along a winding road to the village. Until not many years ago, the last part of the journey had to be done in a palanquin carried by porters.

Captain Peter Hunt arrived in Moganshan at noon. He stayed in one of the village's inns, swam in the club's Olympic swimming pool, and after lunch slept a well-deserved nap. At dusk, he went down to the saloon to drink tea while waiting it get dark. There was still a month to go until the end of the summer and the place was very busy. He avoided engaging in conversation with tourists and left the inn in the dead of the night.

He carried a backpack with a blanket, a couple of cans of food, a canteen, a flint, a compass and his fully loaded revolver. In his hand he held a battery-powered lantern that guided him through the trees as he went into the forest and ascended the slope of the mountain. After an hour of walking, he found a clearing among the trees and spread the blanket next to some ferns. He lit a campfire with the flint, ate meat with canned beans, and drank half of the canteen. The site was silent, and he could only hear the squeak of some insect in the distance.

He stared at the bright stars for a while, while imagining what would happen the next day. Anyway, it would be the end of that damn affair. He had already managed to decipher the rest of the story. Upon arriving in Shanghai, the fake German consul had re-established the networks of his father, a scholar and enthusiast of Chinese culture, to find the ancient scroll containing the spell of the *red typhoon.* In his quest, Kiel had crossed paths with Mei Ling, a member of a brotherhood of warriors who had also become interested in the weapon as a means of gaining power in China.

The conspirators tasked a secret society, the Green Gang, with recovering the scroll and obtaining the items to make the alchemist explosive, but the gang's boss had decided to sell the secrets to the highest bidder. To top it off, the henchman who had been tasked for the job decided to act on his own and after an assassination attempt managed to alert the English to the plans of the attack. The man had paid with his life for the betrayal. That's where Mary Ann Taylor and then Hunt himself entered the story.

On the way had been left Chester Peng and the beautiful warrior. Two useless deaths, the captain told himself. Thinking of them, he shuddered involuntarily. Although each had departed in very different circumstances, the false consul had to take responsibility for both.

Hunt gave a sardonic smile knowing that soon the man would have to give an account of his actions. With that thought in mind, he lay on the ground, wrapped in the blanket. As the bonfire slowly extinguished, he set out to spend the night in the woods.

The villas that dotted the slopes of the mountain varied in size and style, but they were all luxurious. There were in the form of an English castle, such as the one built near the top by a Scottish missionary and doctor; Mediterranean style, reminiscent of the Riviera or Tuscany; or even others that imitated classical Chinese architecture. The villa belonging to the German consulate in Shanghai, erected by the diplomatic representative before the Great War, was an exact replica of the summer residences located in the Bavarian Alps.

After breakfast, consul Herr Rudolph Kiel settled into the back veranda to read a book by Goethe but failed to concentrate on the text. He had been staying in the villa for more than a week, apparently on vacation, accompanied by an assistant, the driver and a bodyguard. In addition, in the villa resided a butler and his wife, who cleaned and cooked. Kiel had established a daily routine. In the mornings, he would listen to music on the gramophone in the living room or read a book from the library's vast collection. Then he would have lunch alone in the dining room, drink a glass of brandy, and then go for a walk in the surroundings. Every day he went to bed early.

However, routine and waiting were getting him mad. The real reason for his trip to the mountain was the encounter he had arranged with Mei Ling for after she had captured that damned Englishman Hunt and retrieved the spell scroll. Kiel still felt dizzy just thinking about the destruction of the factory in Pudong and the possible loss of the valuable document. Hunt had turned out to be a cunning and persistent adversary whom he had to eliminate if he wanted to press ahead with his plans for Germany's resurgence.

Kiel's agents had been on the verge of capturing Hunt and his companion before they boarded a steamer bound for Hong Kong. Mei Ling decided that she would intercept them during the trip and promised the consul that she would be back in no more than five days. The consul had suggested that the meeting take place in Moganshan, a remote place and much more discreet than hectic Shanghai. The warrior agreed and immediately set off south. One of her companions of the brotherhood would put her in contact with some pirates that ravaged the Strait of Formosa, where the ship of the fugitives had to pass.

But the girl was several days late, and he had not heard from her. Kiel was becoming impatient. The meddling of the English was costing a huge sum of money and a considerable delay in planning the operation. He couldn't help but wonder if he had done the right thing by partnering with those Chinese he knew little about. When he met Mei Ling, he was impressed with her and had no trouble convincing himself of her abilities. At the time, he found her a valuable ally in his quest. In addition, he had to recognize that she was very beautiful.

No, he thought. Hunt would not be able to escape. Maybe he was a cunning guy, but he was at a total disadvantage to Mei Ling. The girl's network of informants was impressive. Hundreds or perhaps thousands of coolies, dockers, *amahs,* and all kinds of local employees reported to the brotherhood of warriors on the activities of Westerners who usurped China's riches. Kiel suspected that even his servants in the village were allied with the nationalist movements, so he kept them out of his official affairs and forbade them access to his office.

The consul put aside the book and concluded that he should end his relationship with the Chinese. Mei Ling and her people only helped him to get money and weapons, including the *red typhoon* itself. No doubt the warrior would try to make a copy of the spell, or even test its effects, before handing it to Kiel, but she had to remember that it was the consul who paid for her search. Once the spell was in his hands, Kiel would make sure that his secrets only belonged to him. He gave a damn about the fate of China and its inhabitants, but he did not want their rebellious attempts to alert the English or the rest of Europe.

He got up and strolled along the veranda in a hurry. If the girl didn't show up within a couple of days, he would have to return to Shanghai. Would there be another copy of the spell somewhere? Heck, he'd have to start the search again! He could not return to Germany empty-handed. The industrialist Gerber had spent a fortune financing the operation and former General Kemnitz had half the army waiting for orders for an uprising. Both would be furious if the miracle weapon finally didn't show up. Kiel stopped walking and leaned on one of the columns that supported the ceiling of the gallery. If only he could...

A shadow caught his attention. The veranda opened to a well-kept garden surrounded by hedges. Beyond these, there was a bamboo forest that ended in a cliff cut on the slope of the mountain. Kiel looked back at the trees and found that a dark figure was silhouetted against the thin, long trunks. He sharpened his gaze and could make out the outline of a cape swayed by the breeze. It was Mei Ling's unmistakable silhouette.

"Eckert!" He called.

Instantly the bodyguard appeared beside him, a tall and stocky man with his head shaved.

"At your service, sir!"

"Are you carrying your gun, Eckert?"

"*Jawohl, Herr Konsul!* Certainly!"

"Come with me."

Kiel approached the chair where he had been reading and bent down to grab his cane. He went down the staircase of the veranda and crossed the garden in the direction of the forest. Eckert followed him at a marching pace, like the soldier he had been.

Both men immediately reached the trees, but the girl had disappeared. Kiel hesitated for a moment, but he looked around and discovered the silhouette that beckoned him from inside the forest. Then it disappeared again. Kiel went among the bamboos, always accompanied by the bodyguard, and began to ascend the slope of the mountain. The terrain soon became steeper, and the consul had to use the cane to help himself with the climb.

Where the hell did the damn girl take him? He ruled out that it was a trap or an ambush, because she always acted alone. He had seen her in action, and she didn't need help from anyone. With her combat skills she was able to defeat several enemies at once, as Tony 'the Mountain' Lu's men had discovered. No, Kiel thought. That mystery meant something else. After thinking about it for a moment, and while panting to continue climbing the slope of the mountain, he concluded that it must be money. Mei Ling had recovered the spell roll and now intended to renegotiate their agreement. He decided that he would haggle a little, but in order to get the document he was willing to pay anything.

The air was getting colder, and an intense breeze was blowing. They were getting closer and closer to the top of the mountain. The terrain had become rocky, and the bamboos were beginning to be spaced out. A moment later, the two men reached the cliff that marked the edge of the forest. Kiel shuddered from the cold. The girl was waiting for him on a rocky ledge. She wore her black outfit and had the hood on, hiding her face. The hilt of the *jian* sword poked out of the edge of the cloak, above her waist.

"I guess we didn't come here to admire the view," Kiel said annoyed. As she didn't respond, he added: "Come on, Mei Ling, stop playing."

Behind the figure, the mountains formed extensive greenish valleys shrouded in fog. The sun shone high in the sky, but its rays barely warmed the air. The blowing of the wind forced him to scream to be heard.

"We have an agreement, Mei Ling!" Kiel insisted, loudly.

The girl put her hands to the hood and slowly took it off, revealing her face. Kiel first saw the blonde hair in an uproar in the wind, and then noticed the blue eyes and European features of the woman.

"What does this mean?!" He asked with a

scream.

Behind him, the bodyguard sensed the danger and approached his boss.

"We finally know each other, Consul Kiel," said a voice behind them.

The two Germans jumped back. Peter Hunt came out of the last bamboos of the forest, with the revolver pointed at his enemies.

"Sorry, I meant 'Count von Dahlen'."

Kiel tried to keep his composure, but his eyes betrayed him. For a moment the pupils narrowed in surprise, but Hunt became aware of the reaction.

"The visit to your apartment in the French Concession was very helpful," Hunt said. "Your personal documents told a very... interesting story".

Kiel gritted his teeth and his cheeks twitched in a rictus of fury.

"What happened to Mei Ling?" The consul asked after a moment.

However, in his mind he already knew the answer. He went pale and his pulse accelerated.

"She succumbed to her temptations, Kiel. She was destroyed by the *red typhoon.*"

"Liar! You killed her, Hunt!"

The captain lowered his head and shook it in a gesture of denial. Then he stared back at the person responsible for all those deaths.

"It was the fault of her own ambition," the captain insisted. "Mei Ling wanted to master a power too great for her... and she failed!"

"So, the spell..."

The consul was not able to finish the sentence. Fear gripped his throat.

"Lost forever, Kiel. Just like your plans."

Hunt wanted to smile but abstained. He just looked at the German harshly. Kiel looked dejected, but the captain did not wish to be overconfident. He held the revolver up.

"Surrender, Kiel. Come with me back to Shanghai."

"And then, what will happen?"

"You will be arrested and sent to London for trial."

Kiel let out a bitter and dry laugh.

"I will never have a fair trial in your country, Hunt. After Versailles, I know how you treat the defeated."

"As on the previous occasion," Hunt replied contemptuously, "it is you, the Germans, who wish to start a war."

As his boss spoke, Eckert had slowly pulled away to the side. Hunt, who had his attention fixed on Kiel, did not notice. Mary Ann, for her part, followed the exchange between the two men with increasing anguish. The bodyguard put his hand inside the jacket to extract his pistol.

"*Es lebe Deutschland!* Long live Germany!" shouted Eckert as he charged toward Hunt.

The captain saw a blurred image out of the

corner of his eye. His trained mind told him it was a gun emerging from the bodyguard's jacket. He turned to the attacker and pointed his revolver. For a terrible moment both weapons shone in the morning sun, but only one spit out their flash. Eckert had rushed to act and shouted before he was ready. Hunt, for his part, had his finger on the trigger.

The bodyguard was hit in the chest and fell on his back. Hunt took a step towards the fallen opponent to check that he was incapacitated. Mary Ann sounded an alarm. Hunt felt, more than he saw, something speeding across in front of him and falling on his arm. A sharp pain numbed his right wrist as the Webley burst out of his hand. Only then did he understand that Kiel had just beaten him with his cane.

He leaned back sharply and dodged a new attack from the consul. He shouted furiously and made the cane swing like a sword. Kiel was enraged and kept carrying forward. Hunt had to jump and crouch as the stiff wooden rod whistled over his head. Still avoiding the cane, Hunt looked all over the ground in search of his revolver but did not spot it.

"Mary Ann, look for my gun!" He shouted in despair.

Kiel managed to deliver a couple of blows to his torso and shoulder. Hunt's sight was clouded with pain. He had to admit that the damn German was brave and, moreover, a good fighter.

Eventually, Hunt gave up looking for the revolver and threw himself at his opponent. He avoided another blow to the head and clung to the consul with both arms, in a hold. Kiel crossed the cane over his back and squeezed it with both hands, burying the rod against his body. Hunt groaned in pain and headbutted his enemy. Kiel screamed and a trail of blood flowed from his nose.

"Peter, the sword!" Mary Ann called him.

Hunt looked over Kiel's shoulder. The girl was holding the *jian* sword high. The captain cursed himself for not having thought about it before. He pushed the German away and threw himself towards the girl. Mary Ann threw the sword into the air. Hunt rolled on the ground, jumped up and picked up the flying sword. He immediately turned to Kiel. The false consul looked at him with bloodshot eyes and took the cane with both hands. Then he pulled the hilt and unsheathed a long stiletto.

"Damn you!" The captain muttered.

The two blades collided with a metallic squeal. Both opponents mastered fencing and knew how to attack and defend with long weapons. Between feints and lunges, they danced on the ground, watching the protruding rocks out of the corner of their eyes so as not to stumble. The attacks were accompanied by furious groans and looks as hard as the steel they held in their hands.

Hunt brandished the elegant *jian* from side

to side, taking advantage of the sharp edge of its blade. Kiel, whose weapon had no edge, would stop the blows and then stab by pushing his whole body forward. Hunt attacked hard, charging his arm to snatch the stiletto from the German, but Kiel held it as if it were the extension of his own arm. The two men turned again and again on the grass and among the rocks, without giving each other quarters. Both were exhausted, but they knew that defeat equaled death. Only the adrenaline kept them struggling.

"Beware!" The girl suddenly warned.

A bullet thundered over the noise of the wind. Hunt had instinctively crouched down and felt the hum of the projectile passing over his head. He looked towards the origin of the shot and saw the bodyguard lying on his side, with his pistol raised and a gesture of pain on his face. The gun trembled in his hand, and then fell to the ground. The man tried to sit up, but blood gushed from his mouth and his head tilted until it was motionless. His last effort had been to defend his boss.

Kiel pounced on Hunt taking advantage of his distraction. He entangled the thin stiletto in the Chinese sword and pulled up. The *jian* flashed in the air, and then Hunt lost sight of it. Seeing himself disarmed, Hunt backed sharply and stumbled upon a rock. His body slammed on his back to the ground. The consul gave a scream of fury that tore the air and threw the tip of the stiletto into the chest of his fallen enemy. Hunt cursed himself for dying that stupid way and vowed revenge in some other life.

A new shot echoed on the mountain. Hunt assumed that the bodyguard was still alive, but then Kiel shuddered. The tip of the stiletto deflected and collided with the rock, next to Hunt's body. He rolled to the side and sprang up. Mary Ann was still holding the Webley with both hands, raised before her eyes. Hunt ran to catch the *jian* sword and confronted Kiel.

The consul was pressing his hands against the wound on his abdomen. Seeing the captain, he began to retreat on a rock ledge that ended at the edge of the cliff. Hunt walked calmly towards his enemy; his sword pointed at the front.

"I'll see you on another battlefield, Captain!" Kiel snapped in spasms.

He felt the edge of the rock on his feet and stopped moving. The wind shook his clothes and made him swing to the edge of the precipice.

"You will have to fight in hell, Kiel!"

The thin blade of the sword easily pierced the consul's torso, between the ribs, and emerged from the back, covered with blood. The body scrambled and was left hanging from the weapon. Hunt held on to the rock on his left foot and put his right on the chest of his dying enemy. He pushed hard and pulled the sword back. The gun was released, and the consul's body fell on its back. For a second, he swayed over the edge, spread-eagled. Kiel grimaced, and then rushed into the void.

A week later, the *North China Daily News* published a small note in the criminal affairs section:

> GERMAN CONSUL DISAPPEARED IN MOGANSHAN
>
> *Herr Rudolph Kiel, representative of the German Republic in the city of Shanghai, was last seen more than a week ago in the villa that the consulate maintains in the resort of Moganshan. Herr Kiel is believed to have gone for a walk with his bodyguard, Herr Eckert, but they did not return to the villa. According to the butler of the house, the consul was not a regular visitor to the summer residence, so he was not familiar with the surrounding wooded terrain.*
>
> *So far, Hangchow police believe the two German citizens may have accidentally fallen into a deep ravine while strolling. Locals are scouring the land surrounding the village in search of signs that could alert them to the whereabouts of the disappeared. If necessary, the police will dispatch a larger force of volunteers.*
>
> *The village of Moganshan is renowned for its climate and the most important members*

of the community have their summer houses there...

Hunt left the paper on the table. The lounge hall of the Astor House was very lively. Dozens of guests dined and danced to the rhythm of a cheerful piece of jazz played by a band of American musicians. A waiter approached the captain's table and bent down to make himself heard over the bustle of the crowd.

"Your guest has arrived, sir."

Hunt adjusted the knot of the bow tie and smoothed his dinner jacket as he stood up. Mary Ann wore an elegant dark blue long silk and lace dress. She had fixed her hair, which she held with a matching ribbon, and applied makeup and lipstick. It was almost unrecognizable.

"You look like a movie star, my dear."

He leaned over and kissed her on the cheek.

"Oh, my God, the things you say, Peter!"

However, the girl was delighted. She smiled broadly and showed a radiant expression. Hunt helped her sit down and then occupied his chair, on the other side of the table.

"This place is wonderful," Mary Ann said, as she looked around. "I had never been here before."

"I ordered champagne. We must celebrate."

The waiter showed up with a bottle of Bollinger, which he left in a silver ice bucket after serving two glasses to the diners. They took their own and both raised them in a toast.

"I can't believe this is all over," she sighed, visibly relieved.

"It's not over yet, my dear."

She became restless, but then saw that he was smiling. Hunt pulled two pieces of cardboard from his jacket and handed them to her. The girl's face lit up when she discovered that they were ship tickets.

"A steamer trip from Shanghai to London!"

"And in first class, as I promised. We leave early tomorrow."

"That's fine, but it's tomorrow," Mary Ann replied in a serious tone.

Then she looked at Hunt, and a passionate smile slowly formed on her lips.

"And what will we do tonight?" The girl asked.

Her eyes were shining under the lights in the lounge hall.

Hunt smiled back at her. He then got up from the chair and motioned to Mary Ann to do the same. He grabbed her arm and with a gesture called the waiter.

"Bring the champagne to my room," he ordered.

The waiter smiled slightly.

"Right now, Captain Hunt."

THE END

BOOKS IN THIS SERIES

The Adventures of Captain Hunt

Read more adventures of Department X's main investigator, Captain Peter Hunt

Cult Of The Serpent